Neal Arbic | WHITE

Neal Arbic | WHITE

NEW PULP PRESS

Published by New Pulp Press, LLC, 926 Truman Avenue, Key West, Florida 33040, USA.

For information contact:
Publisher@NewPulpPress.com

ISBN-13: 978-0692521038 (New Pulp Press)
ISBN-10: 0692521038

Cover by Alisdair Jones

Neal Arbic | WHITE

Saturday, August 9th, 1969, 1:45 AM

Black. No moon. The three-week-old smog smothering LA hid the stars. A police strobe flashed red across the large gridiron gate. The Bel Air mansion's grounds seemed abandoned, only an empty patrol car at the end of its long sloping driveway on Cielo Drive. Then, emerging from the shadows: Officer José Delgado, his service revolver drawn down with both hands. His black boots cautiously climbed the asphalt drive, his eyes locked on what lay before him.

A white Rambler appeared to be parked haphazardly, but as he neared, it became clear the car had rear-ended a large oak. Its engine choked on its last drops of gas. The interior light was on, the driver's door – wide open.

Rivulets of blood met Delgado's boots. On only his third day of active duty, he raised his revolver. Eyes wide, he scanned the dark as he moved steadily toward the car door. Something hung from it.

He froze. It was the body of a teenage boy, short blond hair, glasses, short sleeve shirt, his head and arms sprawled on the asphalt. Delgado drew near, leaning over the body, squinting. The poor light from inside the car revealed a small piece of skull missing just below the hairline. Blood trickled from the back of his head. Officer Delgado was about to squat by the victim when he saw her.

Pivoting towards the front door of the mansion, his eyes were drawn to her body. The bright porch light made the scene pale and ghostly, a distant vision in the absolute dark. She lay halfway out of the doorway. His gun rose to chest level.

Sidestepping the young man's body, he made his way across the lawn. His eyes flickered nervously from window to window, watching for any movement inside, sporadically surveying the young woman with long blonde hair, her yellow summer dress drenched in blood. A worried mantra filled his head – *first officer on scene, first officer on scene* – summoning his academy classes: *As initial patrolman on a crime scene – render immediate assistance to any living victims, preserve the evidence.* He took his first step onto the stone path leading to the front door and stopped again. Slowly turning his head he saw another body a few feet away: a man, medium height, face down on the lawn, a large knife sticking out the back of his neck. The blade gleamed.

Keeping his eyes on the windows, the officer slowly made his way towards the man. His pulse drummed in his ears. He tried to remain calm, but could not help notice his pistol trembling in his hands. Squatting to feel for a pulse on the facedown man, he accidentally touched the large carving knife. His hand jumped back. A strong wind came up, breaking one of LA's longest heat waves. It swung the front door. The girl's body blocked it from closing. And now the officer could see it.

Written on the mansion's door, in blood, was the word PIG.

10:45 AM

In the morning sunlight, a black 1941 Packard Formal navigated the narrow canyon street of Cielo Drive and came to its dead end. Vehicles choked the cul-de-sac: a dozen patrol cars, deputy photo cars, Crime Lab, LA County Coroner and news vans.

The press was held at bay by a line of police sawhorses and patrolmen. Bleary-eyed officer Delgado paced the mansion's gate nervously, smoking a cigarette, waiting for a ride back to the station. He wearily tipped his hat back to view the vintage vehicle pulling up to the gates – a popular high-end car in the 40s, a rare sight in '69. "Now that's a jalopy."

A nearby officer gave a knowing smile. "Yeah? Well, wait to you see the fossil who's driving it."

Jack Middleton edged out of the car looking like a retired boxer gone to seed: big, squashed nose broken in places, ruddy complexion from a lifetime of booze, pockmarked skin, deep mean wrinkles around his eyes. The dog tags under his shirt and all-gray crew cut were homage to buddies lost in World War II.

His hard pale blue eyes squinted in the sunlight, quickly counting the number of cut telephone wires that hung around the gate.

Young patrolmen leaned against the gate smoking and giving Jack skeptical looks. Closing in like a bouncer on underage drinkers, he grimaced and pointed to the gate's electronic opener. Decades of cigar smoke and hangovers had left his throat a deep rasp, "There's a bloody fingerprint on that button."

The officers turned and stared. Jack picked a patrolman. "You! Don't just stand there like an idiot with your jaw hanging. Fetch someone from Forensics, will ya!"

The patrolman disappeared up the drive.

Up the long oak-lined driveway Jack's legs loosened, his back straightened, revealing the vigor of a much younger man. The estate grounds were eerily quiet: no bird calls, squirrels, not even a cricket. His eyes roved the perfectly manicured lawn, well-trimmed shrubs and a distant in-ground pool.

Jack spied the white Rambler rear-ended into an oak. Six technicians from Scientific Investigation Division swarmed the car scraping goo, measuring trajectories and blood spatter. Jack hated the SID crew. He still carried his own evidence kit from when detectives lifted their own prints. SID guys could mess up, miss evidence or misplace it. And the more men on a crime scene, the better chances important clues would be trampled.

He passed the body of the teenage boy hanging from the car door with a glance.

Jack called to an older tech, "Lloyd!"

A bald man dusting for fingerprints on the car's door handle looked up.

Jack grinned. "Hey, make sure you don't get your own prints on there, or I'll have to arrest *you*." Jack whispered to himself, "You dumb fuck."

Lloyd shook his head and went back to work.

He left the SID team with a dismissive wave. "You're wasting your time, Lloyd. That windshield says the shots came from outside the car."

Jack's eyes shifted to the lawn, the body with the carving knife in its neck, now being covered with a white coroner's tarp. He made his way up to the mansion, negotiating pools of blood on the flagstone path.

It was a French country style mansion, the second floor a large sloping roof with dormer windows extending out of it. The ground floor had large wide windows and beautiful stone walls. A patrolman hunched over just outside the porch, vomit on the ground and bushes. Another patrolman, hand on the crouched man's shoulder, offered moral support. It was a safe bet there were more bodies inside.

He stepped over the young woman's corpse in the doorway as if merely avoiding a garden hose. But then he paused and stepped back over her. He stood over the corpse, his head bowed, not at her, but at the door.

Jack read the bloody letters under his breath, "Pig."

Inside the house, a young photographer appeared, tripod in hand, hair down over his ears. He yelled at Jack. "Hey, man! You're standing on my crime scene!"

Jack looked up, and stepped over the body into the hall. Passing the young photographer, he gruffly advised, "Get a haircut."

In a high-beamed living room, bodies lay everywhere. It was ramshackle and grisly: blood matted into the white plush carpet, streaked across the French doors, splash marks on huge bookcases and elegant chairs, streams soaked into frilled drapes and pillows, sprayed couches, a smudged handprint across a toppled lamp shade. Messages were scrawled in blood across the white walls: Rise, Piggies, Helter Skelter. A twisted corpse laid at Jack's feet, a young woman, her abdomen chopped up: deep, raw and open. An equally bloodied woman had been hacked a few feet away, another by the stone fireplace. Jack counted seven fatalities. A group of officers and techs had gathered behind a long couch draped in an American flag. They stared down at something.

Jack made his way over. There she lay in a blood-drenched bikini. She was beautiful. She was young. She was a bulging eight months pregnant. And dead.

A young tech and two patrolmen spoke in hushed voices, "Who would stab a woman when she's pregnant?"

"Who would stab her in the belly ... with a fork?"

"The same guy who stabbed that man out on the lawn...107 times."

Even Jack, after decades of murder, felt like he had just been punched in the back of the head. The way the light fell on her face, her naked protruding belly, the way it had been mutilated.

An orderly from the Coroner's Office smoked a cigarette. "Why do I know her?"

A patrolman squatted beside the body. "It's Sharon Tate."

A young tech squatted. "The actress?"

The patrolman nodded. "Hollywood party – all these people were sort of famous."

Jack's grim eyes surveyed her for a moment, not as a detective, but as a man looking at a crime. His teeth clenched behind tight lips, his fists tightened.

When the anger passed, he took a deep silent breath and began to notice the room again. There were too many people in it, mixed in with the techs and photographers were patrolmen walking about disturbing evidence; one had stepped in a pool of blood and was tracking it out the back door onto the patio.

Jack yelled, "I want every sumbitch patrolman outta my crime scene!"

~ ~ ~

While younger detectives studied the bodies, Jack's practiced eyes kept returning to bloodied walls, studying the messages scrawled in blood: Helter Skelter, Piggies, Rise.

The young photographer with hair over his ears squatted, adjusting his tripod over the punctured corpse of a handsome man in a tux. He kept glancing at Jack's perplexed face. Finally, he could no longer resist the urge to enlighten him. Brushing back his hair, he called across the room, "The Beatles!"

Jack turned his head, irritated. "What?"

The photographer came up from his squat and repeated, "The Beatles." He made his way through the bodies; a large lens compact swung at his neck with every step.

They met halfway, facing each other. Scrawled behind them in blood along the white wall was *Helter Skelter.* The young man pointed to the bloody letters, "The words. They're lyrics."

3:15 PM

The Spiral Staircase on the Sunset Strip was LA's most notorious record store. Pot deals were done in the back room, hippies congregated out front. Sarah Wilkinson, known as Sister Sunshine to friends, worked the afternoon shift. Jack's black Packard pulled up front. Sarah smiled at the vintage car through the plate glass. She expected to see some far out rock star step into the bright sunlight, but her smile evaporated when Jack emerged. His grim face and drab suit said it all. Her eyes widened. Running to lower the volume on the store's stereo, she yelled, "Cop!"

Customers made for the back door. A commotion broke out in the backroom: tables skidded, chairs fell over, swearing and then the scuttling of feet, the metal door opening, more feet, and then the heavy clack of the door falling shut – as Jack opened the front door.

Sarah's head turned towards him and she smiled. Jack acknowledged her with an impassive nod.

He stood scanning the store: the walls painted in swirling colors; incense curled through the air and multi-color psychedelic posters covered the ceiling, hanging beads where doors should be. The music seemed like liquid, ever morphing: *She's like a Rainbow* by The Rolling Stones.

Sarah approached him. "Can I help you?"

He paused as he looked her over. She was a medieval princess: straight golden hair hung down to her waist, a flowery gown of colors. Her blue eyes shone from over-mascaraed lashes. A small golden heart hung from her black velvet choker.

Jack dug into his jacket pocket, pulled out a tiny notebook. "I'm looking for The Beatles' ... " He deciphered his notes, reading in a halting manner, "The ... White ... Album?"

She tried not to laugh at the old man. "It's our biggest selling record, for a year now."

She led him through a maze of racks displaying endless rows of brightly colored psychedelic albums and pointed at a blank, all-white album cover. "This is it."

Jack stood stunned, thinking she was joking. Noticing his pause, she lifted the 12x12 inch album from the rack and handed it to him.

Jack stared at its blankness like it was beyond his comprehension. "Why is there nothing on this thing?"

He flipped it over, the back was also blank. White. No title, no song listings, no picture.

"What is this?"

"Cool, huh?" She pointed to the front cover. Jack flipped it back. "See. It's embossed on the front."

Jack squinted. In the lower right corner, raised on the surface of the jacket, without any ink: The Beatles.

Sarah's curiosity won out. "You buying this for your kids, I mean, grandkids?"

Jack handed her the album, dug out his notes again. "I'm looking for a song." He found his page. "A song called...Helter Skelter."

Sarah's face lit up, lifting her heels in excitement. "That's a great song. It's on the record."

She bounced back to the counter, pulled out the store's copy of The White Album and slid out a black vinyl disc.

As she placed it on the turntable, she thought of the badge under Jack's jacket. "Look, can I ask you a favor? My boyfriend was busted last night for a little grass – only a couple joints. I don't get paid till next Friday, so I can't bail him out. Could you help me? Since I'm helping you, maybe you could get the charges dropped?"

Jack's eyes went blank like he didn't see or hear her. He looked away with a perfect not-my-job expression.

She got the message. Her face dropped; eyes watered. She turned to put the record on. Placing the turntable's arm over the spinning disc, she carefully dropped the needle. The scratchy hiss of the needle riding the empty groove filled the store. In a moment of anger, Sarah cranked the powerful stereo's volume to full. She would blast the old man's ears off.

A distorted electric guitar stabbed the air. Breathless vocals broke in screaming, then burst into psychotic laughter. The drums boomed, the beat thudding like bodies hitting the floor. The music flayed madly, the sound of the world falling apart. Grating, out-of-tune guitars swirled from speaker to speaker. The girl spoke, but Jack could not hear over the din. The last record the old man bought was an old 78rpm in 1953: Hank William's *Your Cheating Heart*. The satanic screams, frantic guitars, relentless smashing cymbals made his skin crawl.

Suddenly, he saw the murder scene: the blood soaked carpet, the blood spattered furniture, the massacred bodies, the butchered pregnant woman.

The bloody words dripping from the white walls were the very lyrics screaming at him now: HELTER SKELTER! To Jack, the song sounded like one thing, and one thing only: Murder.

Monday, August 11th, 1969, 9:02 AM

The sun crept up on East LA and a faded, blue bungalow. Stepping out onto his porch, unshaven and in pajamas, Jack gazed along the narrow rundown street of former working-class houses. His tattered slippers whispered against the pavement that led to his morning paper. A picket fence leaned in and out, its white paint peeling. With a groan, he bent for the newspaper. The headline, if Jack had bothered to read it:

POLICE SHOOTING SCANDAL
Fourth Unarmed Black Man Killed This Year
LAPD Claims Shooting Justified

Jack turned and smiled at the crabgrass and the home he had mortgaged with the GI Bill. He sighed and squinted in the warm sun. Enjoying the feel of the *Los Angeles Times* in his hand; he closed his eyes and slipped into bliss.

The sun on his face reminded him of desert horseback rides with his father – a ten-year-old Jack pretending to be an Old West sheriff on the lookout for bad guys. Jack smiled. One memory led to another: his first patrol in '38 and a pair of brass knuckles. He punched a pimp so hard the guy's eye popped out.

13

His sergeant told him brass knuckles were not standard issue, took them away, yet hung them high on the precinct's wall like a trophy. Crime on Jack's beat dropped to almost nothing.

The incident earned him the nickname 'Knuckles.'

An old Plymouth Convertible passed Jack's house. A blackbird landed on his roof. But Jack was somewhere else: the 40s, where the violent side of his nature made him the go-to interrogation man when confessions needed to be expedited. The Department soon discovered his hidden talents, an ability to hunt and to smell a lie. This combination of cruelty and cunning made him a valued asset in the LAPD.

Jack's shoulders relaxed, remembering his favorite part: rubbing elbows with senators, congressmen and movie starlets in the 50s. They often needed hard-to-get information quickly and problems disposed of quietly. Jack's violence occasionally spilled over to uncooperative witnesses and even fellow officers, but grateful 'friends' squashed mentions of these in official reports.

In the press, Jack became LA's poster boy for law and order – taking down major headlining cases, on the QT, Jack's less-than-admirable talents were utilized by the powers that be.

But the 60s brought change.

Laughter shattered Jack's memories. His eyes opened. He sneered. "Fuckin' hippies."

The flowery-dressed teenagers didn't notice him. They giggled and strutted down the street.

He retreated and slammed the door, jarring the picture on the wall: a black and white of his wife, dead for six years. From his gloomy living room he tossed the fresh paper into the kitchen. It landed on yesterday's paper still wrapped in its elastic, surrounded by all of last week's papers – still unopened. The pile of papers stood next to another pile and another. Stack after stack of unopened newspapers covered the whole kitchen floor.

Jack slumped in a faded club chair. The small end table beside him was crowded with empty scotch bottles, the closest: near-empty. He stared at the blank glass screen of his small TV.

There was a knock at the door. He groaned. On his way, he caught a glimpse of an afro out his window. Jack stopped. Through the blinds, he inspected the young black man in tight slacks, a white t-shirt and red windbreaker with racing strips. His afro was high and wide with pride, complemented by long sideburns. Jack cursed under his breath, "F'christsakes."

Jack swung open the door. "Get off my property!"

The door slammed in the young man's face. Jack stormed back to his chair.

The young man gave the closed door a *fuck you* with his eyes. Born in the Alabama, hitting adolescence in an LA ghetto, enrolled into an all-white college; he was used to frosty receptions. He fished a folded paper from his pocket, flipped it open and checked the address. This was the place. It was little comfort. He knew how to play it cool, but his gut danced. Taking a moment to restore a skillful poker face, he adjusted the gun under his jacket. The greatest risk was just coming here, so he might as well play it out. He took a deep breath of morning air, then knocked three times – loud.

Before Jack could sit, he heard the knocks. Jack reached for the holster slung over his chair, pulled out his .38 and popped open the cylinder. It was loaded. He swung the door open and pointed the gun. "Get lost! You goddamn-"

The young man held a police badge. Jack paused, his eyes examining the police shield designating rank and number.

The black man's wide eyes examined Jack's gun with disbelief. "You Detective Middleton?"

The gun lowered. The old man's eyes lingered on the badge. "Yes."

"I'm Officer Hicks. Delware Hicks. You requested a detective applicant from Narcotics?"

"You're black."

Delware detected fresh scotch on the old man's breath. "Yes, I know."

Jack withdrew into the house. The young man stood eyeing him.

Jack glanced back. "Well, come in. Shut the door, will ya!"

The living room smelt like stale cigar smoke. Dust covered a battered table, a bulky Victor Victrola gramophone, a pile of heavy 78rpm platters leaning against its clawed legs. A grimy radio with myriad dials still had its art deco charm. The place had a woman's touch: faded flowered curtains, yellowed laced table top dollies, but their condition said she was long gone.

Jack lowered himself into his chair and pointed to a sofa. "Sit!"

Delware noted a shelf of World War II memorabilia: an Air Force insignia, a Good Conduct Medal, a Purple Heart, a glass vial holding what looked like shrapnel – Delware blinked –a Congressional Medal of Honor, its starred blue ribbon wrapped around tarnished brass knuckles.

Jack scratched his unshaven face. "Why the hell did you come here? Couldn't you wait 'til I got to the station? And which idiot told you where I live?" Jack didn't wait for answers. "Let's see your ID."

From the edge of the lumpy sofa, Delware handed over a wallet. Jack inspected the LAPD laminate, stared at its young black face. "I asked for the youngest applicant they had, didn't know they'd send me a coon."

Delware winced. Jack caught it and challenged him with a purposeful stare. Delware flinched. Jack's face was solid granite, his eyes *spooky*; there was an almost supernatural concentration in them. Under that unrelenting stare, Delware was forced to speak his mind. "I'm a *black* man."

"I don't care what you are...as long as you're not a first prize dummy with a lousy attitude. I just didn't know they were sending me a coo-" Jack stopped himself.

Delware pushed a clenched fist into the sofa; his voice trembled. "I'm a law officer like you. No different. And if you're going to refer to my race: I'm *black*."

Not even a minute in and Jack had already found the kid's soft spot. He congratulated himself by poking it again. "Well, let's not get all emotional about the fact you're a spook."

Blood pumped into Delware's ears. He detected the slightest smirk on the old man's face. *Is he goading me?*

Jack handed the wallet back. "So you want to be a detective? You know there are no...*black*...detectives in Homicide?"

Delware rose, surprised to find his legs a little shaky. "I need to use your bathroom."

Jack's eyebrows rose. He had grown old in a segregated army and police force; his Louisianan roots were a world of drinking fountains clearly marked White and Colored.

Delware's defiant eyes stared back. He had grown up in a state of white-only restaurants, white-only theatres, white-only bathrooms. Legally, segregation had ended only four years earlier.

The change in the law tipped the scales for Jack. His eyes relented. He gave a reluctant, "Sure," and pointed his thumb blindly over his shoulder.

When Delware reached a door, Jack jumped with a violent, "Hey!"

Delware spun around.

Jack yelled. "Not that door! The one on the *left!*" He muttered as he sat. "No one goes in there ... not even me."

~ ~ ~

In the cramped bathroom Delware found an unwashed toilet: rimmed dark brown, speckled with black dirt. He grimaced at the stench. "Goddamn. To think brothers marched and died for the right to share this shit."

Delware leaned back on the door for a long minute. He didn't unzip his pants. His bathroom ploy had paid off. He had pegged the old geezer: Jack was no die-hard racist, not if he let a black man use his bathroom. At some point, the old man may have had a black friend or co-worker, maybe even feelings for a black woman. His new partner was like all old timer cops – a real cowboy, trigger happy, pistol-whipping confessions, breaking a hundred laws to enforce one, talking like it was still 1947. Delware despised racial trash talk, but this old man could be his ticket to something higher.

Looking in the mirror, smiling at his dark African good looks, he slid his hands into his pants, pulling back his jacket just enough to reveal the tip of his badge and holster. Delware nodded approvingly and whispered, "Baaaadd mothafucka."

He flushed the toilet with his boot and went back into the hall. He eyed the stacks of unwrapped newspapers on the kitchen floor.

Delware flopped down on the couch, a smiling Black Power stud. He leaned back and asked with ambitious eyes, "So what do you need me to do?"

Jack's dull eyes saw the kid was thinking about making the Detective Bureau: no more patrols or uniforms, having the inside track on headlining murders and every other cop in LA stepping aside when you arrived. But sooner or later, you were left with the bodies. And every day brought more: the five dead children who played with dynamite, the two week old boy with his head cut off by his mother, the fifteen year-old boy who blew his head off with a shotgun, the husband's face staring at his 70 year-old wife who had been raped and murdered, and over the weekend, the severely mutilated body of a pregnant Sharon Tate. Jack knew LA seduced young cops, not its bright sunshine or tanned beach beauties, but those midnight murmurings over the police shortwave, the weird intimacy of walking into a stranger's bedroom in the middle of the night, their half-naked body lifeless at your feet. You saw those chaotic moments, not sentimental casket death, but raw, violent, never pretty death. But in Homicide, when those cases remained open, unchecked, unsolved – *those* victims became your children. The faces you thought about between sips of coffee and swigs of scotch.

For the briefest moment, Jack wanted to tell the young man to forget about it. Go back to a foot patrol and handing out tickets. Where you checked in at four and left the winos behind at midnight, because there was no checking out of Homicide Division. No end to thinking about open cases. Those bodies followed you home, from that day forward, for better or worse, for richer or poorer. Delware's eyes shifted to the gramophone's giant horn, its metal logo of black and white dogs listening intently to a giant Victrola horn. A Hank Williams 78rpm record lay beside it on the worn fake Persian rug. "You from the south, Detective Middleton?"

Jack snapped, "What?"

"I don't know many white men in California who eat grits." Delware's eyes edged toward an old cereal bowl beside Jack's chair.

Jack glanced at the crusty bowl. "My father was. We'd visit...family, vacation."

"Your TV's unplugged. There's a lot of dust on that cord."

Jack grinned at the kid's attempt to interrogate. "I pulled the plug in '63, kid."

Delware raised an eyebrow. "You don't read newspapers, don't watch TV...do you know the first man walked on the moon last month?"

"Ask me if I give a damn." Jack snorted. "I'm not as hep as I use to be."

"Hep?" Delware held back a laugh. "You mean *hip*."

Jack sneered, leaned over and pulled something from the other side of his chair. Delware was shocked by what was handed to him: The Beatles' White Album. Nothing could be more contrary to this room and man: the pristine glow of the all white cover, its modern pop art starkness. Delware owned the album, but seeing it here, touching it now, made no sense at all, as if someone was playing a joke. He muttered, "What is this?"

Jack's gruff voice snapped, "Evidence."

"I don't understand."

"Neither do I. That's why you're here. I need to understand these lyrics. It's all screaming to me. Goddamn noise you kids listen to. Can't understand a word they're saying."

"Why do you need to understand the lyrics?"

"They were written in blood on the walls of the crime scene."

"The Tate murders!"

"Yes, how do you know?"

"It made yesterday's front page – in every newspaper across the country." Delware leaned towards the kitchen of unwrapped papers. "I'm sure it's in there somewhere."

The mockery in the young man's voice was not lost on

Jack. He frowned, staring at his kitchen. "I got a psychopath. And he listens to that record. It's important to him. I think he's one of yours."

"A black?"

Jack glanced at him. "A hippie."

Delware looked doubtful. "That's pretty far out."

"And I say it's even money that drugs have something to do with this."

Delware looked back at the album. "So *these* are the words written in blood."

"It reminds me of a case in '48 – a satanic cult. Ritual murders. Now this psycho – left messages from *that* record. If he kills by it, he'll live by it. That's how I find him. But I need to figure out the message. I need to understand this horseshit you hippies talk."

Delware rolled his eyes. All these old-timers thought anyone under thirty was a hippie.

Delware weighed the album in his hands. "You think the motivation is...from this?"

"This guy's motivation is he's a *psycho*. I've seen these types of murders. It's got the signs of serial murder all over it; it's only a matter of time before we see another. I want you to listen to this record, write out the lyrics. Start with the song Helter Skelter. I want that song by tomorrow. I need to understand what the hell you kids are up to."

Delware placed the album down beside him. "Do you know anything about hippies?"

Jack picked his nose. "I know one when I see one: he looks like Tarzan, walks like Jane, and smells like goddamn Cheetah."

Monday, August 11th, 1969, 12:05 AM

Out of the downtown haze at Spring and 1st rose the white tower of Los Angeles City Hall – a monument from the 1920s boom and an LA icon ever since. Inside was housed LAPD Central Division Headquarters, and above them, the District Attorney's office.

Jack led Delware to the third floor and down a maze of corridors. Here Jack made sense. His old fedora hat and worn tweed suit shared the same era as the dull black speckled floor and decades-old lockers crammed along the walls.

Jack looked back. "Ever been to the third floor?"

Delware shook his head. Black officers were largely segregated and relegated to foot patrols. Delware knew he was one of the few blacks to pass these halls. The Detective Bureau: Vice, Robbery, Bunco had a token black officer each, but Homicide was an all-white inner sanctum.

Fear and fierce pride sparked Delware as he entered. Homicide buzzed with ringing telephones and clacking typewriters. Officers shuffled amidst narrow aisles of old desks piled high with bloated files. Delware kept a cool exterior, yet his pulse raced. He was stepping into the coziest power structure in the LAPD, on the biggest case of the decade, hoping to be the Bureau's first black Homicide detective once it was all over.

Jack turned, his hand stopping Delware. "Just sit tight and keep your nose clean." He waved a finger. "And *don't* draw any attention to yourself."

Walking straight through the chaos – Jack stood out again: the oldest man in the room. Around him were middle-aged men in bright polyester blazers, slacks and sport jackets, a few had hair down to their collars, sporting mustaches and sideburns.

Delware tried to occupy himself with the cork bulletin boards, scanning wanted sheets, procedural bulletins, mug shots. He turned his head to a large board crammed with color photos, the predominant color: red. His legs went numb. These were the Tate murders, the once beautiful people of LA, now butchered, chopped, drenched in their own blood from head to toe. He had seen death, but this was more than murder. This was sadistic, psycho slaughter. His eyes traced their flesh – hundreds of stab wounds. His pupils went wide; his throat dried. Those famous faces draped in blood, their cheeks, foreheads, noses disfigured by gaping slits. On the swollen belly of one victim was carved in long straight strokes: WHITE.

A pale, young detective in a white shirt and black tie confronted Delware. "Can I help you?"

Delware snapped out of it. "Excuse me?"

The young officer's hair was almost in his eyes. "Are you *supposed* to be here?"

Delware puffed his chest, flashed his badge. "I'm with Detective Middleton."

The detective glanced at the badge, then the pictures of the Tate murders. "Oh, you're with the old guy." Connecting the dots, he leaned in and whispered, "You want to make detective?"

Playing it cool, Delware shrugged. "Sure."

The detective gave him a clandestine smile and whispered, "Cool man. But ... heads up. The old man hasn't solved a case in six months, a real bum run, or he's just getting senile." He pointed to a marker board across the room. "See those open cases in red?"

Delware nodded.

"Twenty are his." The detective turned back to Delware. "There's no way he's going to remain lead detective on *this* case. He has to take forced retirement at Christmas anyways. That's how long he's been with the Department."

The young man lit a cigarette. "And watch your back, the guy's a psycho too. A few years ago, he punched the shit out of his partner, put him in the hospital. Now no one on the Bureau wants to be paired with the guy."

"How's he still here then?"

"Chief Parker. They were best friends, but now Parker's gone. Still, be careful, Pat Boyle's got the old man's back." He gave Delware a slight parting wave. "If you ask me, they're just letting him ride it out till Christmas. So don't get your hopes up."

~ ~ ~

Captain Patrick Boyle couldn't believe what he had read and didn't like it. Inside his cramped office, he stewed, his old eyes straining behind horn-rimmed glasses, his enormous belly pushing into the desk, hairy arms protruding from rolled-up sleeves. He stared down at Jack Middleton's First Summary Report for a third time. He moaned. It had been a shitty month. Two of his best detectives were on holiday, leaving a long line of open cases and complaints from the DA's office. The whole Department was getting roasted alive in the press for a number of police shootings of unarmed black men. It was a PR disaster. The black community was up in arms and the Black Panthers were coming off as the good guys. All-white juries acquitting the officers involved only made things worse. The LAPD were fast becoming the most hated cops in America.

Pat tossed the report aside and rubbed his eyes, wishing he could wake up from this nightmare. He heard Dirk Benedict talking with his team just outside his office. A hush fell over them. He knew Jack had arrived. Pat kneaded his gray stubble scalp like a headache was coming on. Dirk was still silent. Pat could just see a sneering Jack at his door, drilling Dirk with his eyes. Pat yelled from his desk as if calling off a bulldog, "Jack, get in here!"

Jack lumbered inside, humiliation and rage stirring him. Before he even saw Pat he knew what he was going to say.

Pat did his best to not look at Jack. "I read your initial report." He shook his head. "What is this garbage?!"

Jack closed the door. "What?"

"This summary report! Your conclusion! Jack. Hippies?" Pat held up the report. The form was neatly typed except the twelve empty lines under Suspect Description, scrawled across the blank lines in huge letters: DAMN DIRTY HIPPIES!

Pat's eyes bulged with anger. "A bunch of crazed hippies killed these people! If I didn't know this was from you, I'd laugh."

"That's what the evidence says."

Pat dropped the report on his desk. "I can smell you from here."

"What?"

"From behind my desk, Jack. You smell like a boozehound."

Jack looked down at his jacket and sniffed.

Pat rose. "You've been the town drunk for eight years, showing up for duty looking like you've been sleeping in your car and *now* you're getting ambitious? Your summary reports are always late and usually unreadable." Pat couldn't help it; he let out a small laugh. "Look at this!

Except for your suspect report, I can actually read it and I find it on my desk first thing in the morning!" Pat sat again trying to calm down. He lit a cigar, then looked at it like he wondered how it got in his hand, then stabbed it out absentmindedly. "I've been slip-routing you skid row cases for years now and you haven't said squat."

Jack yanked a chair over and sat. "I'm sick of this low priority shit."

Pat's fat hairy fingers curled into a fist. "Well, you'd never know it! You've been coasting like a slow boat to China."

Jack sat with an impassive, arrogant smirk. "You know, Patty...I liked your dumb Irish ass so much better before you became one of the brass."

Pat hated that look. They had been partners since '47, drinking buddies since before that, but for the last decade Jack had just been nothing but a poor example of a police officer.

Pat's fingers pushed Jack's report off his desk blotter like it stank. "Hippies? Anti-war, peace-loving hopheads! What do we book 'em for? Drugs, Jack, maybe a fist fight. Now you're saying – just overnight – they've become multiple-murderers ... a group of them. Thrill killers? For Christ's sake! Why are you still here, Jack? You've done your twenty – twenty years ago, and earned that pension twice. Do you actually believe this crap you wrote?!"

Jack slouched deeper into his chair. "C'mon Patty, look at those kids, will ya! They're filthy! Immoral flag-burning draft-dodging communists! Hell, the Reds could invade for all they care. They'd pass Khrushchev a marijuana cigarette as long as they can walk around with long hair – looking like women, dressed like homos and talking like eastside coloreds!"

"Jack! Multiple-murders are done by two people – at the most. Serial killers are secretive loners. Your report outlines a *group* of serial killers! I've never seen – or *heard* – of a case of serial killers ... joining forces."

"Patty, all those runaways coming in to the city, all the drugs they're taking. It's possible. In '48, there was-"

"Jack, this ain't twenty years ago. You're not bombing Berlin and I ain't storming Normandy. I got a second opinion from Dirk. He looked at the photos and we agree. This is a revenge murder – possibly a drug deal gone bad. Ray Claborn, the grounds keeper who lived out back in the guesthouse, has dropped off the face of the earth." Pat flipped open a file on his desk, "Ray Edward Claborn is a three-time loser. This young Okie has an outstanding warrant on drug charges and is a known associate of motorcycle gang members trafficking drugs. It's simple. A definite drug, gang-related murder anyway you look at it. Since Dirk's been on the motorcycle gangs for a while, I've designated him to be chief investigator and detached detectives to him."

Jack jumped to his feet, his face flushing red. "You're kicking me off! I caught the squeal!"

Pat launched from his chair, came around his desk like a bull. "You just happened to be on Day Watch when this was just another one-eighty-seven. This has made headlines around the world. Maybe if you'd been sober over the weekend you'd realized what a panic the city is in. There's a run on the gun shops, locksmiths and alarm companies. Everyone's out buying watchdogs, f'christsakes. Upstairs is going ape-shit and they're looking at me for answers!" Pat started laughing, almost hysterically. "And you come in here hung-over telling me dope-smoking peaceniks are suddenly transforming like werewolves into multiple murderers!" He snatched Jack's report from his desk. "You think I should show this to the District Attorney! What do you think Vince is going to say to me?"

Pat spoke more angrily than he had intended. He regretted it. It broke his heart to say it to his friend: "I think you need to work another case."

Jack felt the floor slipping away beneath him. He looked to the closed blinds that hid Pat's office from the rest of the Division. "Patty, every detective on roster will be assigned to this for weeks. What are you saying, I'm the only one on regular rotation?" Jack shook his head. "Patty, don't let me go out this way...like a disgrace."

Pat made his way back to his desk to avoid Jack's eyes. "Jack, there's a lot of unsolved on that board and most of it belongs to you. I know you think this case will be your big redemption, but-"

"Patty, you know that's luck, I been picking up losers." Jack tried to find his friend's eyes, forcing himself into his gaze. "You know, you've been routing me cases that usually go unsolved no matter who works them. You've had as many over the years; I'm just getting all mine in a row!"

Pat sat. "Jack, times have changed. People are different. These victims, and probably their murderers, are young enough to be your grandkids."

Jack leaned over his desk. "I have a lead into the hippie community. I've got a secret weapon on this one."

Pat had learned to tolerate slovenly Jack for the last six years, but the return of ambitious Jack scared him.

Jack ploughed on. "He's out there in the office, right now." He pointed towards the window. "He's by the door."

Pat gave the Venetian blinds a distrustful look. Reluctantly, he leaned towards the glass and used two fingers to scissor open the slats.

Out in the office, he saw one of the older detectives confronting a young black man. Pat could not comprehend what was transpiring, but then, the frowning black man pinned a badge on his jacket.

Pat suddenly recognized the young officer and let the slats flap back.

"Oh, Jack, you've got to be kidding."

Jack smiled. "That kid's gold."

"No, Jack, he's black."

Jack's smile grew wider.

Pat frowned and shook his head. "You sonvabitch, Jack! Do you know that kid at all? It's Delware Hicks!"

Jack's eyes popped. "You know him?"

"Yes, Jack, I do! When you're Chief of Detectives you have to know who's applying for the Bureau. Not like you who gets to lay back playing private dick."

Jack smiled, enjoying Pat's rant; he was familiar with its opening line.

Pat's anger got him out of his seat and pacing. "That kid's applied five times. He aced the detective's exam three times. He doesn't get the message: No Negros in Homicide."

Jack shook his head. He knew the unspoken rule, but didn't care.

Pat dropped his hands on the desk and leaned over it. "And that kid almost got kicked off the force."

"Why?"

"He got assigned to Waylon."

Jack laughed and kicked his feet up on Pat's desk. "Mr. Ku Klux Klan?"

Pat resented anyone on the force being referred to like that. Jack could be smug and loose-lipped; public relations was not a factor in Jack's job. Pat stood straight and sneered. "Waylon's no Klansman."

Jack's eyes gleefully watched a vein on Pat's forehead begin to pulsate. "Yeah? Waylon Hampton? Christ, the guy's actually got a Confederate General on his family tree! He ever tell you any stories about his Grand Dragon daddy? Or tell you any Martin Luther *Coon* jokes?"

The remarks made the vein bulge purple. Pat dropped his elbows on his desk and his head into his hands.

Jack knew that gesture was a bad sign. Jack's smile disappeared. He took his feet off the desk and pretended to care. "So what happened between Delware and Waylon?"

Pat spoke through his hands. "Waylon insisted on calling him Officer Nappy in front of his whole squad. On the day Martin Luther King was shot, the kid just cracked, pulled his service revolver on Waylon."

"Ahhh, I remember hearing that, so *that* was Delware. Would have loved to seen Waylon's face."

Pat came up with a slightly amused grin. "The problem is that the LAPD have to recruit from the human race. Waylon's far from an exemplary officer, but he's a good tactical officer. I wouldn't go on a raid without him."

"How did Delware get out of it?"

"Said he'd go to the newspapers with a detailed account of Waylon's MO."

Jack laughed, "Smart cookie!"

"Yeah, Delware wouldn't accept a transfer to an all black unit. He actually had the brass so nervous they promoted him, giving him rotations into Narcotics – as undercover when needed."

Jack sat back, impressed. "He leveraged an expulsion into a promotion. That kid can turn shit into clover."

"Yeah, and now you bring him in through the front door."

"He's not *in*, Patty, he's assisting. There's a big difference."

"You don't think that kid's been all ears for an opportunity like this? You're the sucker now, Jack. No one would assign a Negro to you. Bet *he* approached *you*, right? Bet his sergeant doesn't even know where *he* is."

Jack's eyes widened. He let out a laugh. "That's why he

came to my house! Sneaky sumbitch." Admiration sparkled in Jack's eyes. "Well, I got to say...the kid's good."

Pat frowned. His jowls formed new chins.

Jack leaned forward in his chair. "Patty, he pegged me for a southerner by just looking at my cereal bowl. And get this. The kid's at my house and asks to go to the bathroom."

Pat laughed against his will. "In your house?"

"Yeah, and I let him."

"Hold on, I still can't believe you had a colored in your house: you're saying you let him use your bathroom?"

"Yeah. And you know what I hear? Nothing. No pissing, no shitting. Not even a fart. The kid's testing me! Seeing if I'm a Klansman or something...what do the kids call that?"

Pat's eyebrows rose. "A racist?"

"Yeah, see how much of a *racist* I am."

"Good God, Jack. *Racist*? Never thought I'd live to hear a commie word like that come from *your* mouth. You sound like a damn dirty hippie."

Jack grinned. "Yeah, I'm hip."

Pat's eyes rolled.

Jack bent forward waving an earnest finger. "That bathroom stunt – that's good police work. I didn't even see it coming. That's why I want him. He's colored. *They'll* never see him coming."

Pat leaned over to the window and flipped the blind again, taking a long look. "Jack, that's the first time I seen a Negro up here that wasn't in cuffs. There are Bureau boys who won't stand for this." He let the blind go with an agitated flick. "*This* is what I hate about you, when the heat is on – you raise the ante!"

Jack did his best impression of an innocent, deserving man. "Let me stay on it. Look, I'll keep the kid on a tight leash. I don't need to be primary. The Department owes me that much. *You* owe me that much."

Pat sighed. He disliked seeing Jack come as close to begging as a man like Jack could. Pat felt strangely ashamed.

Jack saw him wavering and jumped in. "It's a big case and you know City Hall will be pouring huge resources into it. Then you can stand up and honestly say you're following every possible lead...doing everything we can."

Pat leaned back and pondered the offer, his thick fingers absentmindedly pinching his chin. "I'll have to talk to Dirk."

Jack snapped. "Fuck Dirk! I just need access to the evidence. Let Dirk run around in fuckin' circles like a chicken with its-"

Pat's face soured. Jack softened his tone. "I mean. I'll stay out of his way. I know I'm right. A month, that's all I need. I'll pin this maniac. He's right under our noses; all I ask is a chance."

Pat frowned.

Jack found Pat's eyes. "One last chance?"

Pat sighed. On Jack's rise to the top, he had always taken care of Pat as his younger partner. In Jack's decline, he had never asked for favors. Now that he had, it reminded him of Jack's glory days. Pat realized his frustration with Jack over the last ten years was watching so much talent go to waste. He took a deep breath and pointed a judge's finger. "You buy some mouthwash so you don't come in here stinking like booze! And the colored kid ... fine ... on the street, but not up here. Keep him out of the office. And for God's sake, don't go on a bender and beat the kid up like your last partner! We don't want any *incidents*. If you hurt the kid, they'll have to goddamn make him Chief of Police! *And* I'm the only one left covering your ass, Jack, and I'm sick of it. Any shit and you're off the case! I'll throw you out of the Department myself."

Jack was trying his best not to smile as he made a quick escape out the door. "Sure, sure, Patty, don't worry."

~ ~ ~

Jack emerged from Pat's office, flipped off Dirk and his team, and strode through the maze of desks. Delware stood at the door, no longer harassed, but looking defensive. Jack brushed by him. "You're with me, kid."

The pair entered the hallway. Jack donned his hat and headed downstairs.

Delware tried to keep up. "So we're cool?"

Jack grunted. "If you mean, are you assigned to me? Yes, tomorrow, Day Watch."

Delware grinned, a bounce in his step.

They hit the second floor and Delware's swagger and smile died. "Where we going?"

"Narcotics."

"Why?"

"Why? 'Cause I said that's where we're going."

Delware's face crinkled with worry. "Listen I-"

"Shut your yap. Don't question my authority! You're giving me a headache. I want to talk to your sergeant."

"But-"

"Quit your squawking, will ya! You're bothering me. I'm trying to think over here."

In a split second they were in Narcotics.

Jack shouted, "Who's in charge!"

A red-haired, mid-size man turned and spoke with a southern drawl, "Lieutenant Smith is out, I'm Sergeant –"

"Detective Middleton, Homicide, I sent a request for an assistant."

"Yeah, Officer Jacobs was sent upstairs, he couldn't find you. Do you want-"

"Don't bother. I'm here to tell you Officer Hicks here showed up at my house this morning and I'm assuming he missed roll call."

The sergeant's eyes damned Delware with a glance. "Yes, he missed roll call."

"Well, he pretended he was sent by your Department to assist me."

The sergeant's jaw dropped. His face turned red. He was about to yell when Jack cut him off. "Well, I've accepted him as my assistant on the case, so you can tell this Jacobs to go to hell. Is that clear, sergeant? I want Officer Hicks detached to me as of tomorrow morning."

Jack eyed Delware, but spoke to the sergeant. "But I won't be needing him till then so...I'll leave him in your command. You can do whatever you want with Officer Hicks for the rest of day."

Jack smiled and tipped his hat at Delware. "Now stay at your post, report to me tomorrow morning: 0800."

Jack slipped out the door.

All the way down the hall Jack could hear the sergeant yelling at Delware. He grinned.

Tuesday, August 12th, 1969, 8:00 AM

The next morning, Delware made his way to Homicide only to be stopped at the door. The same young detective who had questioned him the day before stood in the doorway smoking a cigarette. He leaned an arm on the doorframe, blocking Delware. "The old guy said to meet him out front. Look for a black Packard – *real* old-fashioned."

Delware descended from the third floor and emerged out the main doors of LA's white-towered City Hall. He stood by a column looking for the Packard.

Inside his car, Jack glanced at the young black man and honked the horn.

Delware sauntered over and opened the door.

Jack grinned. "How are you this morning?"

Delware sat, looking frustrated. "I'd be a whole lot better if you hadn't set me up in front of my sergeant yesterday."

"Yeah? You woulda figured a way out of it, huh?"

"Yes."

"I bet you would have too. Let that be a lesson to you: don't *fuck* around with me." Jack started the car. "You can fuck around with your sergeant. You can fuck with the whole Department for all I care. Been with the

Department for over thirty years and I'm sick of its bullshit. *But* you fuck around with me...I'll kill you...and make it look like an accident. And that's no figure of speech there. Back in the Forties when we couldn't close a case because of weak evidence, we didn't bother with no judge and jury. We shot the sumbitch and made it look like an accident. And that's what I'll do to you, if you fuck around with *me*."

Delware sneered, defiant. "Yeah? Well, what do I get if I don't fuck around?"

Jack pulled the car away from the curb and into traffic. "I'll teach you how to shoot someone and make it look like an accident."

On Spring Street, Jack sped through a red light, then ran all the stop signs along Temple. He only glanced before speeding through a red that lead to the highway where he raced through traffic.

Delware looked over at Jack, amazed. "You just went through three stop signs and two red lights. Don't you ever stop?"

Jack stomped on the brakes. Tires squealed. Delware flew forward, bracing the dashboard. The car skidded, stuttering to a stop in the middle of the 101. Jack turned off the car and took the keys out of the ignition. He stared at Delware. "Is this what you want?"

Speeding cars came from behind, swerving, tires screeching, horns blaring. Delware looked at Jack like he was crazy.

Jack eyed Delware with an eerie calm. "Happy now? Have we stopped long enough? OK? Can we get to where we're going?"

Delware looked nervously behind at the oncoming traffic doing its best to miss the parked Packard. "Yeah! Go! Go! GO!"

Jack pulled out a large silver flask from his inside

jacket pocket, casually unscrewed the lid and swigged.

He handed the flask to Delware. "You look like you need some of this."

"GO!"

Starting the car, Jack punched the gas petal down to the floorboards. The car jolted forward. In seconds, they were flying past other motorists.

Jack kept his eyes on the road as he weaved through traffic. "Look. I get it. Youse blacks want to be equal with us whites. Fine. But you ain't *my* equal. I don't care if you're white, black, or fuckin' blue; I'm your senior officer. You can ask questions, but I don't want an earful of *your* thoughts on how I do *my* job. Do what I say and leave the rest to me. I'm going to solve this case...and *you're* going to watch and hopefully goddamn learn something."

~ ~ ~

Pulling off the 101, the Packard slowed onto Santa Monica headed for the Hollywood Hills. Jack hung an arm out the window, took a side street to enjoy one of LA's most affluent neighborhoods. Soon, towering palm trees lined the road. White Spanish mansions passed in the windows: tiled roofs, long driveways, sculptured landscapes.

Delware sulked, but played it like indifference. Jack surveyed his silent, slouching partner: tight white t-shirt over his muscular chest, a wide belt with a brass buckle shaped like an American eagle, a brown leather vest covering his clipped holster and tight blue jeans with flared bottoms. In Jack's eyes, his partner looked like he should be cuffed in the back seat.

Underneath Delware's cool exterior, he was watching his plans go to shit. Forget senile, the old man was insane, even *deadly*. With every glance out the window, he sunk lower in his seat, embarrassed to be on the street with this fossil. The car might pass as vintage cool, but the old man was as square as they came in his brown 1940s three-piece tweed suit, tie and matching fedora hat.

Jack glanced at Delware's Afro. "So you don't get your hair processed? You like it all nappy like that?"

Delware drilled Jack with his eyes. "Yeah, man, haven't you heard? Black is beautiful. I let it grow natural. I'm black and proud. I don't want to look like no white man. Dig?"

Jack pointed to an outline in Delware's pants pocket. "What's that?"

Delware pulled out a comb. "You never seen an afro comb before?"

Jack frowned. "I have, but never got a chance to ask what it's called."

Delware looked away. "Well, now you know."

"So, you into that Black Power horseshit?"

Delware glanced at the old man. "What am I? A suspect?"

Jack shrugged. "Hey. We're just talking...right?"

"OK." Delware shrugged. "Yeah, man."

"Then let me ask you something, kid. You support that cop killer Huey Newton?"

"If you ask me, and you are... Newton's a political prisoner. I don't see any real evidence that says otherwise. He's in jail because he's a Black Panther, not a killer." Delware slipped on big black sunglasses. He oozed black militant cool. He slid down in his seat, adjusted the bulge in his tight jeans and...*relaxed.*

Jack eyed him with disgust. "Take those things off."

Delware sat up. "What?"

"Take off your fuckin' sunglasses!"

"Why?"

"You look like a Panther, f'christsakes. You ain't a narc on the street no more. This is plain clothes, not undercover. You dress decent. Tie and jacket next time!"

Delware laughed, "Decent, man?"

"Yeah, like a cop." Jack dug in. "Jeans are for *farmers.*" He shook his head. "How can you go around looking like that?"

Delware grinned behind his thick shades and spoke smooth and slow, "'Cause I look gooood." He slid back down in his seat. "Look man, people aren't so uptight anymore." His eyes drifted to a young blonde in a mini-skirt and low-cut blouse walking a dog. Delware leered. "And the ladies like to let it all hang out."

Jack caught Delware's eyes on the white girl. He sneered, gritting his teeth behind tight lips, glancing at the girl now in the rearview mirror. "It's getting hard to pick out the prostitutes. Don't girls know they look like hookers?"

Jack fumbled in his jacket for a cigar.

Delware grinned. "If you weren't so old, you'd dress a little better yourself, get out of those raggity ass threads."

Jack gave a vicious smile, holding back his rage. "You're fuckin' lucky I need you. I wanted some fuckin' hippie cop and now I'm sitting beside one. Fuck, it's shittier than I thought."

Delware bit back. "I ain't no hippie."

Jack wasn't buying it. Pulling out the cigar, he nodded sarcastically. "Oh yeah. You're not into that peace and love?"

"No man, I'm into loving myself a piece of ass."

"How can you be a cop and support the Panthers?"

"Hey, if a white man can carry a shotgun, why can't a brother?"

Jack tossed the cigar into his mouth and talked around it. "Yeah, but you're a cop, you want that shotgun pointed at you?"

When Jack glanced away to turn onto Sunset Blvd, Delware gave him the finger. "A brother won't have no reason to point his gun at me. Shit man, you don't get it. When a racist cop rousts someone because he's black and then that brother shows up shot-in-the-back, what's a brother to do? What's LAPD ever done to stop it? Nothing! A community has a right to protect itself. No black man is going to the seventy-seventh crying '*Police brutality.*' What do you think is going to happen to him? What all-white jury is going to believe a brother over a white cop? Hell, they're turning dogs and fire hoses on my people for exercising their right to *free speech.*"

Jack took the cigar out of his mouth and waved it at Delware. "Listen kid, you better decide which side you're on."

"Justice. That's the side I'm on. Like all cops should be."

"Then why you dress like an eastside nigg-"

Delware whipped off his sunglasses. His eyes could have left two smoking bullet holes in the old man's head.

Jack blinked. The deadly look in Delware's eyes was unmistakable; the kid was dangerous, maybe even a killer. Jack smiled. "You got a good stare, kid. I'll give you that. That actually got my heart pumping."

Jack turned his eyes to the road while he fished for matches. "I know it ain't fashionable to talk about youse – *blacks* – like we used to. But I ain't fashionable. See?"

Delware shook off the adrenalin, sat back and gave Jack's rumpled suit a once over. "Yeah, I see."

Jack turned off Sunset onto Benedict Canyon, a winding canyon road above Hollywood, uphill all the way.

They passed three teenaged white girls under a palm tree selling *Maps to the Stars*. Delware's head turned, eyeing the attractive scenery. The back of Jack's hand slapped him across the chest. "What the fuck are you looking at?"

Delware's natural instinct was to return the blow, but

his mind was so stunned by the sudden burst of violence that he just stared in disbelief.

Jack's face was turning all shades of red. "I won't stand for that! Listen, kid, I'm not into that *free love* horseshit! That's where I draw the line: the mixing of the races! I don't care if the Supreme Court did strike down the miscegenation laws last year. You ask me, the races don't belong together. Every time they are, there's some sort of trouble. And who do you think ends up in the middle? *Us.* I got all types of tolerance for youse people, but if you ever leer at a white woman in my presence, I'll fuckin' pop your eyes out of your head."

Delware was jumping in his seat, his hands clutching the dash and his seat so his arms wouldn't start swinging at Jack. "You're unbelievable, old man! You got some serious hang ups. Man, you ain't got issues ... you got the whole damn subscription! You gotta get with it. Get where it's at, man!"

"I ain't asking you to believe me and I ain't getting with anything. Just do what I say!"

Delware shifted in his seat. "You need to get laid, gramps. And why should I? Why should I do what you say?"

Jack grinned, playing the card he had been holding back so long. "'Cause I know you're tired of pounding the pavement, walking that beat in that sweaty wool uniform – that goddamn Sam Browne belt digging into your back! Think you'd be happy in Narcotics, but no, you got to be at the top of the food chain with the white boys in Homicide. Well, you ain't got a snowball's chance in Hell, *but* if you do: I'm it! I'll fuckin' write you up so bad you'll be back in uniform directing traffic. And the only way you'll ever get near the third floor again is if you become a *janitor.* That's why you're going to do *exactly* what I say."

Delware slouched deep in his seat. "Sh-iiiitt."

Jack dug in a jacket pocket and smiled at his matches. "Stop talking eastside, kid. I heard you talk normal yesterday. What's the matter with you?"

Delware muttered, "I been undercover for six months, man. You just can't wash the streets off you in a single day."

The truth of those words hit Jack. He spit out his window, lit his cigar and left the car to steer itself for a dangerous moment. After three long puffs, he looked over at the young man and softened his tone. "You been working undercover a bit too long ... but you're in a car now, not on the street."

Jack turned onto Cielo Drive.

9:02 AM

Police sawhorses corralled the gate at Cielo's dead end. A lone black-and-white stood guard. A bored officer leaned against the car, cigarette butts circling his feet.

The Packard pulled up.

Jack got out and slammed the door. He leaned in the window. "We're going up."

Delware remained slouched in his seat, his defiant eyes following Jack to the gate. He muttered, "Up yours, you crazy fuckin' fool." He shoved his door open.

Delware followed Jack up the long driveway. The grounds were peaceful, normal. Jack glanced over at Delware. The kid looked edgy. Good. Jack liked his partners on their toes.

Jack stared up at the mansion. "There were far too many dicks and techs here the other day. It's like sending in a football team to commit a burglary. Can't really think or see with so many people around. You and me, we're going to take our time. You know drugs and all that hippie shit; that's our key. You tell me what you see. OK, kid? We'll find something Dirk and his team missed."

Delware, hands in pockets, kept a pace behind. "Yeah, you're sure of that? We're going to find what thirty other detectives missed."

"I guarantee it."

"Why you so sure?"

"'Cause they always miss something."

~ ~ ~

Jack circled around to the back of the house following a low hedge. A guest house came into view, then the lawn sloped down to the service entrance. "They came in through here."

Jack pointed to a window above a stone stairway with a slashed screen. The pair paused before the torn mesh.

Delware stared unimpressed. As a patrolman, he'd responded to plenty of burglary calls. A slashed screen was typical and indicated an experienced burglar who knew better than to jimmy a door – hardly the work of a madman. If anything, this weakened Jack's theory. The only thing that stood out was the shape of the cut – unusual. It was L-shaped.

Jack tilted his hat back with a finger. "You ever see a screen cut like that?"

Delware shook his head. "Can't say I have."

Jack walked away. "You should see this. It's a bit of a mystery."

Turning a corner, a large in-ground swimming pool came into view. The majestic oaks gave way; the lawn dropped, revealing a sweeping view of a desert canyon.

Jack led Delware to a patio door; the white curtains behind the sliding glass were spattered with blood. He pointed to the ground. "Those bloody shoe prints belong to goddamn patrolmen, but look at this one."

They squatted. There on the stone step was a bloody barefoot print.

Jack asked, "What can you tell by that?"

"Female. Small. Maybe even a teenager."

Jack nodded.

Delware's fingers touched the stone and traced the

bloody print. "One of the victims?"

"Doesn't match a single one."

"Someone got away?"

Jack and Delware's eyes followed the fading trail of barefoot prints on the patio. They led across the manicured lawn to the wild desert beyond.

Jack studied the wilderness. "Perhaps there's a living witness."

"Any idea who?"

"No one's come forward. We've searched the brush and the desert. No bodies out there. The guess is: someone got away, maybe only slightly wounded."

Jack scanned the trees on the western slope. "She's out there somewhere. I just can't figure out why she hasn't made contact."

"Do you think they might have kidnapped her?"

Jack stood and stared into the canyon. "Maybe."

~ ~ ~

They checked out the guesthouse where Ray Claborn once lived. Jack wasn't interested. His gut told him the missing groundskeeper wasn't their man. They circled around the house, passing the swimming pool.

Jack snapped his fingers at Delware. "You got those lyrics?"

Delware pulled a folded dog-eared paper from his pocket, held it out.

Giving the rumpled page a dirty look, Jack snatched it. His voice a perfect mix of disgust and sarcasm, "Well, Officer, this sure looks like some Grade A – Number One paperwork here." He waved the sheet in Delware's face. "Thanks for this."

Jack stopped and read. Delware braced himself as he tried to look causal.

Finishing the page, Jack looked at Delware, then down at the page again as if someone had crapped in his hands.

His face turned red, but he spoke restrained, "Is this right? Are these the lyrics to Helter Skelter?"

"I listened to them all night, again and again, that's what he's singing."

Jack crumpled the page with one hand. "Is it all in slang? Does it mean anything at all?"

Delware shrugged, "The one phrase: *coming down fast.*"

"Which means?"

"Bad things are about to happen."

Jack's eyes asked for more.

Delware shuffled in place. "As in: 'the shit's coming down.'"

"So this is what passes for lyrics today, absolute nonsense: no story, just random words?" Jack jammed the ball of paper into his pocket. "This is what drugs have done to your generation."

"So, you giving up on your theory, that there's some deep meaning in it?"

Jack headed for the mansion. "Hell, no. It's always a jumble at the start. First, we sort out the pieces, *then*, we fit them together."

~ ~ ~

Jack and Delware stopped at the front door. Its bloody message was still there, each man reading it inside his head. They entered.

They paused before the living room. The bodies were gone, their outlines remained.

Jack stared calmly at the blood spatters and stained carpets. After a couple thousand cases, he knew that almost all the clues he needed were right here...*if* he read them right.

For all the crime scenes Delware had seen, nothing compared to this. This was a dozen murders in a single room. A real battlefield. Large areas of black dried blood covered the white carpet. Every wall and piece of furniture was splashed. Delware's eyes were drawn to a blood sprayed American flag draped over the couch. He pointed, "Was that left by the murderers?"

Jack shook his head. "No, victims' idea of home decoration."

Jack held his breath and then let it out slow. "A crime scene is a story, but there's always a couple pages missing. So we have to read in between the lines and figure out what's missing." He took a small step into the living room, his eyes deliberately reading the room. "One reason Patty wants to find a drug deal angle is 'cause then there's a connection between victim and perpetrator. It's always the lover, family member, business colleague...or dealer."

Jack stepped over an outline like the body was still there. He had memorized every corpse and for him they were still in the room. "It's very difficult to find a serial killer because there is no personal relationship with the victim. A psychopath kills for the sake of killing. He doesn't need a reason, just a victim."

In the middle of the room, Jack paused to reconstruct the crime. He stared a moment, then closed his eyes. A moment later, he opened them slow and careful like lifting a coffin lid. In his mind's eye the dried blood on the walls turned red and shiny, suddenly it was night and every light in the room was on. In his mind the scene now played in reverse: knocked over tables and lamps righted themselves, bodies rose from where they fell. The blood on the walls flew back into still struggling victims. His calculated trajectories showed their last movements before they collapsed. Jack could see the knives plunging in, the directions the blades came from. The only thing missing: the killers. In Jack's mind, they were empty air. He saw only knives floating and plunging down as if held by ghostly hands.

Then it ended. The crime scene had spoken. Now, he played it forward. He followed the victims in their final moments, heard their screams and the heavy thuds as they hit the floor. He read their dying faces, wishing they could whisper to him from beyond the grave: what they saw, who they saw. Delware watched Jack following a trail of blood. Jack was following Sharon Tate and ended up behind the couch where she fell. He squatted. Delware came up beside him. Jack watched Sharon's last breaths. His wide eyes saw Sharon slip away – the struggle leaving her: eyes closing, face muscles slacking, her nightmare evening finally ending.

The vision ceased. Jack was back in the sunny room, before him lay only carpet dried hard with black blood.

He stood up and scanned the room. "It's in here somewhere. A psycho always leaves a signature. Like when a man marries a woman, he puts a ring on her finger. So every nut leaves ... or takes ... something ... to make this, his."

Delware's eyes roved the large bloody letters on the walls: Helter Skelter, Piggies. He whispered, *"Ma-tha-fucka*. These are some freaked out maniacs."

Jack looked up at the walls and smiled. "Patty and Dirk think it's a ploy the killers wrote to throw us off. So we won't look for direct connections to the victims. It's a bad bet. Never discard a piece of evidence or ignore what's right in front of you. Never drop anything till it's been thoroughly examined." Jack waved around the room. "If the writing was staged, there would be more staging." His eyes hunted. "Murder's a primal act. Cool heads never prevail. Staged murders always read funny: bodies are moved, blood spatters don't line up. Clues come up *way* too easy."

Delware surveyed the outlined carnage. "Well, it certainly looks like the work of hardcore freaks."

Both men moved slowly, floating over blood stains, contemplating random objects.

Minutes later, Jack stopped at a cherry-wood bookshelf, expensive leather-bound books from floor to ceiling, a few scattered at his feet. "Delware come here."

Jack pointed to a high shelf. "Look at the books."

Delware tiptoed through the evidence. "Yeah?"

"Notice anything?"

Delware placed a hand on his cocked hip. "It's a mess, like everything else."

"Yeah, it is, but *look* at the bookshelves. And then, look at the rest of the room."

Delware studied a moment, then it dawned. "It's only that one shelf that's disturbed! All the tables and chairs are knocked over like signs of a struggle, but the rest of the shelves are in perfect order, no signs of impact." He stepped closer and pointed. "Only these few books from this one shelf...second from the top. These books weren't knocked over in a struggle. They were pulled off on purpose."

Jack smiled. "Now, if we didn't have a football team in here the first day it would have been more obvious, but now these books on the floor have been kicked about by patrolmen."

They scanned the scattered books.

Delware asked, "Was there something behind the books? Was this staged?"

"Maybe." Jack tiptoed through the books and stopped. He whispered as if his very breath might disturb evidence, "Delware."

Delware's eyes followed Jack's. There, on the white carpet, was a black Bible.

Jack squatted.

Delware squatted beside him. "What is it?"

"Look at the books, then the Bible."

Delware's eyes jumped from books to Bible, again and again. He saw it. "Jack! There are pages hanging out. Someone was ripping pages."

"That's right, kid. You see any other books ripped up?"

Delware checked again. "Not one."

Jack took a pen from his jacket pocket to open the Bible. He carefully flipped pages to where they were torn out. It was from the very back, the last book of the Bible.

Delware leaned over Jack's shoulder. "Why would someone rip pages out?"

Jack's pen shifted through the torn pages. Thinking aloud, he whispered, "Wonder if it means anything...the missing pages are *all* from The Book of Revelation."

"The Apocalypse of Saint John?"

Jack looked up at Delware, "You know your Bible, kid?"

Delware nodded. "My mother never missed a prayer meeting or Sunday service."

"My wife was the same way. Use to drag me to church every Sunday." Jack looked around at the bloody room and then to Delware. "Does this look like the final battle of Armageddon to you?"

Jack's eyes returned to the black Bible, his face almost Buddha-like in its calm, his eyes lucid as if contemplating the face of God. He whispered and did not even hear himself say, "A good book always hides something."

Then he flinched. He stood and walked briskly to the wall, his feet treading through the outlined bodies he had so carefully avoided just moments ago. Gazing up at the bloody letters, his rough fingertips touched the white wall. He whispered to himself, *"Look at that."*

Delware navigated over. "What?"

His voice startled Jack out of the reverie. Jack pointed to the letters. "See the strokes?"

"Yeah."

"Notice anything?"

Delware strained his eyes, but came up with nothing.

Jack asked, "What would you say they were written with?"

Delware looked puzzled, "Too wide to be fingers. A cloth, small towel?"

"A blood soaked cloth could write many strokes, a whole letter. Notice how each stroke drips? That means whatever was used – didn't hold the blood and had to be soaked again and again – for every stroke. You wouldn't need to do that with cloth."

Jack glanced back at the Bible. Delware followed his stare.

Delware turned back to Jack and questioned with his eyes.

Jack just smiled.

It hit Delware like a brick. "The pages. The missing pages from the Bible!"

Jack corrected, "Pages from The Apocalypse." He looked up at the wall. "And what is the Apocalypse?"

Delware was surprised his mother's sermons had at last become useful. "The end of times, Judgment Day, the revenge of God, divine destruction and chaos."

Jack smiled. He tapped his nose and pointed at Delware, signaling he had hit it right on the nose. Like a teacher to a blackboard, Jack pointed to the letters. "It's slang. How would you describe divine chaos? Apocalyptic anarchy? What's a more modern word for chaos?"

Delware could see where Jack was going. He looked up at the bloody letters. "Helter Skelter."

~ ~ ~

They walked down the long oak-lined drive from the mansion.

Delware asked, "So, what's the plan?"

"Dirk is lead investigator and in some ways that's to

our advantage. Even with his theory, he's still gotta run in a dozen different directions, knocking the case down the totem pole: burglary gone wrong, mob hit, revenge, drug freak out, drug burn, lover's quarrel, until he narrows it. Even then it's likely he'll miss the mark, 'cause I doubt he'll like the conclusion. He's already dismissing the evidence that leads right to it...because it's too incredible."

"That hippies did this?"

Jack nodded and instructed, "Suspect everyone."

He shook his head. "This whole crime scene stinks, kid. It's not a normal murder. And there's nothing even remotely remarkable about this missing groundskeeper, or his record. Yet Dirk's still gotta track down Ray Claborn who will be on the top of his short list of suspects. That could take weeks, maybe months." Jack spit, lit a cigar and looked back at the mansion. "Hell, even motorcycle gangs – who are bat-shit crazy – don't fit this. No. This is some psycho Judgment Day horseshit we're looking at. And all the rules and procedures go out the window with it."

They got to the gate. The lone patrolman stamped out another finished cigarette.

Delware stopped in his tracks.

Jack got a few steps ahead, before he noticed and turned. "What is it, kid?"

Delware's eyes went *wide*. "I saw something."

He dashed back to the house.

Jack watched him go, then slowly followed.

He found Delware in the living room.

What Jack saw seemed a strange vision: the way the sunlight fell on the red and white stripes of the American flag draped over the couch, the white wall dripping with the bloody letters: Helter Skelter, the black man in the foreground, with his back to him.

"Delware?"

"I remembered this plate on the edge of the coffee

table, yet there's no tea cups, not even a coffee mug in sight."

Delware slowly turned, in his hand a black plate with three white sugar cubes.

Jack looked down at the cubes. "What?"

Delware held the plate high as if offering it to Jack. "I think this is LSD."

3:14 PM

The rattle of pipes haunted the LAPD basement. The evidence room was a floor to ceiling cage. Inside its chain-linked walls, a dirty light bulb illuminated Jack and Delware staring down at a scuffed wooden table. There, three white sugar cubes glistened under a bright desk lamp.

Jack looked irritated. "I don't get it, what the hell is this stuff doing in sugar?"

Delware's dark eyes never left the cubes. "LSD is a potent liquid. You won't want to take even a half teaspoon of the stuff. You only need a few micrograms to send you out on a very long, weird trip. Because the dosage is so low and the liquid clear and odorless, you need something – something to absorb it: a tiny piece of blotter paper, a gelatin tablet, a sugar cube."

"How do you know it's there?"

"I'll show you." Delware flicked off the light and turned on a set of overhead black lights used to detect minute traces of blood. Delware smiled as the room flooded with an ultraviolet hue. His eyes surveyed the eerie glowing haze. "Humans can't see this part of the light spectrum." Delware leaned in close and pointed at small bluish-white patches now glowing on the cubes. "See that? Just like blood and semen, acid – I mean, lysergic acid diethylamide, glows under black light."

Jack's eyes focused on the glowing spots. "I've heard of this, but never seen it."

Delware gave a smug, "I doubt you would have. Hippies don't go around murdering each other. LSD isn't a typical drug you'd find at a homicide."

Jack pulled out his silver flask and took a swig. He had seen arrogance in younger officers before, but never a black officer. Restraining his irritation with Delware's tone, he wiped his mouth with his sleeve. "So what's the big deal? Why do hippies love this so much?"

"It's a hallucinogen: it distorts your perceptions of time and space, and your usual way of thinking – screws up your senses: you taste music, hear colors. Solids appear like liquid, inanimate objects come alive; patterns on rugs and wallpaper are set in motion. Things close by appear far away, a gaping canyon can look like a small ditch. And it's all very convincing. When you're on it, it's hard to tell the difference between reality and illusion."

"How does it work?"

Delware shrugged. "I've heard it fries your neural pathways, kills the nerve endings, so your brain has to reroute your senses. Another theory is it causes your brain to hemorrhage, the blood trickles down so the different sides of your brain can't communicate with each other. No one knows."

"So why the hell would anyone take it?"

Delware grinned, defiant. "Why the hell would anyone drink poison?" He pointed to Jack's flask still open and in his hand. "That alcohol is poisoning your blood stream right now."

Jack looked down at his flask. "Booze is different." He took another swigged to prove his point. He smiled at Delware. "See, still standing, walls ain't moving."

Delware shook his head at the old man.

Jack frowned. "So stop fucking around and just tell me why the hell would anyone take this shit?"

Delware squatted by the table, his eyes level with the cubes. He whispered, "Heightens your perception. People have experiences, like they're at one with the world, feel they see the divine in everything." Delware's voice portrayed personal experience, "Music sounds amazing; colors are vivid. It's all very intense, everything's alive."

"Wait a second!" Jack's accusing eyes turned on Delware. "You took this stuff, didn't you *boy*!"

Delware shot up, his face menacing. "I ain't your *boy*!"

Jack grabbed him by his collar and pulled him in. "You doping?"

Their nostrils were so close they felt each other's breath. Delware shouted into Jack's face. "I ain't your *boy*!!"

An angry Delware in the glow of black light made quite a specter, that raw killer look in his eyes. Fascinated by those eyes, Jack got control of his temper first. He released his grip, pushing him away. "Take it easy, kid. You'll blow a gasket."

Delware straightened out his shirt. "I ain't following you around with no mop and shine rag! I ain't no shucking and jiving Uncle Tom gonna tap dance for you! I'm not into your hang-ups old man! This ain't yesterday! Get with it. That white man scene is over. I'm a man! I'm black and proud, mothafucka!"

Delware took a step back, his eyes still locked on Jack.

Jack's eyes followed him suspiciously. "Just show some respect, will ya."

"Show me some respect you pasty ass hillbilly."

They felt the fight itching to get out, but knew better. In the tense silence, the eerie light, they stared each other down.

Jack was restless, but with no room to pace. He put his

flask to his lips and upended it. Wiping his mouth with his sleeve again, he let out a long breath. "OK, kid. Calm down. When you take this shit?"

Delware shook his head. He leaned back on the table eyeballing his partner. After a deep breath, he spoke. "I dropped it in '65, before it was illegal. Dig? I wasn't a cop then."

"OK, I believe you. Go on."

"It was in college, a friend of mine gave me a hit."

"What happened?"

Delware knew his confession would disturb the old man, so he spoke frankly, "It opened my mind, gave me a whole new perspective on my life. I used to hate cops, I mean, really hate. The cops in Alabama would lynch you; the cops in LA would shoot you. If it wasn't for that acid trip, I would have probably joined the Panthers. But on this trip, I had a vision. I saw myself in uniform." Delware slowly shook his head, the memory still poignant. "It blew my mind. That vision helped me. It was like something I never imagined, but it seemed right. You know, to change the system from the inside. It got me out of this rut of hate I was in."

Jack gave a sarcastic, "Well, that's very heart-warming."

"You know who would benefit from an acid trip?" Delware pointed his finger. "You. You're in some deep ruts, old man. You got to free your mind."

"I ain't freeing nothing. And you." Jack pointed his finger. "You need to get control of *your mind*, and realize you're a cop now, not a hippie."

Jack returned to the plate and lit a cigar without ever taking his eyes off the cubes. "Well, let's say the victims were on this stuff. So what?"

"LSD makes concentrating and communicating pretty hard. Depending on the dose, even finding the front door could be impossible. It explains why so many were killed. Even a few victims on acid would mean a high body count by a small group of killers."

Jack contemplated the answer.

Delware added, "Its presence in the house does reinforce Dirk's theory of a drug deal gone wrong."

Jack found an old wooden chair in the dim unworldly light and slouched into it. "Dirk's reports are fragmented, zigzagging from one point to another: this evidence he claims is staged, that evidence...he just ignores. What's confusing Dirk is he's never crossed a goddamn sumbitch, playing the psychopath game."

"What's the psychopath game?"

Jack looked at Delware in the black light. "A man...playing God."

Jack stood up, flicked on the lights. The white bulbs vanquished the eerie gloom. Jack approached the plate and picked up a sugar cube. "Murder is straightforward, kid, a primal act; the simplest explanation is usually the right one."

"But your conclusion is anything but ..." Delware shook his head. "Your theory is so far out, man."

Jack held the cube up to the light and grinned. "In this case ... the simplest answer is also the most incredible."

Wednesday, August 13th, 1969, 2:08 AM

A hooked moon hung over the dark, silent neighborhood. In the shadows of his living room, restless dreams haunted Jack's sleep. His body twitched and jerked in his chair. He muttered. Suddenly, his eyes shot wide open like he'd seen a ghost.

Friday, August 15th, 1969, 10:10 AM

Jack weaved through downtown LA, running stop signs, ducking down alleys and side streets to avoid traffic. "This goddamn city – too many people in it!"

Delware wedged his elbow in his window and gripped the roof. Jack turned sharply, spinning out of an alleyway in Chinatown. An old lady shouted angrily in Cantonese. Jack smiled and flashed his badge out the window.

He reached into his jacket and pulled out his silver flask and smiled at it. He turned to Delware. "Almost there, kid. The good old morgue."

Jack took a swig and then slammed on the brakes, his eyes wide with disbelief. "Goddamn!! How could I be so stupid?"

"What is it?"

Jack held up his hand, silencing his partner. The Packard idled in the middle of the street, cars honked behind. Jack closed his eyes and made a quick calculation. Delware's scalp prickled with excitement and fear. Jack had realized something. A bottomless pit opened up in his stomach, the old man was solving the case right in front of him. It was over before he even had a chance to do any real detective work. Jack's eyes shot open. "Gotcha!"

Looking behind, Jack pulled the car into reverse. He dented the bumper on a '55 Olds sedan. The family inside looked scared. Jack's bumper: not a scratch. He spun the Packard around and hit the gas, his eyes fixed. "I know where you are, you sumbitch!"

Jack threw a police strobe on the roof and opened up the engine. Honking on top of the siren, he swore at the pedestrians he almost hit, taking wild turns down Alameda, Hill and Grand.

Delware shouted over the siren. "Jack! Maybe we should call for back up!"

"Shut up, will ya! I'm trying to think!"

Jack took another sharp turn. "This is it!" He stomped on the brake, skidded across the lane and rode the front tires up onto the curb. The Packard blocked half the street. They jumped out of the car.

On the sidewalk Jack shouted at Delware. "Where do you think you're going? Stay here!"

"But-"

"I don't need you, kid. STAY HERE!"

Jack burst through the front door of the store holding his badge over his head. "LAPD!"

The three figures in the narrow liquor store froze. A black man held his hands in the air. The bald cashier behind the counter stepped back. The lady at the counter dropped her change and coins rolled across the floor. Jack stepped forward. She stepped back. He leaned over the counter and whispered. "You got a mickey of Black and White scotch?"

The cashier stood stunned for a moment, then nervously handed over a 26oz bottle of Black and White. "This is all we got."

Jack smiled. "Well, the more the merrier." He twisted the cap, took a long drink like it was water, and then wiped his mouth with his sleeve. "Ahhh, that's the stuff, *right there.*"

Delware paced the sidewalk outside. Large posters and

window displays blocked his view. "Goddamn it!" He kicked opened the door with his badge in one hand and gun in the other. "Hands where I can see them!"

Everyone in the store threw their hands into the air, except Jack.

What Delware saw stopped him dead: Jack filling his large silver flask.

Jack looked up. "I told you to wait outside, kid! I'll be a minute."

Delware stared, stunned as everyone else.

Jack glanced up again. "I said, OUTSIDE! I'll see you in the car."

Delware slowly turned and stepped back onto the sidewalk. Traffic clogged both sides of the street, the Packard's flashing strobe held motorists at bay. An ever growing crowd of children and gawkers circled the store and blocked the sidewalks, muttering, rubbernecking to see what was going on.

Holstering his gun, Delware waved his hands high in the air. He had said it many times before, but this time he actually meant it. "Stand back. Nothing to see here!"

Inside the store, Jack's flask overflowed. Scotch splashed on the grimy floorboards. His feet jumped back, avoiding the spray.

Jack smiled. "There we *go*." Placing the bottle on the counter, he sealed the flask and hid it in his jacket. He winked at the cashier. "One more for the road." He upended the bottle and took one last long drink. Looking at the occupants of the store, their hands almost back down, he eyed the black man. "Hey you!" He slammed the bottle down on the counter and sauntered towards him. "You're black and proud, aren't you?"

The man made no reply.

Jack grinned. "Hey, I understand." He did his best Delware impression, "Black is beautiful. Right on?"

The man nodded and croaked, "Right on."

Jack raised his brows, pleased with himself. "You know how I know that?"

The man shook his head.

"Because *I'm* hip."

Jack made for the door. As he opened it, the bald cashier called out. "Officer!" The man behind the counter pointed to the cash register, gesturing for payment by rubbing two fingers and a thumb together in the air.

Jack smiled at the near empty bottle on the counter and gave the cashier an amused glance. "Police business. Thanks for your co-operation."

Jack strolled to the car and yelled at the crowd. "Nothing to see here!"

He jumped in and smiled at Delware. "*Now,* we're good to go."

He pulled the police strobe from the roof, reversed and sped down an alleyway, clipping garbage cans, leaving them spinning and rolling.

~ ~ ~

Jack swigged from his flask, steered with one hand and hummed Hank Williams' *Honky Tonkin'*. Smiling, he offered his flask to Delware. "Morning bracer?"

Delware just turned his head away.

Jack liked silence. He hated chatty partners. Even though he planned on giving Delware a hard time for showing up in jeans and a T-shirt again, he decided to lighten up. Jack pointed with his chin. "So you got a backup piece down there, don't ya...in those hippie pants?"

Delware smirked. "They're called bellbottoms. And they're not hippie pants. Everyone has a pair."

Jack eyed the road. "Still can see your back-up piece, even with those wide hippie bottoms. I'm sure no citizen or shitbird criminal would see it. But I can. An experienced crook would too. Make you for police."

"Never happened yet."

"Ankle holster's a real cop thing – never seen a criminal with one of those." Jack glanced at Delware. "So how do you like the Department so far, kid?"

Delware gave a snide, "I like to lock up white folk."

Jack tried to hold back his laugh, but it escaped. "Well, you came to the right city. LA's got no shortage of bad guys. We got 'em in every color."

Delware smiled.

Jack spoke through a grin. "So, you're kidding me, right? That's the real appeal – slamming jail house doors on whites?"

"And the thrill."

"What thrill would you be talking about?"

"Walking around with a badge and a gun. Throwing anyone you want up against a wall. Taking names."

Jack was still grinning. "So that's it? And cuffing white men?"

"And the money."

Jack shook his head. "Cops don't make much money."

"They do for a black man."

"I thought you went to college."

"That don't change the color of my skin."

Jack shrugged his shoulders, conceding the point. He turned onto Pasadena. "Well, I'll tell you. I looked at your detective exams. Not bad, kid. But that doesn't mean you can be a real dick like me."

Delware smiled to himself. *Yeah, you're a real dick.*

Jack cleared his throat. "You see, a killer really worth catching don't leave his address lying around. When there's not enough of a trail, you gotta sniff 'em out."

Delware waved off Jack's advice. "What you trying to lay on me, man? Later with the lectures." He turned to look out the window. He hated lectures, especially from some old-timer drunk.

Between swigs, Jack continued on his merry way. "This racket ain't logical. As a kid, I used to listen to Sherlock Holmes on the radio. That show was better than all that crap that came out with TV. I used to think 'I can be like Holmes – reason it all out.' But it's not like that: working cases. You can't trust your mind." Jack licked a drop of scotch from his lip. "Sometimes, you know who did it – by pure instinct."

Delware rolled his eyes.

Jack swigged. "It's an unmistakable feeling – to know how to hunt. That's what you need. Exams might get you into Homicide, but they won't keep you there. A lot of bright guys get busted back to Robbery, Vice ... Patrol."

Delware gazed out the window. "Well, it looks like you also need white skin."

12:45 PM

The Packard ran the stop sign at Macy and turned south onto Mission, a long canal road that passed under the freeway. The flask had never left Jack's hand and after each ran stop sign or red light he took another swig. Delware watched the reckless drinking game in silent apprehension. With a liquored up grin and a shiny highness in his eyes, Jack did his train conductor imitation, "Next stop: County Morgue!" He whistled through his teeth like a train leaving the station.

Delware looked over at Jack. "I don't like hospitals."

"Yeah, then you'll love the chop shop. It's twice as creepy and smells ten times worse."

Delware grimaced.

Jack grinned. "It's all part of the job, kid. And it's your last chance to see one of our victims. Once they leave the medical examiner they go under *ground*. You need to see at least one...and you can pitch Sal your LSD hunch."

They pulled up in front of a grim brick building. Delware looked over at the Los Angeles County Morgue, then at Jack's gleeful mug. Jack spoke in a hush, "I should warn you ... the medical examiner-" He held up his hand and let it fall with a limp wrist.

Delware asked, "He's gay?"

Jack flinched. "Is that what you kids call it? Well, if

you mean he's a homo-fruit, yes. I'm just telling you 'cause some of the guys get ... uncomfortable around him."

Inside the building, the two officers descended a flight of cement stairs leaving the last of the sunlight behind. In the bleak cinderblock corridors, naked fluorescents buzzed overhead. The windowless labyrinth smelled of formaldehyde and bleach. Their steps echoed down the narrow halls. As they moved deeper into the maze, the overheads flickered, some were just dead. They moved through patches of darkness and uneven light.

Delware's jaw was tight, his mouth dry.

Jack swaggered. "Don't worry, kid. Think of it as a laboratory – a postmortem examination with your friendly forensic pathologist." He nudged him with his elbow. "If nothing else, it makes great padding for reports."

They came to a steel door. Jack pulled it open and held it for Delware with a cruel grin. "All aboard."

The narrow room was dim, except for a bright circle of light that illuminated two men in white smocks. They looked up from a slab. To Delware, they looked like a pair of grave robbers caught in the act. Then he realized the place was crowded with dead people: silent, still, horizontal. Their dim outlines stretched off into the shadows.

The coroner stared at Delware. His voice was hyper-feminized and slightly ghoulish. "Weellll ... "

He stepped out from behind the slab and the bright light. Walking slowly towards them, he was just a shadow. His face reappeared under the door's weak EXIT light: a pale, balding man with hollow cheeks, bushy brows and dark, deep set eyes beneath thick black-rimmed glasses. Smiling sweetly at Delware, his pencil thin mustache curled on his upper lip. "This is a pleasant surprise." He held up a bloodied gloved hand with a scalpel still in it, his voice full of enthusiasm, "A *Negro!*" Stepping a little closer, he looked Delware over and peeked behind at his buttocks. "I've never had a Negro in here before...*standing*, that is. You know, I prefer my men *vertical*."

Jack tried his best not to smile. "This is Officer Hicks."

Trapped in the close confines, Delware gave an awkward, yet defiant, "I prefer to be referred to as 'black.'"

Sal cocked his hip to rest a hand on. He pulled his head back, reframing the young man. "Well, Officer Hicks. I've seen a lot of bodies come through those doors. Black *and* white. They are all tagged, bagged, and weighed. I dissect, then remove their skin. And do you know what I find underneath, Officer Hicks?"

Delware shook his head.

"Red. So you see, underneath our skin, we're *all* the same color."

Jack interrupted, "Is she still here?"

Sal turned to Jack. "Yes, I kept her locked up just for you."

The coroner turned his attention back to Delware. "You missed the official autopsy, Officer Hicks, but Jack insisted I hold her on ice for you."

Sal tilted his head and in the dim light his pale features became gruesome. "I'll get her out of the freezer."

He walked past a panel of steel lockers, one on top of the other. "We've been swamped. Always on the full moon, especially when it falls on a weekend."

Sal opened a large door to a walk-in cooler. A black body bag appeared, rollers beneath it that would allow him to slip it onto a metal gurney. "This is the one we had trouble identifying. Not related to any of the other victims, seemed to be at the party alone – just off the bus – in the wrong place, at the wrong time. Only family is in Nebraska. They're bussing in later today. So you're just in time, Officer Hicks. You beat the hearse. She'll be taking her last drive soon."

The corpse rolled on the gurney. The detectives followed. Sal joked, "Table for one!"

His attendant gave a snicker. He was a short, thin Mexican with a goatee and a glass eye that did not move, but stared slightly off-center. With a grin, he flipped a switch creating a second circle of light and helped slide the body onto a porcelain slab.

In the harsh surgical light Sal looked pale as a ghost, his bald scalp shining beneath his comb-over. "She has 89 stab wounds. 'Cause of death: a deep incision to her chest severing the aorta, the internal bleeding in her chest cavity caused sufficient pressure to stop her heart from beating."

Jack raised a finger. "My partner here has a theory he wants to pass by you."

Delware reluctantly stepped out of the shadows. "We found LSD at the crimes scene. Did you find any trace of it in the bodies?"

"There's no toxicology test for LSD because it's a relatively new drug, Officer."

Delware met Sal's dark eyes. "Well, did you notice anything unusual? Say in the size of their pupils?"

The two white clad men gave each other a meaningful glance.

Jack caught it and stepped in. "Was there something unusual?"

The attendant answered. "When we lifted their lids, I said 'Sal look at these pupils.'"

Sal nodded. "Some of the victims did have enlarged pupils when they first came in."

Delware looked to Jack. "So, they were on LSD."

Jack shrugged. "Maybe."

Sal nodded to his attendant, who put on rubber gloves. He unzipped the bag, revealing an ashen female face.

She was gaunt, her pale beauty barely visible through

her clay-like lifelessness. Delware winced. He had seen bodies sprawled or crumpled on the street, but their blood was still liquid, their skin lifelike, not like this ghostly white leather.

Delware detected a faint expression on her face, as if her soul, down some infinite well, was still screaming for help.

Sal looked at Delware. "Three different blades were used on almost every victim." Unzipping the bag farther, he revealed a savagely butchered torso.

Delware winced and stepped back.

Sal turned to him and spoke softly. "The large Y-shaped incision across her chest is mine." He pointed to the sown up wound that spanned the torso. "I sawed through her ribs, removed her breast-plate to lift out her organs."

Delware glanced at a metal tray with a white electric autopsy saw on it. Its handle was lettered in red: Stryker.

Sal's eyes never left Delware's face. "You see, a dissection of the heart, liver, lungs must be done to check for disease, deformity, wounds. Also, sampling fluids from her liver and bladder can measure alcohol and drug consumption. I sawed open her skull to remove the brain. The contents of the stomach were analyzed. All samples and swabs are marked and bagged for toxicology tests that can be used as evidence." He smiled at the young officer. "The autopsy protocol is very efficient."

Sal turned back to the corpse. "Now look closely at her other wounds – all stab wounds of various depths. The blades were all single-edged. The type of knives you'd find in any kitchen drawer."

Jack nodded. "Yup. The drawers were all opened in the kitchen. They didn't bother to bring their own murder weapons, *very rude.*"

Delware frowned at Jack's gallows' humor; Sal smiled.

"All three blades are found on her: a serrated edge, a medium 6-inch and a very large carving knife. On the other victims there were even fork punctures."

Sal's finger floated from slashes to gaping cuts. "Tracking the wounds, they started in her back. The serrated edge came first. From the jagged tears, your victim was probably running away. But then she fell." He pointed to a long ragged slash on her shoulder. "See here. This laceration is the serrated edge coming around the front now." Sal's finger lowered to her chest. "The large carving blade joined in then." His finger stopped. "Here. See this deep wound in the chest?"

As Delware's eyes were directed to the wound, he felt his stomach turning. The drying skin looked bleached and crusty at its edges, the tissue inside poison-yellow, the dried blood deathly black.

Sal fingered the wound. "The knife went in up to the hilt. The blade was 10 inches long with a 1 ½-inch width. This large carving knife cut the aorta."

Jack interrupted. "Tell him about the other types of wounds."

"Gunshots on the young male found in the car and the man out on the lawn. Seems like a baseball bat was also used, a total of 27 times. He really put up quite a fight."

Jack nodded. "Good for him."

Sal turned to Jack. "So what's your guess?"

Jack stepped closer to the examination table. "From the wounds – most of the larger ones from the bigger blade are on this side, and the smaller wounds are on the other. Looks like they swarmed their victims."

Sal nodded. "Yes, that's my read. But since the killers preferred their blades and swarmed one victim at a time, it's surprising no one got away?"

Delware, still eying the dozens of deep cuts, tried to keep down his lunch. "They were on acid. LSD. It's a disorientating, debilitating drug. Most likely they ended up running around in circles unable to even find the front door."

Sal wondered, "So they were not sure of what was happening?"

The question silenced Delware for a moment, the scenario spun in his head. "Sometimes LSD can bring on some pretty horrifying hallucinations ... rooted in deep subconscious fears that can give way to intense panics. But being murdered on...that would-" After a hard swallow, Delware answered, "LSD's not a narcotic. They would have been aware, in fact, they would have felt it all –" he shuddered, "– more intensely." Glancing at a large wound, he turned away. "LSD would have exaggerated their perception and sensations."

Sal stepped back. "Jesus."

Jack shook his head. "A fuckin' nightmare."

Sal returned to the body. "In the last few moments of her life this third blade came in on her lower abdomen." He unzipped the bag farther revealing a huge gaping wound beneath her belly button. Her intestines hung out. They had been shredded like minced meat. Sal saw the look of horror on Delware's face and spoke apologetically, "I will sew her up before her parents come, I only left this open for your examination."

Delware lurched out of the room, a hand over his mouth.

~ ~ ~

Delware stooped over a metal sink, staring at his regurgitated lunch. He was surprised he could distinguish the hotdog from the fries.

Jack came out of the examination room. "You finished puking yet?"

"Ah, I can't, Jack."

Jack eyed him, amused. For the first time, Delware

had addressed him by his first name. "You calling me *Jack* now?"

"Man, I don't wanna go back in there."

"Oh yeah? Well, neither do I, but it's my job. What? You think that stuff in there don't make me sick. Well, it makes me plenty sick, but you don't see me out here whining, now do ya?"

"No, I mean it. I can't."

Jack approached him from behind. "You know, you had me fooled. I thought you were a cop, and even more – I thought, just maybe, you *might* be a detective."

Delware turned, still looking faint. "Look, I ... I've, my stomach ... had enough for today." He hobbled towards the exit keeping one hand on the wall for balance.

Jack lunged at him. "No, you DON'T!"

He twisted Delware's arm behind his back. Delware jumped onto his toes and froze. The young man's face twisted with pain, his lips let loose an excruciating moan. Jack whispered in his ear. "Do you remember this police hold from the academy? The Come-Along? Well, this is the unofficial version." He gave a quick, sharp kick to Delware's shin. Delware howled and hopped, losing control of his leg. Jack spun him around. "They're trying to throw me off this case downtown, three months before I retire! They got me halfway out the door and you, you want to go home 'cause you're feeling queasy!"

Jack kicked open the door to the examination room and squeezed Delware through, pushing him across the floor. "Look! Look at her, will ya!" He shoved Delware's face down towards the cadaver's intestines. "That's a fuckin' clue! Right there." Delware's free arm caught the edge of the slab and stopped himself with his face just inches away. Jack kept pushing. "That's the evidence you need to examine. You can't look away even if it sickens you." Jack kicked Delware's legs apart so he couldn't get his balance and got Delware's face just an inch from the shredded intestines. Delware's eyes went wide, he choked on the stench. Jack kept pushing, he was all red with effort. "You don't get to choose between beautiful and ugly in this job. It doesn't matter what you see – YOU NEVER TURN AWAY!"

Sal ran over. "What in god's name are you doing, Middleton!"

Jack held him off with a threatening glare. "Leave me alone, Sal!"

Delware kept trying to regain his balance. Jack kept kicking his legs apart. "*Your* eyes are *her* only hope! Better get used to looking, 'cause that's the only thing you've got!" Delware's sweaty palm began to slip. Jack edged him closer. "Look! Look at her!"

Delware's face was right up to the intestines.

Jack kicked Delware's legs apart again. "You look and look and look until you see – until you see!"

Delware's sweaty palm finally slipped. The intestines made a squishing sound as his face plunged deeper into them. The attendee turned away in disgust. Jack, surprised he had actually overpowered the kid, quickly pulled him up and threw him to the floor.

Delware shook and coughed. Jack turned away in disgust; he had not meant to push Delware's face *into* the corpse. He just wanted to teach the kid a lesson – not get *himself* kicked off the force. With a frustrated swipe, he knocked tools from a tray, scattering them across the floor.

Sal frowned. "Middleton! You're a crazy son of a bitch! Get the hell out of here!"

Jack turned on Sal. "I'm not finished yet, Sal! You understand?!"

Sal turned to his attendant who was now running for cover. Sal and Jack turned. Delware was on the ground, his back against the wall, his gun pointed at Jack.

Palms raised, Sal tried to speak calmly, "Son, think about what you're doing."

Sal's warning did not cut through the rage and humiliation that burned in every cell of Delware's body. He raised the gun to Jack's head, snarling like a vicious junkyard dog, murder in his eyes. Delware's mean streak was now in full bloom and on display for all to see, and it was a mile wide. Jack stood fascinated. Had Delware murdered someone in the past? Maybe. Would he kill someone in the future? Probably. Would he shoot him now? 50/50.

It was Jack's face that threw Delware. There was no fear in it. The surging urge to pull the trigger, to send this insane bastard to hell, rolled back. Jack's eyes looked beyond the barrel of the .38. Like a trapper who had accidentally caught his prey, Jack stared with a mixture of astonishment and awe at his prize: Delware's breaking point. The look undid Delware. An impossible calculation went through his head. His days at the Academy flashed before him with the answer he had been looking for – Interrogation Techniques 101: keep the suspect off balance with threats, erratic behavior, unpredictable mood swings. The wheels that had been in endless motion trying to figure Jack out now clicked into place. Jack had been shaking him down the whole time in one long, endless interrogation.

Delware jump up. The gun shook in his hand, "You honky mothafucka!"

Jack gave him an insane, eerie smile, absorbing every line of rage in Delware's face. "Hey Sal, looks like we found the kid's back bone."

Delware headed for the door, keeping the gun pointed back in Jack's general direction. "I'm outta here! Fuck you, you psycho fucka!"

Jack came after him. "Where do you think you're

going? Kid! If you walk out that door, don't come back!"

Delware spun around, the barrel of his gun pointed perfectly at Jack's forehead. "You stay away from me." He began to squeeze the trigger. "You touch me again and I'll blow your brains out!"

Jack didn't move, but he didn't retreat. His eyes never left Delware's. Delware squeezed harder, the .38's hammer began to pull back, that killer look returning to his eyes.

Sal stepped back in horror, turning his head. "Please, don't shoot him!"

The attendant squealed from his hiding place, "They'll send you to the gas chamber!"

Jack remained calm, even defiant, knowing he could play the kid any way he wanted. "You pull that trigger...and you'll never, ever, wear that gold Detective badge."

The words hung in the air.

Delware lowered his gun. His eyes gave Jack one last *fuck you*. "You're going to regret this, old man." He stormed out.

~ ~ ~

The sun was setting when Jack emerged from the morgue. Mission Road was so quiet he could hear the canal water running and the faint roar of the distant highway. He half expected an ambush, but more, hoped his partner would be cooled off. Jack scoped both ends of the street. Delware was gone. Only the empty Packard stood waiting. He stood a bit longer, pretending to read a billboard, to look at cars on the freeway, the sunset. The sky turned a deep golden brown. Still, no Delware.

Jack took a long, slow walk to his car. He slid in and pulled out his flask, but stopped before it touched his lips. He gave it a recriminating sneer, then tossed it into the back seat.He looked up at the empty street. "Shit!"

Friday, August 15th, 1969, 7:57 AM

Pulling up to the curb of City Hall the next morning, Jack parked in front of the white tower. He sat sober and clean shaven. His face appeared causal, but his eyes flickered towards the sidewalk with each passerby: patrolmen, kids on their way to school, lawyers, office workers. No Delware.

After twenty minutes, he'd had enough. Getting out, he leaned back on the hood and didn't hide it now. His head turned in all directions, tossing glances across the street. "Where is this kid? What is he, a sissy? Can't take a little roughhousing? How long does he need to cool off anyways?"

Five minutes later, he sighed and headed up the stairs of City Hall. Delware won't be inside Homicide, but he might be close by. Jack took a slow, roundabout route through the station. His stroll led him to the open door of Homicide Division. Delware was nowhere. Jack even took the long shot and looked inside.

He headed down to Narcotics and found the same red-haired sergeant at his desk. "Officer Hicks report in today?"

The sergeant looked around like someone had just farted. "Here? No."

"Wasn't at roll call?"

"He's not with you?"

Jack shook his head.

Grabbing a pen, the sergeant pulled a file. "AWOL, again!" He started to fill in a form. "Another infraction."

Jack cocked his neck. "Is that a transfer request?"

The sergeant looked up with a satisfied grin. "In case he ever comes back. Lieutenant Miller don't want him in his squad and the captain ain't happy he's up here."

"Why?"

"The guy's not a team player. No one trusts him, so no one wants to work with him. He's out to 'reform' the Department. We don't need no reformers. We ain't looking for no superstars up here neither. You did the guy a favor – taking him. He was just a hair's breadth away from being busted back to patrol."

Jack walked away, leaving the sergeant to write his report.

~ ~ ~

Jack found Waylon in Patrol, his two hundred and fifty pounds crammed in a tiny office, dozens of clipboards hung on the walls, feet up on his desk as he read the paper.

Leaning against the doorframe, Jack cleared his throat. "You seen Officer Hicks?"

Waylon raised a single suspicious eyebrow. "Why you wanna know?"

"Has he been down here or not?"

Waylon went back to his newspaper, grinning. "Haven't seen him in a *coon's* age."

"Heard he put a gun to your head. You called him Officer Nappy to his face, until he broke, huh?"

"That's what *you* think. Hell, you gotta get a better breed of informant."

"Yeah?"

Waylon looked over his paper. "The full story is the kid was tailing my boys in Watts, when he should have been patrolling the streets."

Jack came off the doorframe. "Your boys have been having a pretty good time shooting unarmed black men. How many this year?"

Waylon tossed the paper aside. "What? You taking the side of those damn dirty hippies? My officers were acting in self-defense!"

Jack switched up. "Who's Delware's buddy down here?"

Waylon laughed. "Shit, he ain't got no friends! And for the record Jack, he called for back up and none came. That's why he put the gun to my head, 'cause he blamed me. But no one came 'cause no one cares. That coon don't know his place. And he'd better stay wherever he is, 'cause if he comes back down here – he's dead. One way or another."

Waylon grabbed his newspaper, shook it straight. "That boy is just obsolete farm machinery to me."

Jack walked away, glanced around the muster room, squad room, change rooms, and left.

He found a small bench in the main hall, lit a cigar, but didn't enjoy it. Jack kept looking at the main doors. He needed a partner, someone who could understand hippie culture, and now he understood why he had gotten Delware so easily – no one wanted him. He needed a drink, and then, got angry with himself for wanting it. Jack snubbed out his cigar.

Taking off his hat, he slowly shuffled his fingers along its brim. Like a clock, the hat made its way around again and again.

Behind the massive watch desk young officers logged in prisoners and checked arrest reports. To Jack, they looked like boys in school uniforms. Back in the day, everyone knew him, but to these kids he was just a leftover cop from the past. If he had played it straight, who knows, maybe he could have been Chief of Police. But instead he gave the LAPD the finest crime stats in America – by rigging crime scenes, destroying files, beating confessions and arranging accidents for criminals who got lucky with judge and jury.

Jack stared at the door. No Delware. His hat stopped. He placed it back on his head and left. The kid was gone and he wouldn't get another, especially once Pat found out why.

Stepping out into bright sunshine, he stood by the main door and lit another cigar. "Fuck this, fuck Delware."

Heading back to his car, he saw an afro in the Packard. Jack tossed the cigar with a mixture of relief and pity. Poor kid had nowhere to go: it was either up or out.

Jack walked slowly, keeping his eyes on the afro.

In the car, Jack found Delware looking away from him, then in a single motion Delware flicked open a switchblade and placed it squarely between Jack's legs.

Jack looked down at the gleaming blade. "Nice, kid. You got the drop on me, in my own car, right outside City Hall. You got some *balls*."

Delware hissed, "And you won't have any left soon." Jack saw Delware's eyes. They were looking at a dead man.

Jack smiled at the knife. It was normal life that made Jack uncomfortable; danger had a calming effect, gave him a focus: get out of the situation. This calm had saved his life countless times. Others panicked, impulsively acted – leaving the potential killer no choice but to strike. Jack knew if someone wanted you dead, they just killed you. If they didn't, they wanted something. All you needed to do was understand. The only rule: stand your ground. Never let them take you to where no one can find you.

Jack took his eyes off the blade. "Did I ever tell you about the Middleton Curse? My father was shot in the line of duty, responding to a liquor store break-in. My grandfather was shot in the back, just outside the police station. Both my dad and grandfather were buried in their uniforms."

Delware shoved the blade into Jack's trousers and Jack felt a breeze from the tear.

Delware whispered, "I seen the way you drive, old man, and how you treat me, so I know you sure as hell don't care if you live or die. But I know you don't want to walk around with no dick your pants. Listen mothafucka, I was planning on knifing you right here and taking a bus down to Mexico."

Staring into Delware's eyes, Jack could see he wasn't lying. "OK, kid, but you've got a helluva lot more brains than that. So let's hear Plan B."

The blade went deeper, piercing Jack's boxers and pricking his scrotum. Jack's hips jumped back, his lips jerked into an uncomfortable grin.

Delware sneered. "You listen: *no one* disrespects me, especially not *you*, you drunken hillbilly. You cannot imagine the amount of *white man bullshit* I've had to go through to get here! And I'm here to stay, so let's get this straight: I ain't no quitter!" His panther-like eyes locked on Jack's. "You may be incapable of relating to people outside of your interrogation skills..." He whispered fiercely, "Fine! But you EVER lay your honky hands on me again I'll castrate you!"

Jack nodded carefully. "OK, kid."

"A black man don't come this far by being stupid. I want to see those files! I want to know everything you do." Delware pushed the blade and its prick made Jack sit up STRAIGHT. "Get me in that office."

"OK, kid! You've made your point. Just gimme time to come up with a plan. You'll get a crack at this case."

Delware searched for deceit in Jack's eyes, but found none. Folding the blade back into its handle, he turned his head, unable to look at Jack a moment longer.

Jack resisted the urge to pull his gun and beat the shit out of the kid. He was sober. Too sober. Besides, the whole point of Delware getting the draw on him was to humiliate and even the score. Jack owed the kid that much; he couldn't deny it. He reached for his flask and remembered he had purposely left it at home.

After inspecting the new hole in his pants, Jack thought about saying sorry, but knew that word would never cross his lips. He turned away, staring off into the distance. "Kid."

Delware would not look at him.

Jack spoke soft. "My dad ... sometimes, he'd take me to the airfield. When I got old enough, he taught me to fly.

"When he died, I kept flying. The Japs attacked Pearl Harbor and the Air Force needed pilots. I got in right away. I flew missions – dropped the 101st over Normandy, later over Holland, did secret mission for the OSS. The war was almost over when I went on my last mission ... there were all these wounded men on board. We flew into flak. It was popping all around us. Smashed the windshield on one side ... I looked over at my co-pilot ..." Jack smiled. "We used to call him Bullets, 'cause he wore bullet belts across his chest like a cowboy. He was a real joker. Well, I got some Kraut shrapnel in my leg, but Bullets got all torn up. I mean shredded, his guts fell out ... like that girl.

"The engine was hit so bad it took us four hours to get back to base. That whole time, he was screaming, moaning, crying. Strapped in, he wasn't sitting any farther from me than you are now. He died as I landed."

Jack was silent for a long time.

"He begged me to shoot him, you know? Begged for hours, but I couldn't. The gun was out of reach and I couldn't let go of the controls. There was no autopilot back then. I had to fly that plane every second or, in the condition it was in, it would have gone down. Those wounded men would have died, we all would have...if I let go.

"So I sat there. Beside my best friend, and I listened to him die – for hours."

Delware turned and studied Jack's face in the morning sun.

Jack looked away. "I never flew again. I was carried to the hospital. He was carried to the morgue. The war ended a few weeks later, before I even got out of the hospital.

"Sometimes when I hear a plane, I think of Bullets. I've never been back to an airfield."

Jack turned to Delware. "Kid, *this* is your job. Your *duty*. You got to understand ... if you let go of the controls, if you look away, even for a second, more people could die."

Friday, August 22nd, 1969, 5:45 PM

The glowing jukebox cranked Johnny Cash's *Ring of Fire*. The LAPD dayshift was out of blues and filing into O'Malley's Pub, a dive jammed with tiny tables and overflowing ashtrays. Off-duty officers yakked it up by the pool tables and ordered draft over the long polished counter. Pat Boyle sat at the mahogany bar on his favorite stool – just one of the boys.

He looked up from his beer through the smoky air and saw in the bar mirror Jack Middleton wading through the crowd, avoiding fiery cigarettes and teeming beer mugs.

Pat swiveled on his stool. "What the hell are you doing in this stinking joint?" Pat waved at the bartender. "Danny, two beers and two double scotch!"

Jack sat beside him and hollered, "And I'll have the same!"

Pat laughed. "Jesus, Mary and Joseph! The world must be coming to an end." He guzzled the rest of his beer. "When Martha was alive you'd stay out all night. But now, you go home right from the office, and never drink with anyone."

Jack pulled a cigar from his jacket. "Guess, I'm trying to make it up to her. Not leave her alone so much."

Pat raised an eyebrow. "Jack, she's not at home anymore."

Jack lit the cigar and frowned through the smoke. "She is to me."

Pat pondered his friend, then sighed, staring down at his empty mug. "I know what you mean. When Lilly died...I made her a spice rack. She was always nagging me to make her one. I said I would, so she waited and waited. You know, I don't know if I really meant to build it or not. But when she passed-" He crossed himself. "*God bless her.* I built the damn thing – hung it right over the stove too. Still sitting there, empty." Pat pushed away his empty mug. "I don't cook, never been any good at women's work."

Jack half-smiled, lost in his own thoughts. Pat examined his friend's expression. "So, how's the colored kid working out?"

"Delware? It's been hell. And goddamn, he's a touchy sumbitch – this 'black' horseshit. I try to be polite: call him a Negro and he starts yelling." Jack did an angry Delware impression, "I'm a man! I ain't your nigga' and I ain't nobody's Negro. I'm black and proud, mothafucka!"

Pat forced a laugh and shook his head. The LAPD was struggling to put on a new face amidst controversial racial shootings. Now, here was a senior detective doing public Negro impressions for laughs. Pat was caught between official policy and reality.

Trying to steer the conversation, Pat leaned in. "Hey, remember when we were the only two Irish guys on the force? They treated us like dogs."

Jack nodded.

Pat pretended not to remember, "What was that joke Captain Wylie used to make?"

"Why did God create alcohol?" Jack grinned, "To keep the Irish from ruling the world."

Pat laughed. "Remember that night we were pinned down by those strikers throwing bricks? What did he call the bricks again?"

Jack laughed, "Irish confetti."

The drinks arrived: four beers and four double-scotches. Pat slipped the bartender a few bills and handed Jack a shot glass. "It's on me."

Jack hadn't had a drink all day. He smiled at his glass.

Pat raised his. "Bombs away!"

Both men upended their shot glasses. Jack banged his on the bar and frowned.

Pat caught the expression. "What?"

Jack took a moment to brace himself for what he was about to say. "I need help."

Pat fell silent.

"I'm in trouble, Patty. I got evidence, a good hunch..."

Pat snapped out of it. "What's the problem?"

"It's like there's a big white wall in front of me. There's nothing on it. It's just blank. But all I need to know is just on the other side." Jack pulled a paper from his jacket and unfolded it on the bar. "Delware typed up the lyrics to this song: Piggies. Look at that, will ya." He slipped the page along the bar.

Pat slipped on a pair of reading glasses and read it through. "*Piggies.* It's about us, right? Cops. The pigs. Says we need a *whacking,* mob slang. But how does this fit in with the murder of a pregnant starlet? None of the victims were cops. It doesn't match. Shouldn't they have killed a cop?"

Jack nodded. "I know. I've been pouring over these and other lyrics from the album. I see bits and pieces, but they don't fit, don't form a picture that could be our psycho's plan." He slumped over his drink. "I got a big fat zero."

"What does Delware think?"

"Thinks I'm a maniac, leading him on a wild goose chase." Jack drew closer. "I feel this sumbitch, Patty. He's a hippie. I know it. He's not far, but these kids – they live in another world, speak another language. All I need is a glimpse of how they see, then I'll bring him in, I know it. I know it!" Jack clenched his fist. "He's following some kind of map. Psychos always do. It's right in front of us, Patty!"

Pat knew Jack's hunch was nonsense from the start, but wanted to be gentle now. "You still think it's a psycho?"

Jack nodded. "I was wrong about Delware. He's got connections with hippies all over town, but with every question to him, or his informants, all I get is stupid looks." Jack eyed himself in the mirror behind the bar. "He took me to a record store – showed me a poster right up on the wall. The Beatles – four guys with long, long hair. Looked like a bunch of women. The most faggy goddamned thing you could ever imagine."

Pat gave a bitter laugh. "It's a different world, Jack. I remember the draft for World War II. I knew a guy who got a 4F and committed suicide because he couldn't join the fight. Today ... kids dodge their duty, burn their draft cards *and* the flag."

"I can't believe what's happened to our country. It's all gone to hell." Jack lit a cigar. "Marijuana used to be for homos and jazz musicians, *now*, teenage girls smoke it in public parks."

Pat smiled wistfully. "Remember you'd have to wine and dine a dame to get a crummy kiss goodnight?"

Jack started to boil. "Girls today run around – no bra, no panties. We used to take pride in a nice new suit, not these kids. They wear rags and they're proud of 'em."

Pat muttered, shaking his head, "Damn dirty hippies."

There was genuine anguish in Jack's voice, "Sodomy and porn used to be illegal! Goddamn Supreme Court! And *their* Miranda Rights! It's like no one's on the side of law and order no more!"

Pat contemplated his beer. "It's the world today – civil rights."

Jack downed his last scotch. *"God!* I hate that snotty Dirk."

Pat poured beer down his throat until his mug was empty. Catching his breath, he felt drunk enough to say it. "Jack, this damn Dirk thing. *Why are you taking it so personal?* I mean, kid thinks he knows everything 'cause he's been on a long lucky streak. But he's hitting dead ends too since all the prints came up empty. But Jack, you're trying to beat *him.* Didn't we use to laugh at the old timers trying to make their last big case? Well, you're making this your 'last big case.' That's your mistake: skipping the small steps. You want to go out with a bang. Jack, your whole theory just feels like ... a stab in the dark."

Jack gave a small frown, thought about it and yelled at the bartender, "Another scotch over here!"

Jack turned to his friend. "So what odds are you giving me?"

Pat seesawed his hand. "These victims were rich *and* famous." He shook his head. "Psycho killers are rare. They choose loners for victims, people no one will miss. And lure them off the street. I give you – hundred to one – that you found the first serial killer in all of history that picks celebrity victims the whole world will miss...*and* makes house calls."

Jack's scotch arrived.

Pat turned back to the bar. "Dirk's even money. I don't have to tell you, Jack. Killers usually know their victims."

Jack stared at the amber liquid in his glass and sneered. "That kid, Dirk – thinks he's a real detective. It's beginner's luck, Patty. He's not a real dick."

Jack picked up his glass, swirled the scotch and tossed it down his throat.

Pat thought of Dirk's rise in the Department. Jack was

right, he didn't fit in. He wasn't a Bureau boy yet. He'd been *too* lucky. Pat fingered his empty mug and let the words slip out. "I know what you mean, he needs a Gwynette Sanders."

The juke box played; the younger detectives laughed it up over a dirty joke. But for a moment, Jack and Pat were somewhere else. First, to an alleyway they had walked twenty-three years ago. Once again the two detectives were young and at their feet was the body of an eight-year-old black girl laid out on the pavement, a drizzle of soft rain beading on her forehead. Her eyes closed, as if she were merely sleeping.

Internally, both went over the eight month investigation: the many leads, the different suspects, all leading nowhere – how slowly her case files were moved off their desks or covered by other files. Lastly, they remembered the photo of Gwynette that stayed on the bulletin board for years, her grade three school picture, her missing-a-tooth smile like a benediction over the office: Gwynette Sanders – the patron saint of unsolved murders.

Jack recalled the day in June, 1953, when he walked into the office and noticed the picture was gone. He realized then, the killer had gotten away.

The hunter voice in both men whispered: *maybe ...* if they opened the files again, they'd see it now. *Maybe after all these years?* Both men brushed the voice aside. They had already done that countless times on many a slow night.

The music on the jukebox returned. The gaggle of voices brought them back to the here and now.

Pat sighed. "Yeah. You're not a real detective until you get a case...you never solve."

The two men were silent.

Pat's eyes lit up. "Jack, you got someone in your family, your granddaughter. She must be a teenager now. You could talk to her."

"I haven't talked to them since Martha's funeral."

"The funeral? Why so long?"

"My daughter, Lynn, had just got divorced, showed up with her kid and...a coon boyfriend. A coon! She held his hand as they lowered Martha into her grave."

Pat shot straight up with wide eyes. "She was dating a colored?"

Humiliated, Jack spoke softly, "Yeah. Should have seen it coming when she got pregnant in college and never married *that* guy. She went wrong long ago."

Pat's eyes were still wide with disbelief. "A colored? Your own *daughter!*"

Jack nodded, deflated.

Pat hunched back over the bar. "Well, she was a wild one, Jack. Hanging out with beatniks and all." He put a comforting arm around his friend. "Jack. I'm *sorry*. I really am."

"After the funeral, I swore I'd never talk to her again."

"That's rough." Pat pulled his arm away. "What do you think the chances are your granddaughter's a hippie?"

"She'd be about nineteen. Yeah, I'm sure she's the barefooted type, if she's anything like her mother."

Pat shook his head. "Well, you need a real hippie – hundred percent – a pot smoking, cop hater – who's not afraid of you, who doesn't see *you* as the law. Delware may be young, but he's still a police officer. No one can be a full fledge hippie with a badge and gun. Cops see the world in a certain way. You need to talk to your granddaughter. Give her an unofficial visit, off the record, just family stuff." He swigged his last beer.

~ ~ ~

The night was misty and the streets abandoned. Jack weaved under the glow of a street lamp, fishing for coins in his pockets. A few drunken off-duty cops stumbled out from O'Malley's across the street. Jack lurched into a phone booth. He tried to drop a coin in, it took him three tries. Finally, he dialed, very slowly.

The operator came on. "You'll need to deposit another nickel to place your call."

Jack grumbled.

The female voice returned. "Sir, are you still there? You'll need to deposit another nick-"

"Yeah, yeah, you stupid broad! Shut up, will ya!"

Another nickel disappeared into the slot. Jack listened to the phone ring at the other end. Then a sleepy voice questioned from the other side. "Hello?"

"Hi Lynn."

"Dad?"

"Yeah, it's me."

Then came a startled panic. "Is everything all right?"

Jack gave a slurred, "Yeah, yeah."

There was a pause on the other end. She had caught the slur and was already rolling her eyes. "What is it, dad?"

"Where is Julia?"

"Julia? She's in San Francisco. Frank was just out there."

"Yeah, I don't give a shit about him."

It hadn't even been a minute and already she was exhausted by her father. "So what do you want, dad?"

"Her address."

"Why?"

"I'm going to pay her a visit."

"Why?"

"Can't a man visit his own granddaughter? Are you going to give me her address or not?"

"Hold on."

Jack listened to his daughter's breathing, drawers opening, paper rustling. He had loved Lynn as a child. She was sweeter than sunshine – a fine young lady. Jack worked hard and broke a lot of rules to get the money needed to give her what he and his family never had: a college education. But she came back pregnant by a beatnik boyfriend. She was another person then. She spoke about equality for coloreds and women, criticizing the way Jack treated Martha – *his own wife!* Lynn started calling him a fascist, a male chauvinist. He hadn't sent her to college to come back a goddamn communist.

Jack felt betrayed by his daughter, his country, the crummy college he had given all his money to. *What the hell are they teaching these kids in school today anyways?*

"Dad, are you ready?"

Sunday, August 24th, 1969, 6:45 PM

From LA, Jack tore up the I-5 into San Francisco in less than six hours. The sun began to sink behind the Golden Gate Bridge as he headed towards The Haight: an abundance of cheap student housing gone mad. By the time he hit the stop sign at Haight and Ashbury all types of music filled the air: rock, jazz, folk. He couldn't believe it. Hippies were everywhere: long hairs sauntering down the streets, bare-foots sitting on the sidewalks, beards inside tiny vans, girls with flowers in their hair hanging out of windows, young women in saris, mini-skirts and big floppy feathered hats, bare-chested guys riding down the streets on motorcycles. Blacks and whites laughed, walking together like there was no difference between them. It was a world upside down.

He turned onto Page Street. The low rent Victorians on the sloping side streets were painted up like rainbows. The Packard pulled up in front of a broken down mansion painted lemon yellow. Black spray-painted letters across the second floor declared: Yellow Submarine.

Jack made his way up multi-colored steps and knocked. Music blared behind the door. It opened revealing a young black man wearing nothing, but a stoned smile. Jack took a step back, trying to comprehend. The stoned smile vanished. Even in plain clothes, Jack's gray crew cut and grim face were more conspicuous than any badge.

The man tried to close the door, but Jack's foot wedged it open.

His voice came from behind the door. "Hey, look, man. You need a warrant to come in here. I know my rights!"

"Relax, this isn't business. I'm looking for Julia Middleton. She's my granddaughter."

The door stopped pushing on Jack's foot. "There's no Julia here, man." He peeked out at Jack, his eyes lit up. "Aaahhh, Julia. You mean *Missy.*"

Jack didn't like the way he said '*Missy.*'

The door opened, the music became clearer. *Somebody to Love* by Jefferson Airplane spun on a turntable inside.

"Come in, man." Smiling and nodding, the man was amused to see someone so straight enter the Submarine. "I'm Coyote."

The smell of marijuana wafted through the foyer. A three-legged hound scampered across the elaborate parquet floor. Two Siamese cats eyed the strange visitor from a broken sweeping staircase.

Jack took a step, but Coyote held up a hand. "Wait! I wish there was a hip way to say this, but there are some preliminaries. I know you're off-duty, so you shouldn't mind this."

Coyote began to frisk Jack. "You see. We don't know where your head's at...and...no one enters the Submarine with firearms."

Jack smiled at his amateur pat down.

Finishing Jack's legs, Coyote rose. "Sorry, man. After those murders in LA, the whole scene is pretty uptight."

They passed a crowded living room of hippies sprawling on pillows, couches, and windowsills. Walls were painted with florescent colors in abstract shapes. Stuffed animals littered the floor. There were blacks, Asians, white kids, all lounging together, huddled like a family – laughing and whispering; rolling, passing and smoking joints.

Jack stopped and counted the illegal activities: a line of coke on a handheld mirror, a bowl of colored pills and capsules, loud rock music way above the noise ordinance. Their faces turned concerned at his appearance. Coyote interjected, "He's cool, man. He's looking for Missy."

One kid pointed a bitter finger. "He looks like a cop!"

"Cool it, man. He's her granddad."

Coyote led Jack past a kitchen where longhaired guys played guitars and beaded girls drummed on pots. Leading him up the backstairs, the black man's big naked buttocks were right in Jack's face. The second floor was a maze of rooms, each doorway revealed strange new scenes: a dope fiend's pad, a meditation loft with candles and hippies doing yoga, a dim den of naked hippies spacing out to soft, sensual jazz.

Looking back at Jack, Coyote smiled proudly. "Some real shit is happening here." He led him around another corner. "So what's your scene, man?"

Jack frowned. "What? Speak English, will ya."

Coyote glanced back at the confused old man. "I mean, why are you here...to rap to your granddaughter about?"

Jack didn't answer.

Coyote shook his head. "You scared me, man. I'm about to leave. I'm dodging the draft and headed down Mexico way. I thought you were coming to drag my ass off to Vietnam. Man, I'm not going 10,000 miles to murder people so the white slave-masters can dominate dark people on *that* side of the world too. Fuck that! This is the day and age when that evil shit comes to an end, dig?"

If Jack had his cuffs, he would have slapped them on

and dragged the kid to the nearest army base. Jack growled, "You afraid to fight?"

"Hell, no! I was raised in the ghetto, man. It's just that I ain't got no quarrel with the Vietcong ... no Vietcong ever called *me* nigger."

Coyote stopped before a purple door. He motioned. "That's her room, man." Smiling at Jack, he sauntered away.

There was music on the other side: Coltrane's *A Love Supreme*. Jack stood outside the door for almost ten minutes, staring at the floor, trying to picture his granddaughter, the last time he saw her, what she was wearing, how old she was. But he couldn't picture her now. He whispered to himself, "Six years."

He opened the door.

Before him was a large room with high ceilings. A hippie was on his knees painting circles onto a young woman's naked breast. She stood completely naked and smiled at the stranger in the doorway. The hippie on his knees turned and squinted. "Can I help you, brother?"

Jack barked. "Yeah, you can get the hell away from my granddaughter, you fucking pervert!"

The hippie jumped to his feet backing away, waving his arms. "Hey man, I'm an artist. Everything is righteous. No need to flip out."

Without a hint of shame, the woman cocked her hip to one side. "Granddad?"

Jack lowered his head and covered his eyes with his thick shaking hand. "Goddamn, Julia, cover yourself, will ya!"

The young woman took her time slipping on a summer dress. The artist took advantage of the old man's blindness to make his escape, closing the door quietly behind him.

She smiled at her grandfather's embarrassment. "You can look now."

Jack lowered his hand and a woman appeared before him. He shook his head. "You were just a kid last time I saw you."

Julia smiled. "I was twelve."

Jack thought of Martha's funeral and whispered, "Six years."

His granddaughter pointed to an unmade mattress on the floor. "Sorry, I don't have a chair, but we can sit on the bed."

Jack made his way over and awkwardly sat down. She sat beside him, brushing the hair from her face.

Smelling hashish smoke in the air, Jack looked at the grimy floor and the second-hand dresses draped over milk crate bookshelves. "How the hell can you live like this?"

Julia shrugged her shoulders and smiled. "We're not hurting anyone, Grandpa."

Jack frowned.

Julia straightened her dress. "We share everything. It's really beautiful."

Jack shook his head. "That's pinko, commie talk."

Julia's smile only widened. "No, it's not, Grandpa. It's *love*."

Jack waved her words away. "You kids should be ashamed of yourselves."

She frowned. "Why shouldn't people be free to live as they choose? We're not judging each other here, we listen and create a space where everyone can find themselves. What's so wrong with doing your own thing?"

"It's immoral. It's illegal!"

Julia's face hardened. "Grandpa, don't be so uptight. If more people turned on, the world would be a peaceful place."

Jack didn't know it, but he was entering a debate that raged in living rooms, bedrooms and classrooms across America: young versus old, tradition versus freedom. A generation gap so wide one side could barely hear the other. It remained relatively civil for the first twenty minutes, after that, they began sniping. Jack was immovable. "All I'm saying is, get a job, get a haircut and grow up, will ya!"

Julia's voice turned hot and cold. "You're just part of the establishment; telling us how to live, how to think. Young people are experimenting, looking for new ways, new doors into reality. Why should we copy you?" Julia got up and paced. "Your generation labels everyone. All you care about is profits. There won't even *be* an America if we don't change. We're poisoning the earth! The cold war could wipe out the whole human race in seconds! Why would we want to be like you? We're not free in America. We're judged by our sex, race and wealth. Well, we don't want your cold war, gray suits, and little box houses in the suburbs...or marriages that end in divorce. We want to get back to what's real, to nature. Is that so hard to understand?"

Jack reached for his flask, but found the pocket empty. He shook his head. "My generation worked hard – *all our lives* – to give you kids the opportunities we never had ... and now you throw it back in our face like it's worth nothing!"

As they passed the hour mark, Julia's young pretty face was red. "Every week a hundred boys come back dead from Vietnam, and a hundred more are drafted. You say that's the price of freedom, well, where was their freedom?"

Jack's temper boiled. "Hey! Watch your mouth. This is America, love it or leave it!"

They moved on to family history: stories Jack would rather forget. Arguments that had started with his daughter decades ago returned. Now his life was on trial and his daughter, granddaughter, sat in judgment. Julia raised an accusing finger. "You think women should stay at home, barefoot and pregnant in the kitchen! Just like Grandma, whose biggest worry was the length of hemlines that year, getting her hair done every week and up in rollers every night. Women have a right to choose their own lives!"

Years of frustration, watching his daughter go astray, came back in a flash. "Is it too much to ask you kids to show some respect and live like decent human beings!" Jack waved an angry finger. "You know your mother is to blame for this – dating that goddamn Negro right in front of you!"

As they neared the two hour mark they were reduced to insults. Jack's arm waved at the disheveled room. "So this is what you want? To live like a bunch of animals?"

Julia stood militant and proud. "Animals? Who do you think you are?" She stabbed an accusing finger. "The police are nothing but the goon squad for the rich capitalist *pigs*!"

The word 'pigs' slapped Jack across the face. He paused, her words replayed in his head. "What did you just say?"

"You're part of the uptight pig power structure."

"Capitalist *pig*?"

"Yeah! Rich, greedy *pigs*!"

It shook Jack to the core. The song Piggies played in his head: the harpsichord, the snide voice. It clicked: 'pig' didn't mean cop. It meant rich. It meant the establishment. It meant anyone living in Bel Air. Jack fell silent –snatches of lyrics whirled inside his head. The White Album started to fit together.

After a long silence, he looked at his granddaughter. The anger had flushed out of his system. She had turned aside, tears in her eyes. Her face at that one exact angle looked just like her grandmother as a young woman. The light from the window gave a soft glow to those features Jack knew so well. It was an arresting vision. Jack's wife was suddenly alive, and young again, like the first time he ever saw her. Every thought fell from his mind.

For a moment, Jack forgot where he was. Martha, fair and lovely, was by his side, their whole lives ahead of them, back in a world that made sense. He felt his dreams of youth, his hopes of being a good cop. Their wedding, the birth of their daughter, a whole life passed within his heart. How he longed for this, to see Martha again. And now, she was so close he could touch her. Unconsciously, his hand slid towards hers and he felt its warmth. He whispered, "Martha."

The young girl pulled away. Their eyes met abruptly. She sneered at her grandfather, but then saw the softness, loneliness and sadness in his watery eyes. "I look like her, don't I? Mom always tells me so. She showed me that picture of you and grandma on your honeymoon. You looked good in your uniform."

Jack shook off the vision, embarrassed. This was his out of control granddaughter! And yet the vision of his wife gave rise to confusing emotions and a confession. "I'm just trying to understand this record. I got these murders and there's an important clue in the lyrics. They were written in blood. I'm just trying to understand them. Then, I can bring these killers in."

Suddenly, she realized why he had come, and because it had been in the headlines for weeks, guessed the case he was working on. She felt a momentary respect for him.

Emotions swirling, he walked to the door. Her hand caught his at the doorway. She handed him a small plastic bag. "Take this. It will help you understand."

Jack barely glanced at the bag, hardly heard a word she said. He looked at his granddaughter and once again glimpsed a perfect reflection of his wife. And yet, he knew she was no longer among the living. Love and death tore at his heart. Bewildered, he stuffed the bag into his pocket and left.

~ ~ ~

Jack entered his bungalow and collapsed into his faded club chair. He stared at the small blank screen of his old TV. Twelve hours of driving had almost killed him, leaving him no energy to even pour a scotch on the rocks. The small end table beside him was crowded with empty mickeys. Finding a near-empty one, he drank from the cloudy brown bottle.

He glanced at his pocket, remembering the bag his granddaughter gave him. Pulling it out, he held the clear plastic in front of him, staring. Inside were four sugar cubes. "Why the hell did she give me these?"

Jack closed his sore eyes and remembered the sugar cubes at the crimes scene, remembered Delware showing how they were blotted with LSD.

His eyes opened. Scowling, he tossed the bag across the room. "Fuckin' hippies! Think drugs can solve everything."

Monday, August 25th, 1969, 2:14 AM

Jack muttered, asleep in his chair. The room was deathly quiet, but some nightmare haunted his head. A breeze wandered through the open front windows, the white transparent drapes now alive in a ghostly dance. He gasped. The old man's eyes shot wide open.

Saturday, August 30th, 1969, 11:59 PM

The Detective Bureau was dark and empty, the halls quiet. The corners loomed with shadows. In Homicide, the only light fell from small desk lamps. The hands on the clock touched midnight: the witching hour, the graveyard shift. Working Joes with a hard week behind them were out on a Saturday night drinking and trying to make it pay. Another heat wave had temperatures rising all week and now they boiled over, leaving dead bodies in tenements, streets and alleys.

A shadow darkened the doorway of Homicide Division and gave a good look around. It whispered, "See, kid, I told you I'd come up with a plan. I'll stand guard."

Another shadow appeared.

The first shadow pointed to Dirk's desk. "Like I said, Saturday night clears the place out. It always does. And they won't be back anytime soon. Now let's see if that college education did you any good."

The shadow slipped out the doorway.

The second shadow approached Dirk's desk. Delware's face slowly appeared in the gloom. He stared at the file-laden desk like a mountain of treasure, a holy shrine of secret knowledge. Noiselessly, he slipped into Dirk's chair. Everything he wanted to know about the Tate murders was now at his fingertips. His hands shifted through pages, his eyes darting as if trying to read them all at once.

Out in the hall, Jack killed the last few lights in the stairwell to slow down any returning detectives. Silhouetted by large windows overlooking the glimmering city, he leaned against the wall. Somewhere in greater LA the murderers lurked. On the other side of the wall was a young man getting his first chance at finding them.

Jack pulled out his flask.

~ ~ ~

Jack's legs sprawled on the marble floor. His head tilted back against the wall, mouth open. Out the large windows, the darkness began to thin. Dawn was close. The empty halls whispered with his snores. The steps of returning detectives echoed up from the bottom of the stairs.

Inside Homicide, Delware had forgotten the dangers of trespassing on white man's land. He was surrounded by files, his head spinning with evidence.

The footsteps on the stairs came closer. Jack's head moved, but his eyes remained shut.

Delware opened the last file. The electric fans whirled overhead. Among the swirling facts in his head, an idea was forming, a picture just on the horizon, a map that would put all these facts in order.

A harsh cough from the stairwell startled Jack. The clack of hard soles on cold marble made him jump.

Catching the echo of the cough, Delware rushed to put the files back into order. The coughing came again, louder.

Jack fumbled to his feet and gave a soft warning whistle.

Delware stood ready to bolt away from the desk, but his hands were still feverishly working to put a night's worth of work back in place.

Jack had only made it down a single flight of stairs before he intercepted two weary detectives. He tried to delay them with inane chatter, but they rolled their eyes and moved passed him.

Suddenly, all three men were looking up. The sound of rushing footsteps was headed their way.

Out of breath, Delware appeared at the top of the stairs, feigning surprise. "Jack, there you are! I was wondering where you-"

Jack shouted impatiently, "Yeah, yeah! Shut up, will ya." He motioned Delware to join him. He turned to the detectives. "Well, gotta go."

Relieved to be rescued from the old man's ramblings, the detectives smiled, but eyed Delware suspiciously as he passed. They stopped and gave the pair a second look, watching Delware and Jack descend the steps.

Jack whispered, "Well, how did it go, kid?"

Delware looked like a man in some exalted dream. "I had something. It was right in the back of my mind. I was grasping for it. In another minute, I would have had it."

Jack gave the young man a knowing glance. *That's how it starts.*

Delware shook the reverie from his eyes and his face turned practical again. "Jack, Dirk has a lot right, at the very least, some good points."

Jack shrugged. "Well, you *were* sitting at his desk. He'd have the evidence arranged in a way that makes sense with his theory."

"His biker-drug-deal-gone-wrong has weight. Multiple weapons, means multiple killers – bikers move in groups."

Jack nodded. "I agree it was a tight-knit group."

Delware's face showed a man reasoning his way through many thoughts. "Bikers on parole can't carry guns 'cause it would violate them right back to prison, so many carry knives."

"True, but why wouldn't they use *their* knives? Why would they go to the kitchen to get other knives?"

Delware stopped on the stairs and thought. "The people at the party were high; it's within reason bikers sold them those drugs."

Jack considered the theory. "True."

Delware played his hand. "Things got out of hand, maybe they didn't pay the bikers up front, the bikers stuck around, got high, got frustrated, and suddenly, a fight breaks out."

Jack countered, "In a crime of passion, people tend to kill with their hands or whatever's in reach."

"It's just a short walk to the kitchen."

Jack shook his head. "I can't see angry bikers walking to the kitchen when they got knives on them. That's why bikers don't work for me. And the telephone wires were cut; that shows premeditation."

Delware shook his head. "Yeah, but that could have been done afterwards, the whole idea is that the bloody messages on the walls, slashed screen, all of that, was staged to throw us off."

Jack was silent. The first rays of the sun broke in through the windows. He shook his head. "That's a lot of maybes and it still sounds out of whack. Staged murder scenes, after a fit of rage, are sloppy. The crime scene doesn't make sense – it tells conflicting stories. It still feels like Dirk trying to put square pegs into round holes." Jack tried to lead his young partner. "The reason no one wants to read the evidence as it is, is 'cause the story it tells is too incredible – a group of hippie killers."

Delware shook his head and that vague hunch came back to him. "That feeling I had ... it had something to do with that."

Jack watched Delware's face, hoping the light in his eyes would see the missing piece. Delware shook his head. The hunch slipped away. He felt it evaporate. Delware frowned; frustrated with himself and the fact Jack was so insistent on his far-fetched scenario when a simpler one seemed just in reach. He decided to come at Jack another way. "OK. Let's say the bikers had a long term grudge – maybe it was *all* premeditated, even the misleading evidence."

Jack frowned. "Calculated murders have an almost business-like MO. The number of stab wounds was excessive. Over eighty stabs per person, that's a long time to be killing *one* person. That allows time for others to escape. *If* it was planned, the overkill doesn't make sense. Why risk someone getting away?"

Delware rolled his eyes. "So Jack, if you're saying it wasn't an act of passion and it wasn't premeditated ... then what is it?"

"Just what it looks like: an act of madness." Jack's eyes met Delware's. "The only way to put the premeditated cutting of the phone lines and excessive violence together is to boil it down: they were predators."

Delware gave Jack a doubtful look and then dropped his head. The last serial killing he could recall in LA was the Black Dahlia back in '43, before he was even born.

Jack turned and looked out the stairwell window. "One Christmas, my dad brought home a radio. We were the first family on the street to own one. It had all these dials and tiny incandescent bulbs glowing inside. We loved The Sherlock Holmes Show. Holmes had this precept: when you have eliminated the impossible, whatever remains, however improbable, *must* be the truth."

Delware looked at the old man staring out over LA.

Jack's eyes were distant and deep. "Once you eliminate the impossible, all you have left is: they planned the murders." Jack turned to his partner. "So they could enjoy them."

Monday, September 1st, 1969, 11:26 AM

Two sweaty, delivery men placed the heavy wood console down. The brand-new stereo made everything else in Jack's living room look older and dustier. Delware nodded approvingly, but Jack frowned in his chair like the mustached delivery men were moving in.

Delware walked up and patted the stereo. "Welcome to 1969, Jack!" He un-sleeved a black vinyl disc from the White Album, lifted the lid of the console and placed the glossy disc on the turntable. "This is the way modern people listen to music."

He lifted the arm of the record player and dropped the needle on the spinning disc. The needle popped and hissed in the groove and then the room filled with music.

Jack was amazed, but hid it well. The instruments were all around him.

Delware spoke over Paul McCartney. "This is Hi-Fidelity!"

Jack gave a deadpan, "Charming."

Like a salesman, Delware waved his hands before the two built-in speakers on either end of the console. "What you're listening to is a stereophonic LP. Long Playing. More songs, better sound. It's not like your old mono record player with one speaker. In stereo, the music is spread across two speakers so it's like the band is right in the room with you."

Lifting the needle, he put on the next song. *Blackbird* gently pulsed from the console. Delware motioned to the inside of the long cabinet. "It even has a space to store your LPs in."

Jack squirmed in his seat. He hated lectures, especially from some punk black kid. "OK. OK. Just turn it off."

Delware lifted the needle and placed the arm back on its miniature stand. The turntable automatically stopped spinning.

Jack shook his head at the stereo. "Goddamn thing."

Delware grinned at the old man's sour mug. "Well, now you can listen to the White Album at home."

Jack pushed himself up from his chair with an expressionless, "I'm thrilled." He closed the door behind the deliverymen and turned to Delware. "OK, kid, been studying the lyrics you typed up." Jack walked to the center of the room. "Now what did we find at the crime scene?"

Delware took off his red windbreak. "The Bible."

"Now what's the significance? What is the Bible?"

Delware knew the answers – they had gone over this ground many times. "A message."

Jack corrected, "A message from God, a series of messages."

Jack paced in front of Delware. "And the pages torn from The Book of Revelations, The Apocalypse, were used to write the messages on the wall. What is the Apocalypse?"

Delware rolled his eyes, reciting his pat reply. "Helter skelter."

Jack nodded. "Yes. And no Bible quotes in blood, only lyrics from the White Album – what does *that* mean?"

Delware took a moment. "He believes they're related?"

Jack increased his pace. "Exactly, now what type of

message is the Apocalypse of Saint John?"

Delware leaned back on the stereo. "Prophecy."

"Right! A prophecy of destruction. That's what the White Album is to him: a warning of things to come."

Delware sat back and looked doubtfully at Jack.

Jack was silent for a moment, his eyes somewhere else, as if he was searching, sniffing at the trail he had found.

Delware interrupted the old man's reverie. "So the messages in blood, we're now going to look for ... a secret code? In the White Album?"

Jack glanced at Delware. "That's it, kid."

Delware shook his head. "I got to say it again ... are we really going to find this guy – looking at lyrics?"

Jack's eyes focused on Delware. "So what you worried about? Your career?"

"Everyone thinks we're crazy."

"You want that gold shield, kid?"

Delware rolled his eyes, the old man knew the answer.

Jack scratched his unshaven face. "Tin shields are for those who follow procedure, an admirable quality, but gold shields are for those with the guts to investigate a long shot. If you're not willing, kid, if you can't play the odds, you don't deserve to be called detective and you shouldn't be hunting killers."

"But what happens if you're just following an elaborate ruse?"

"Then Dirk catches the guy."

Delware looked away, watching that gold shield vanish into thin air.

"Kid, there's no magic in what Dirk's doing. Procedure you can learn from anyone. I'm showing you how to *hunt*. We're going into the wilderness. We're looking for maniacs." Jack approached. "You ever heard of James Brussel?"

Delware shook his head.

"Early 50s, he came up with this idea. It may not be accepted procedure, but I'll tell you, the man's onto something: Criminal Profiling – a way to detect sickos who kill for fun. You don't hunt these guys by usual methods, 'cause there's no personal connection with their victims. So you study the killer's MO. You build a picture of him – his habits. You narrow down who you're looking for. A case like that slipped through my fingers once, 'cause I was looking in all the wrong places. I've been waiting, waiting for years to get a crack at another one. And this is it."

Jack walked over to the battered table where his notes were scattered: white pages, black typed lyrics, some circled in red, others with scribbled annotations cramming the margins. "Now if I went through these lyrics and found nothing, I'd look somewhere else, but I found plenty." He grinned down at the mess of paper. "This is his blueprint. It tells us about our guy and what to look for."

Delware walked to the table. "So we're just following unproven procedure and ... your gut? Like a pair of Wild West sheriffs?"

"Fuck that. I'm the sheriff, you're a goddamn deputy." Jack sat. "So, you gonna join the posse, or what?"

Delware spun a chair around and straddled it, surveying the notes between them.

Jack grinned. "Saddle up!"

He began to organize the pages. Delware glanced across the table at Jack with the same apprehension as when Jack sped through stop signs.

Jack frowned. "This album is full of violence. Look at this song, *Piggies*. It was stumping me." He slipped a piece of scribbled paper towards him, and shook the page in the air. "I always thought this was about cops, but it's about rich capitalist pigs: City Hall, the rich, the Hollywood elite." Jack kept his eyes on the page. "My granddaughter says that all we – the establishment – care about is money and power. Now listen to this, will ya. It says the pigs need a '*whacking*', slang for murder. It even mentions forks and knives – the murder weapons!"

A laugh escaped from Delware. "Jack, you can't be serious."

Jack leaned forward. "*Piggies* was written in Sharon Tate's blood. So, yes, I'm dead serious. Look at these titles: Revolution #1, Helter Skelter, Revolution #9, Happiness Is a Warm Gun – the only time a gun is warm is when you just shot somebody."

Delware leaned back in his chair. "Jack, that song's sarcasm."

"Not to our psycho. He's a true believer, an all-or-nothing type. There's a total lack of sexual fetish at the crime scene. We got ourselves a man on a mission: making a statement, taking revenge on the society that rejected him."

Delware's eyes went wide. "Jack, how can you read so much into this? So you're saying it's political?"

Jack stared down Delware. "Our guy's obsessed with the Apocalypse. This is religious!"

Delware shook his head doubtfully.

"You think I'm outta my skull, don't ya?" Jack sat back, reframing his partner. "Our psycho lives by his own twisted code, and that's what will lead us to him. We need to find that code. It's a riddle, a whisper the sane can barely hear." Jack pulled another sheet. "Look at this song – this is where the Apocalypse comes in. *Rocky Raccoon* mentions the Bible – says *Gideon's Bible* checks out." Jack tossed the page. "And the last word in the song: revival – to revive, to rise, *to rise up*."

Delware blinked at the mad logic. "To revolt? Revolution?"

"Psychos see meaning where no one else does. Our guy

thinks he's a soldier, a Messiah. That murder scene, the moment I saw it, I thought of a slaughterhouse. Think about it: these rich, famous, good looking victims – the establishment – slaughtered with knives like pigs." Jack grabbed another sheet. "The song Revolution, the singer says count me out of destruction, but then he whispers '*in*.'" Jack tossed the sheet aside. "A secret message: count me *in* for destruction."

Delware looked doubtfully across the table. "Jack, the Beatles are not-"

"Revolution #9! This is not even music." Jack plowed on. "It's just sound effects, but listen to it: machine-gun fire, the oinking of pigs. This song *is* the revolution – *underway*. At one point someone screams 'rise' over and over again." Jack starting looking for another page, but couldn't find it. "It also appears in this song Blackbird, the lyrics say something like *this is the moment to rise*."

Delware protested. "Jack!"

Jack raised a finger. "Shut up, will ya!" He glared down at a sheet. "In the whole album only one city is mentioned. *Hollywood*. In Honey Pie, it's sung twice." He glanced up. "Which brings us back to our crime scene: the Hollywood Hills. The only place mentioned in all these lyrics!" Jack stood. "It's a map. The whole record is a plan, a message." Jack slammed his hand on the table. "This is what our guy hears: Helter Skelter, The Apocalypse! It's coming down fast! Gideon checks out, this is the time to rise! To destroy the pigs. To start the revolution!" Jack paced around the table in quick strides. "Somewhere in all this is another clue to where he's hiding, I know it! And he's damn close. He won't run, 'cause he believes God is on his side."

Delware threw up his arms. "This is all *crazy*!"

Jack calmly pulled a cigar from his jacket and lit it. Strolling to his chair, he gave Delware a long side look.

"You're finally catching on, kid." Sitting, he took a big puff and nodded to himself. "*Crazy.*" Exhaling a long cloud of smoke, he gazed through it at Delware and grinned. "*That's* what we're looking for."

Wednesday, September 3rd, 1969, 10:32 AM

The call came in to Pat's desk, Dirk yelling at the other end. Their main suspect, the missing groundskeeper from the Tate residence, had been ID-ed! A snitch had spotted Ray Claborn at a North Hollywood bus station. Dirk was out of county; Pat had to nab him. By 10:43. Homicide was buzzing with plainclothesmen slinging pump-action shotguns. At 10:45, Pat burst out of City Hall's backdoor loading a shotgun. Half of Homicide followed him into the parking lot.

Jack and Delware, newly arrived, hadn't even closed the doors of the Packard when Pat whistled and headed for them. "Claborn's been spotted. We're going *now*. He's in North Hollywood boarding a bus for Mexico."

Pat stepped onto the running board of the Packard and turned to the circling officers. "No uniforms, don't even whisper to any patrolmen who may be at the scene. It's too important. Pack everyone into as few cars as possible; I don't want this to turn into a parade. Everyone follows my car. We'll take the Hollywood Freeway to Chandler. I'll pull over just before Laurel Canyon. Our bus station's right on the corner."

Detectives piled into the Packard before Delware could even take a step. Suddenly, a dozen officers disappeared into three cars, leaving Pat and Delware standing in the lot. Pat looked at the packed cars, then waved to Delware. "You're with me. C'mon!"

Pat felt awkward, sitting beside the officer whose career he had done so much to stymie. He felt a tinge of guilt; Delware's reports on the Tate case had been way above average and, more importantly, showed solid police work. But looking over at how young he was, Pat felt even if Delware had been white, he might not have made it into Homicide yet.

They got onto the Hollywood Freeway. Jack's Packard was right behind them – followed by two unmarked Ford LTDs. Delware sat silent.

The awkwardness got to Pat. "That was a good find at the Tate residence. The LSD."

Delware nodded. "Thanks."

"Jack must not have liked it."

"Why?"

"Well, it strengthens Dirk's theory that it was a drug deal."

Delware shrugged. These old guys just didn't get it. It was 1969. Drugs were everywhere. Dentists, accountants, even lawyers were experimenting. If they started kicking down doors they'd find LSD and pot in living rooms all over LA.

Exits came and went: Flower St., Harbor Freeway, Echo Park. Delware's silence continued.

Pat kept glancing at him. "So how you like working with Jack?"

Taking a long side look at Pat, Delware didn't know how to play this. Should he kiss ass and say everything's fine? But how could the head of Homicide not know what type of cop Jack was?

Delware decide to just say it. "Well, he doesn't fit with all the Department's talk about *the new professionalism*."

Pat laughed. "Jack and I come from another era, the

last of a dying breed. Hell, when we started out, there wasn't even an academy. They just handed you a Billy club and let the streets teach you."

"Isn't it dangerous to keep him in the Department? I mean, I'm pretty sure you don't run Homicide like he works cases."

Pat shook his head. "Hell, he's only got a few months to go." LA passed in Pat's windshield. "He may be just some old cop to you, but Jack was king once. Jack *was* Homicide. The guy started out as one of the toughest street cops I've ever seen, and I've seen 'em all. Served in WWII and came back a war hero, he almost bled to death bringing in a shot-up plane full of wounded men. *A national hero*, that's what he was. Not that anyone remembers now. When he made detective, he solved every major case from the late forties to the end of the fifties. He was a star, troubleshooting cases other detectives couldn't even make headway on – reported directly to Chief Parker himself! Forget about section heads, he was his own section and could get anyone he wanted assigned to him."

Delware remembered an old picture at Jack's house: he was Humphrey Bogart handsome in a sharp suit. Delware had never thought of it, but Jack cut quite the figure in his day. He smiled. It was hard to imagine the old man at the peak of his profession *and* being 'cool.'
"What happened?"

Pat caught the ramp to Chandler. "Time." The streets passed in Pat's eyes. "The Department changed, Chief Parker had his heart attack. Jack lost his political and Departmental connections as the old guard retired. He got older, drank too much, worked too late, slowed down. Yet while everyone else was retiring, he kept at it. But then his wife died. Knocked the wind out of his sails and it never came back. The bottle ruined what was left."

Delware understood the reverence he heard in Pat's

voice. Despite his racism and drinking on the job, the old man still had a touch of that power, that light of confidence. Delware had weighed all his options the night after his humiliation at the morgue. He boiled down everything he knew about Jack and the case. In the end, it was Jack's confidence that swayed him. Even though he couldn't believe Jack's theory for a second, his gut told him that Jack could solve the case.

Pat pulled a file wedged beside his seat and passed it to Delware. "Take a look at that mug."

Delware flipped the file open. Clipped to the first page was a mug shot of Ray Claborn.

Seeing Laurel Canyon ahead, Pat pulled to the curb. The other cars followed. Pat and Delware got out. Detectives filed out onto the sidewalk. Jack led the group to Pat. "How should we take him?"

"We're going to take him as he's boarding." Pat checked his watch. "We got ten minutes." He waved a finger at his men. "He's *not* boarding. We take him *in* the line up."

Pat surprised everyone. "Delware goes in."

Jack looked at Pat like he was crazy. Pat relished using Jack's own line on him. "He'll never see him coming."

Pat turned to Delware in his jean vest and t-shirt. "You look nothing like a cop. I want you to go buy a ticket to Tijuana, sit right beside this ugly sonvabitch. I want you directly behind him as the passenger's line up to board. I'll make the pinch, but I want your .38 in his back the moment I do. Do you understand?"

Delware nodded. "Yeah."

Pat waved a finger. "Don't fuck this."

~ ~ ~

The old bus station was from the golden age of Hollywood: tall swank ceilings, art deco walls and BIG. Forty years ago the place said 'Welcome to Hollywood, the dream capital of the world!' now it just said 'old.' It was packed with grimy drifters, GIs, sailors, long hairs looking lost or hustling. Delware navigated through blacks, Latinos and raggedy white folk. Poor families lined wooden benches. Runaways with stars in their eyes headed for the streets. Then he spotted him: Ray Claborn sitting on a long crowded bench. Without turning his head, Delware looked him over. Ray sat, trying to play it cool, but his foot was tapping and his eyes darted: the guy was high.

Delware walked right past him, so close he could smell the marijuana smoke still on his clothes. He sauntered to the ticket booth and leaned on the counter. "One way to Tijuana."

The fat, bald man behind the counter gave him a grunt and a dirty look. Delware wanted to ask him what his problem was, but thought, *no time for this racist honky now*. Without looking, the man handed him a ticket and gave a resentful, "Dock 13."

Delware turned. Ray was gone. His seat was empty. Delware's eyes swept the station. It was chaos, hundreds of people walking in every direction. He took a few steps from the counter, his heart pounding in his ears.

His eyes raced, but still ... nothing. Had Ray made him for a cop? Did he go for the door? Had he just gone to line up? Delware had to gamble. He headed for the boarding area, moving fast, his eyes doing double time. Delware rounded a corner, still no Ray. He ran to the dock doors, but slowed to enter causally. There were forty buses and hundreds of people and enough diesel fumes to choke everyone on the platform. He made his way through the crowd, bumping into luggage, his feet shuffling and skipping. His eyes scanned the crowd. He saw Ray.

Delware looked with disbelieving eyes. His orders were to be right behind him, but Ray was at the head of a long line of white sailors, probably headed for whorehouses south of the border. Delaware would have to bud ahead of them all and worse, right behind Ray was a pretty white woman and her blonde three-year-old girl. The sailors were all eying her and giving her daughter polite smiles. He would have to cut directly in front of them.

Shuffling by the line of sailors, Delware tried to look casual. A few less than sober eyes followed him. He paused. Two sailors directly behind the young mother and daughter laughed and looked the other way. He nudged in front of the woman. She stepped back with a grunt of protest. Two sailors in midline caught the move and eyeballed Delware *hard*. This was going to blow everything. One sailor elbowed the other. They stepped out of line and headed for Delware. Everything was about to get fucked up. Delware glanced at the woman with a weak smile. She gave him the evil eye. This was no time to be black in America. The little girl started to whine. The sailors were closing in. Delware's mind raced. He had to do something. He slipped his jacket back just enough so the sailors could see his holstered .38. They stopped in their tracks, then retreated towards a uniformed cop on the dock. The uniform would have no clue of what was about to happen.

Tempted to just pull out his revolver and take Ray down right there and then, Delware unclipped his holster.

Like a flash, Jack rounded the front of the bus with daggers in his eyes; coming from the side was Pat, his gun drawn down by his side. Ray saw Jack's gun and turned to run, almost knocking Delware over. Delware pulled his gun, grabbed Ray and pushed him to the ground. He got his knee on Ray's back and his gun to his head and was about to yell 'freeze police' when someone yelled those words at him. He looked up and found the uniform cop pointing his gun at his head. Delware stared down the barrel, his badge still under his jacket. The young cop was panicked, his pistol shaking, his finger *way* too tight on the trigger. Delware winced, expecting a bullet. He could almost hear the gun go off.

Jack yelled out, "Don't shoot that coon!"

The patrolman looked up at Jack and Pat with their gun trained on him. Other plainclothes detectives came running with shotguns and .38s in their fists shouting and waving, "Police! Police!" The uniform gave them the deer-in-the-headlights look.

Delware slapped the cuffs on Ray. Ray twisted his neck to look up. In amazement, he groaned at Delware, "You a cop?"

Delware smiled. "That's right, mothafucka!"

~ ~ ~

The hall outside the interrogation rooms was tense. Every detective in Central Division was squeezed in with the brass *and* the DA. No one would leave. No one told anyone to. The whole Department was on the case and more would be arriving the longer they stood there. A moment of truth was coming and everyone had the right to see it. The air conditioning was out. Men sweated and vied to peer through the one-way glass. The only space was inside the cubical where the suspect was being held. Ray Claborn sat cuffed in a bolted down chair in front of a bolted down table. His face was bruised, swelling and bleeding. He hunched over in pain. The only man in there with him: Dirk.

Vince, the District Attorney, and Pat were at the glass, their eyes locked on Claborn.

Vince looked worried. "What are you doing? Where's the polygraph?"

Pat growled, "We'll polygraph him later! Right now, I want answers and I'm going to get 'em."

Dirk unlocked Ray's cuffs and offered him a cigarette. With a shaking hand the suspect accepted the smoke. His other hand lay limp at his side. He winced. "I didn't do nothing. I told that old cop that beat me in the car again and again. He broke my finger. I need a doctor."

"Then who killed them?"

"Fuck if I know. They never talked to me – why would they? – except if they wanted something fixed. But I'll tell you this, they brought it on themselves. Those Hollywood types, you know?"

"No, I don't know."

"The victims, man, they were into satanic shit! Vodoo! The orgy scene...it's in the fuckin' papers. They got what they had coming." Ray shook his head. "Live freaky, man, die freaky." Ray's squat face sweated. His dark eyes darted. "Hell, the papers know more than I do. I ain't lying!"

"Good. Then tell me what you know."

Ray shrugged. "Nada. I mind my own business. I didn't see shit happening up there. I told you."

"Fine. Tell me again."

"Jesus! Really? I told you and every cop a dozen times now." He protested, "Even thinking about that night makes me piss my pants!" Ray rubbed his wrists. "It's a miracle I wasn't killed with the rest of them!"

The last vestiges of Dirk's friendly demeanor vanished. He eyed Ray. Ray got the message.

Ray slumped back and threw up his hands. "I was smoking reefer."

"Start earlier."

Ray dropped his head and answered in fatigued monotones. "I went down to the strip to get some smokes, and a TV dinner, you see? I got back about ten. I eat."

"Then?"

"Then, I smoked a few reefer, listened to Hendrix on my earphones. My cat starts jumping around, acting crazy and making this strange sound, like crying. I took off my earphones to check it out. It was after midnight and it seemed quiet...very quiet. But then I hear music from the house, scary-like, like when you hear music from far away ... and the cat, she's jumping like a maniac. Then I hear something."

"What?"

Ray started to sweat. "The popping sound. I thought some jerk was setting off firecrackers, so I looked out the window. It was very dark, but then I see 'em -'cause they're running in front of the lit windows. People on the lawn. Well, I opened the door and the cat just scrammed straight into the woods. Then I heard screaming. Lots of screaming. And swearing. Someone yelling, 'Oh god, please don't kill me.'"

Ray's eyes were wide with a hypnotic horror. "I stepped out and around the side of the house."

"What did you see?"

"Nothing, so I keep walking towards the house." He clasped his trembling hands and looked like he might piss himself.

"So what did you do?"

"I go across the lawn. I was so *stoned*, I thought I might just be really high, man. But as I go near the house...I got scared. I mean, the screaming was inside and around me and it was very dark. Freaking me out. I got to the porch step and just froze. I hear like people swearing and things getting knocked over inside. I just stood there, like too afraid, I couldn't move. Then ... then the front door opened and there's a girl standing there. Her face covered in blood. Her arms all cut up...her dress full of blood, man. She just stood there, like trying to scream, but no sound came out.

Ray's face was beading with sweat. "Then she collapsed right in the doorway, like dead. I hear this sound behind me. People running. I turned and I can't see too good 'cause it's ... black, but there out on the lawn – this guy falls and like three other people just stabbing him, but there was one tall dude with a baseball bat or something, he's just beating the guy. They didn't see me, I was being very quiet. I got back to my place and just ran, that's when I heard the gunshot. It was really loud. I turned and this guy on his knees was now down on the ground... and the tall dude stood over him with a gun."

"That's the last thing you saw before you ran into the woods?"

Ray nodded.

"There was a bloody female footprint found that didn't match any of the victims. Did you see anyone get away?"

Ray shook his head. "No, man."

Dirk leaned in. "And why didn't you call the police?"

"'Cause of my warrants. I just didn't want to go back to jail. And I thought the killers might be hunting me! I just ran and ran for miles into the hills, you know, like they were following me. Then I hid. About three in the morning, I saw the police lights down at the house. I just took off. That's all. I only saw shadows, didn't see nothing, not one face. And the police were already there. So I took off."

"You can't give a better description?"

"I told you, I only saw shadows."

"You didn't recognize any voices."

Ray shook his head.

Dirk asked, "Why you run to Mexico?"

"I heard the police were looking for me, then saw the paper saying I did it. I got afraid, man."

"So you bought a bus ticket to Mexico?"

Ray nodded. "Yeah."

~ ~ ~

Delware wandered away from the crowded hallway. It

was still sinking in: his close brush with death. The gun at his head left him stunned and just grateful to be alive. Leaving the interrogation rooms, he found himself looking for his partner. Jack wasn't on the third floor, or the second. Delware found him on the first at the end of a quiet marble hallway. He sat on an old wooden bench near the exit, looking like an old man in a church pew, staring off into nothing. His grizzled head nodding in deep thought.

Quiet and humble, as if attending a funeral, Delware sat beside him. Jack didn't notice.

Delware dropped his head and spoke in a whisper, "You know, you called me 'coon.'"

Jack turned surprised and raised an eyebrow.

Delware quoted, "Don't shoot the *coon*."

Jack spoke softly, "I was trying to save you from getting your damn head blown off."

Looking at the floor, Delware remembered the gun's nozzle just a few inches from his face. "It *was* close."

Jack sat back almost smiling. "Honestly, kid, I thought you were a *goner*. That rookie must have been an hour out of the academy. I've never seen a cop so scared. He was *squeezing* that trigger. I swear, if a squirrel had farted in Arizona, you wouldn't be here now."

Nodding, Delware silently thanked God he was alive.

Jack eyed his partner. "You know, you get a wild look in your eye when you pull your gun. Hell, between the way you dress and that look – *I* would have taken you for a born-to-lose low rider."

Both men fell silent.

Delware glanced up and tilted his head back down the hall. "So, why aren't you in there?"

Jack shrugged. "Wrong guy."

"What do you mean?"

"I mean, our psycho's still out there...and more people

are going to die."

"You don't make Ray as the primary? How can you tell it's not the right collar?"

Jack looked down at his bloody knuckles. Delware guessed Ray's blood, not Jack's.

Jack absentmindedly picked a thread from his wrinkled trousers. "I interrogated the kid on the way over. After thirty years, I can smell a lie like shit on my shoes. The kid's clean, at least of our murders. I knew the moment I saw him. But I beat the shit out of him, just to make sure. I'll know our killer, I'll know him the moment I see him."

"Are you sure?"

"Kid, I've seen it all ... twice. Before you were born I was walking a beat, climbing up through Vice, Bunco and Narcotics; I've busted them all: con men, addicts, cheats, lying pimps, thieves, winos ... bums with no address and whores who can't keep one.

"The most frustrating part is being able to read someone. You just know 'em – the type: that's a thief, that's a rapist. You stop seeing what makes them look normal to everyone else. You read the Braille of their character. I see a kid; I know there's no hope. He's going to murder someone someday as sure as other boys are gonna hit puberty. And there's nothing you can do about it. They don't even know they're going to do it themselves.

"I'll spot our killer – in a glance. I just need to see him. I even know what he'll say."

"Yeah?" Delware stared at Jack with doubting eyes. "What's he going to say?"

"Him? He'll call me a *pig*."

Delware laughed, "Jack – every hippie calls cops pigs."

"Yeah." Jack nodded, then grinned at Delware. "But our guy's going to *mean* it."

1:47 PM

Shoving the back door of City Hall open, Jack winced in the bright parking lot. He headed for the Packard baking in the sun. Delware followed, shaking off another wasted day, another dead end.

Jack felt his age, his knuckles hurt, his eyes burned, hunger gnawed his stomach. "I can't even think straight." He kicked at the ground. "It's been nearly a month and I still don't know Hell's first whisper about our psycho. Maybe I'm dead wrong, kid."

"It might be we're looking in the wrong direction. I mean Jack, I can see the holes in Dirk's theory, but there's one big hole in yours."

Cocking his head, Jack waited.

Delware felt his full attention. "Just one thing that doesn't lay right in your theory – the way they got in: through a window. Now that's the choice of an experienced burglar. A bunch of crazed hippies would jimmy a back door or burst in the front door like amateurs. And if there were four, maybe five of them, they would all have to sneak around to the back of the residence, slit a screen, crawl through a small window, move all the way down the back of the house into the kitchen and pull knives from the drawers – all without anyone noticing or hearing them. Maybe a single experienced burglar could have done that, but four, five of them? So many showing such a degree of experience? Jack, where would crazed hippies learn that type of controlled entry? Where would they gain that level of experience?"

The question stopped Jack, but his stomach growled and he lost the train of thought. "Damn it, kid, not right now. I haven't eaten all day. I'm too hungry to even put two and two together." He glanced at the Mel's Drive-in across the street and headed towards it.

Delware followed. "I can't explain it, Jack. It seems more likely that they *were* professionals." As he spoke, it dawned on him. That picture that had been forming on the horizon of his mind, the map he had almost grasped that night alone in Homicide at Dirk's desk now became vividly clear. "We've been looking in the wrong direction!"

Delware ran back into City Hall.

Jack watched and yelled after him, "Kid!" Shaking his head, Jack gave up and muttered to himself, "He must be high as a kite. They're not going to let him into Homicide." Jack headed towards Mel's. "Ahhh, fuck him. Let him go earn his Junior G-man badge. Kid apprehends a single suspect, and now he thinks he's Sherlock fuckin' Holmes."

~ ~ ~

Mel's Drive-in was a fifties-style diner: big plate glass windows, wrap-around booths, black and white checkerboard floor, steel stools along a drawn out counter. The place smelled of grease and was almost empty. It might look passable at night, but it was grimy in the bright afternoon. Jack grabbed a booth so he could look over the street. Halfway through a cheeseburger and a side order of fries, Jack saw Delware running across street. "Awww, Holy Christ. Here comes Junior G-Man with some harebrained hunch."

Delware busted into the diner, spotted Jack and ran to his table. "Jack, you won't believe this."

Jack calmly sipped his milkshake and gave Delware a cynical stare.

Delware eyes were wide with excitement. "Jack, I found-"

Jack's hand shot up. "Hold on, kid!"

"What?"

He smiled and held up his burger. "You know, there could be a bank robbery across the street right now and I might have to go over there and shoot it out with some shitbirds. But let me tell you something, I would take this burger with me. Between shots, I'd still be taking bites of this delicious cheeseburger."

Delware looked wild with bewilderment. "Jack! I found-"

"Know why?"

"Jack!"

Jack shook his burger at Delware. "Do you know why, kid?!"

Delware gave in. "Why?!"

Taking a bite, Jack talked with his mouth full. "'Cause nothing bothers a cop while he's eating."

~ ~ ~

They jaywalked across Spring. Jack dusted crumbs off his jacket with a hand still full of fries. He waved at cars to stop with his burger.

Delware led the way. "I'll bet you this is it!"

Jack popped a load of fries in his mouth and gave a sarcastic, "You're on, kid."

They entered the main hallway of headquarters. Jack made quick work of what was left of his cheeseburger

Delware outpaced him. "Jack, I thought about it, we've been looking for similar murders, but we should be looking for other crimes with similar MOs."

Jack stopped in the middle of the hallway. With distant eyes, he looked beyond the station: Delware was right. Crimes just didn't happen. There was always a run up, early warning signs that needed to be looked for. Tracking the killers in his mind, Jack followed the marks they had left. For a second, Jack's breath stopped in a moment of pure concentration. He saw four hippies in the dead of night silently slitting the screen, saw them quietly crawling through the window and creeping slowly through the darkened passages in the back of the Tate mansion, entering the kitchen and opening the drawers until they found...knives.

Jack gasped. "They learned it! It was part of their plan!"

Delware turned; shocked that Jack had read his mind.

Jack's eyes went wide. "They practiced beforehand."

Delware jumped. "That's right! We've been looking for similar murders. We went through the city *and* county files. There's nothing like it."

Jack nodded. "Yes, but-"

"But they learned in stages! Like predators – they practiced *tracking* their prey, before their first *kill*. Now, how would they practice something like that?!"

Jack beamed. "Burglaries!"

~ ~ ~

Lieutenant Rollins, a tall gray-haired Texan, leaned back in his chair, watching Jack and Delware enter Robbery Division.

Jack gave him a half salute and swallowed the last of his fries. "Hey Henry, you got something for us?"

Rollins popped a stick of gum into his mouth and spoke in a drawl between chews. "Officer Hicks said he wanted anything strange. Well, this is as strange as you can get."

Jack wiped his greasy fingers on his pants. "Whatcha got?"

"Break and Enters with nothing stolen."

"Nothing?"

"They do everything a burglar does, but don't take a thing. It's plain and pointless."

"So just break and enter?"

"Not exactly, I said nothing is taken, but everything is rearranged."

"What do you mean?"

Rollin's tossed a file across his desk. "They move everything around in the house: furniture, whole living rooms, kitchen sets."

Jack picked up the file. "And how many of these do you have?"

Rollins pointed behind the two detectives.

Jack and Delware turned. The whole wall was a map: greater LA laid out before them. Pins and notes dotted the streets and neighborhood. Jack and Delware approached the wall.

Rollins leaned farther back in this chair. "Red pins are house burglaries. Black pins are car thefts. White are store break-ins."

Delware noticed dried wads of gum stuck in one neighborhood. "What's the gum mean?"

Jack and Rollins laughed. Jack said, "I think those are ours."

Rollins piped in, "Yeah, gum means bullshit that ain't worth a pin, but we still got to write reports on 'em. B&Es where nothing is taken is *bullshit*. I don't got enough pins for bullshit."

Jack grinned. But Delware stared at the near circle of dried gum. They were all in Bel Air and at the center of that circle was Ceilo Drive. Delware gasped under his breath. "Jesus. Jack, all of these are in the Hollywood Hills."

Jack saw it too. Without his eyes leaving the map, he spoke to Rollins. "I think we need those reports."

~ ~ ~

Rollins pulled a dozen manila files from a series of gray metal cabinets. "Yeah, we didn't know what the hell was going on. We thought it was pranksters, you know, college kids having a hoot. I mean, burglars usually break in when no one's home. Well, all of these occur while the families *are* home – asleep, mind you."

He dropped the files. They spilled across the desk. "I've never seen anything like it. Goddamn mansions – can you believe it? Not a thing taken."

Delware turned to Jack "Why wouldn't they take something?"

Jack opened a file. "'Cause they wanted to remain under the radar – no major crime, no major investigation."

Rollins nodded. "Well, *they* got that right."

~ ~ ~

Delware and Jack sorted a dozen reports at a single desk. Every file was not more than a page or two and many were hardly filled out. Rollins sat at his desk, shouting at one of his men over the phone.

Jack dropped a file on his desk. "A real waste of paper! No one saw anything and the one that did –" He pulled out a sheet and held it above his head. "This description's horseshit!"

Rollin's covered the receiver. "Maybe the witness didn't see much."

"Malarkey! This guy didn't take more than a second on this. All it says is the old lady made a sighting; suspect description is BLANK!"

Rollins spit out his gum into a waste paper basket. "Jack, nothing was stolen. What do you expect? We fingerprint the place? Call in the FBI?"

Jack threw the file at Rollins. "Look at that! There's not even a badge number on it! Who's the reporting officer?"

Rollins perused the single sheet report and placed the handwriting. He yelled across the office, "Koufax!"

An impossibly thin detective turned his head and Rollins waved him over.

Delware came up beside Jack. Jack whispered out of the side of his mouth. "This is the best we've got, happened a few months ago. We'll go up and re-interview the witness ourselves after we talk to this clown."

~ ~ ~

Koufax sat at the desk facing them. He shrugged. "You really think this is important? Honestly, I didn't think it was much." Koufax's eyes roamed the scattered reports. "Figured it's just a bunch of kids. They left every window in the house open, every drawer pulled opened in the kitchen – counters filled with every fork and knife, all laid out. Very strange."

Jack grumbled, "A *bunch* of kids? Why ya guys keep saying that?"

Koufax nodded. "Yeah, it's not a one man job, *and* the one sighting: a group of kids."

Jack frowned at Koufax. "Details, Detective!"

"An old lady, gets up real early, saw a group of kids running away in the morning."

Jack growled, "A group! That's not much of a description!" Jack waved the report in front of him. "And *you* left it blank. Why?!"

Koufax shrugged, embarrassed. "All she said was long hair and ripped jeans – very dirty. What was I supposed to write? *Damn dirty hippies?*"

Delware and Jack exchanged glances.

Rollins at his desk shouted, "It's a school project, kids out on a field trip."

Koufax laughed.

Jack turned on Rollins. "What?"

Rollins swirled in his wooden chair. "It's a division

joke. Since nothing is taken and it's a group, we came up with a theory that someone is giving burglary lessons."

Koufax smiled. "A class on how to break into highline mansions."

Rollins grinned. "Yeah."

Koufax grinned at Rollins.

Rollins shook his head at Jack. "It's not burglars. Burglars always make sure no one's home. This group always makes sure owners *are* home. Doesn't make sense."

A passing detective with a loose tie and coffee overhearing the conversation, whispered at Jack, "Creepy Crawly."

Jack turned his head and watched the detective vanish out the door. "What the hell was that?"

Rollins tried not to laugh. "Just another joke. That's what we call this supposed school of burglars. The School of Creepy Crawly."

Delware asked, "Why?"

"A piece of vandalism they left behind. In one mansion, in the kitchen, they took a jar of strawberry jam and wrote on the wall, 'Creepy Crawly.'"

Koufax laughed. "Pretty funny, huh? When I first walked into the kitchen I thought it was blood."

Thursday, September 4th, 1969, 2:15 AM

The moon had completely disappeared. Smog covered the stars. The only light was from the street lamps outside. In Jack's living room, he slept in his chair. There was a sound like someone walking on the old creaky floors. A shadow passed over his face. His face twisted as if haunted by a nightmare. Jack heard ghostly whispering in his dreams. He tried to speak. Suddenly, he shot up in his chair, his eyes spooked.

Thursday, September 4th, 1969, 10:45 AM

The Packard pulled up to a chateau-style mansion, three stories high with a veranda over the main doors. Its white fountain glowed behind the iron rod fence in the morning sunlight. The gate was open. Two landscaping trucks blocked the driveway. Sweaty, sun burnt workmen loaded up their mowers.

Jack and Delware weaved through the workers and walked up the long drive. The front lawn was a carpet of deep green grass freshly mowed in a crisscross pattern. It looked like a vast checkerboard. The smell of clippings still hung in the air. Once off the drive, they passed under palm trees and could see a shaded patio.

Jack wiped his shoes on the mat and rang the bell. Delware stared at the mahogany doors. They reminded him of the huge church doors his mother would drag him through every Sunday. The door opened revealing a gray haired woman in a white gown. She still cut an attractive figure, despite the caked make-up on her wrinkles.

She batted her eyes and looked up, admiring Jack. "I should send my butler on errands more often. Look who shows up when *I* answer the door. My, you are a tall one."

Jack shuffled in place, seeming to forget why he rang.

She turned to Delware, her voice oozing privilege. "You're not bad yourself, but a little young. I'd guess you're father and son, but there's no resemblance."

Jack flipped his badge. "Ma'am, I'm Detective Middleton. We're here on police business."

She studied the badge, impressed. "Are you?"

"Are you Mrs. Eleanor Powell?"

She nodded and stepped back to let them in, whispering "A lieutenant? I like a man who's good...but not *too* good."

Two stairways swept down to a marble floor behind her. She sized up the men. "Wellll, you didn't have to show your badge Lieutenant. You have 'cop' written all over you."

Delware eyeballed the vast branching hallways and a massive silver chandelier.

She stepped close to Jack, her expensive Paris perfume wafted. "Am I under arrest? I hope."

Jack ignored the remark. "Ma'am, we're here to follow up on the burglary report you made."

Her eyes hardened. "Oh yes. They didn't take a thing." Her voice continued to sour. "The other officer took it as some type of college prank. I told him, they were very professional and there was nothing funny about it."

Jack pulled out a pad. "They didn't steal anything?"

Delware pulled his eyes away from the rich decor. "What did they do?"

"They re-arranged the furniture...badly."

She focused on Delware. "Look for hippies with poor taste."

Jack questioned. "Hippies?"

"I'm being rude, please come, have a seat." She led the officers into an even larger living room with even taller doors. Wide plate glass windows overlooked LA. The white walls towered over thick white shag. Delware surveyed the shelves and paintings, and found it hard to believe that anyone could break in and not take a thing.

She motioned to a couch with round red pillows. "Please sit. I've been away. We're just getting back to business around here."

She motioned to a bar. "Wellll, can I get you a drink?"

Jack replied, "No, thanks, we're on duty."

As Jack passed, she smelled the scotch on him. She sniffed loudly and gave him a knowing, "Yes, you are." She turned without lifting her feet and glanced back over her shoulder. "Wellll, I'm not." She sauntered to a decanter and poured a drink.

Delware was doing inventory on the room: trophies and treasures. *Welcome to White America.*

Jack looked at his notes. "Mrs. Powell, was your husband home at the time?"

She frowned at her drink. "My husband? His mother should have thrown him out and kept the stork." She turned, stirred her drink and studied Jack. "Lieutenant Middleton, you were doing so well and now you've just ruined the mood. Isn't it part of your job to make sure witnesses are ... *co-operative*?"

Jack just stared and waited.

She gave up with a sigh. "No. He's never home if you must know. We divorced a few years ago. A senator's life: serves the public day and night. Well, serving *some* ... more than *others* – especially at night."

She caught Delware gawking at her view of LA. As if speaking kindly to a child, she asked, "Do you like what you see?"

Delware snapped out of it, but before he could answer she spoke. "When I look at the city, I think of ancient Rome."

Delware raised an eyebrow. "Rome?"

She turned to the window. "Ancient Rome was surrounded by hills, just like Los Angeles. I often wonder if the senators' wives of Rome had the same feeling about their city as I do mine." She advanced on him quickly. Holding out her hand, demanding, "May I see *your* badge?"

Delware pulled back his vest.

Her fingers curled, beckoning the badge to her. "Can you unpin it from your T-shirt? I'd like to take a closer look."

Delware glanced at his partner. Jack nodded. Delware handed the badge over. Turning, she walked away, staring at its embossed metal.

She stopped at the window. "Officer Hicks. You're not a detective. I suppose you're being trained by Lieutenant Middleton. So you're just a centurion?"

She turned back to Delware. Delware shrugged.

"Oh surely – a colored man in the police force – I'm assuming you went to college. You must have studied *some* history. Do you not know the history of your own badge?" She walked over and showed him the badge. "Your badge, Officer Hicks – notice its oval shape. It's modeled on the centurion's shield of the Roman legion. That's why it's called a 'shield.' The border design is based on the fasces, a symbol of ancient Roman authority." She handed it back to Delware, addressing him, "Centurion."

She turned to stare out over LA, the hills sloping down to the city blanketed in smog, the tops of distance office towers floating above the haze. "My husband, or should I say my ex-husband is a corrupt, but wealthy senator who plays to the mob, placating them by building coliseums for their sports and entertainment. That is his role." She turned back to Delware. "As an officer of the law, I'm sure you're well acquainted with the decadence and depravity of Hollywood. So you see, we still live in Rome, it is just *neon* this time."

Jack cleared his throat.

She snapped around. "Oh, yes." Gracefully dropping in

a chair, she smiled at Delware. "He's not much of a conversationalist, is he?"

Only the corners of Delware's mouth smiled.

Flashing a diamond, she fixed her hair. "You want to *know* about the break-in." She turned her full attention on Jack. "Soooo, Lieutenant, go ahead...drill me."

Jack bowed his head and let the remark pass. He came up sober as a judge, his eyes locked on her like a pair of handcuffs. Even Delware could feel the air pressure in the room increase. If he had not seen Jack sneaking shots on the way over, he would have sworn the whole drunk policeman was an act.

Jack's voice rang. "In the initial report it said you caught a glimpse of the burglars as they fled."

The woman stiffened. Delware too had been held under Jack's supernatural stare. You knew if you lied, those eyes would see it. The only way out from that unrelenting stare was to tell the truth, the whole truth, and nothing but the truth.

She cleared her throat and straightened up. "Yes, I did. I didn't hear them, but I do get up frightfully early." Trying to escape Jack's eyes, she winked at Delware. "Something that comes on with age."

Delware nodded politely.

Jack pressed on. "The description in the report was vague; I'd like to go over it with you."

"Of course Lieutenant, the other officer did seem to lose interest once I told him nothing was stolen. I believe he thought I was crazy, you know, just amusing myself by attracting the company of younger men."

Jack's voice grew harsh. "Are you saying you got a good look at them?"

She met Jack's gaze. "Well, it was still dark enough, but yes. I had several seconds to observe them as they fled across the back lawn – into the valley. One man was tall, with blonde hair, another shorter with black hair, very dirty looking, and a beard. The girls looked dirty too."

Jack's and Delware snapped a look at each other. Jack said it. "Girls?"

"Yes, Detective, there were two men and three young girls."

Jack leaned forward. "Wait a minute. Are you *sure* they weren't men. Young men today have long hair."

Offended, she gave a cynical, "Do young men also wear dresses now? I hadn't realized fashion had changed so much."

"They wore dresses?"

"Yes, and bare feet. They all had bare feet." She turned her head toward the backyard. "They slashed a screen to get in. It's in the garden shed."

~ ~ ~

Jack headed for the door. "Kid, this is the break we've been looking for! C'mon!" He whispered under his breath. "We got 'em now."

Delware chased after him, but Mrs. Powell caught his arm at the threshold. "You're the first Negro to come in here not dressed as a butler. Be careful. You're walking on thin ice. Listen intently, so you'll hear if it's cracking underneath your feet."

~ ~ ~

Jack and Delware walked to the back of the mansion. Ivy climbed the walls. They skirted bushes and another set of yard workers. Jack led the way with a wild look in his eye. Delware lagged behind, worried.

Jack glanced back. "What's the matter, kid?"

Delware looked at Jack as if the old man had gone mad. But he shook his head and kept quiet.

"Kid, don't listen to that dame, calling you a centurion. Does the LAPD look like a legion of Roman soldiers to you?! Jesus Christ! Imagine us walking around in sandals?" His lips curled with a vicious distain. "Ha! *Centurions* – now I've heard it all! Goddamn lefty with a college degree talking some horseshit about ancient history." Jack held up his head proud as a true patriot and looked over LA. "This is America, kid. This ain't Rome, it's the goddamn Wild West!"

Delware couldn't hold back any longer. "Jack, this makes no sense."

"What?"

"Teenagers! Girls! Young girls are not exactly your typical multi-murderers, let alone psycho killers."

"Are you kidding? That finally explains the bloody female barefoot prints at the scene! There is *no* missing witness. It belongs to one of the killers."

Delware's jaw dropped.

Jack marched on.

Delware yelled after him. "What's next, Jack? Flying saucers? Some mad man controlling their minds?" Delware gave a tense laugh. "This is getting too far out, man! I mean, science fiction far out!"

Jack kept marching, but grinned to himself. "Why? Because it doesn't make sense?"

Delware waved an arm, catching up. "Yeah, that's exactly it, Jack. It doesn't make any goddamn sense!"

Stopping, Jack looked down at his shoes. He turned on Delware. "That's why you can't understand...you think *all this* should make sense!"

Jack shook his head. "You were a rookie. You must have done prisoner transfers to Folsom. You've seen how full the jails are. You know how many low-life punks we find dead in the gutter every morning. How many people we incarcerate daily? Gangbangers, whores, pushers – they crowd the emergency rooms every night of the week maimed, scarred for life by other hustlers. How many get away scot-free? What percent? What are the odds of success in their racket? Even a degenerate gambler won't put money down on their type 'cause sooner or later, kid, criminals fuck up – or get fucked up." Jack rolled his eyes to the sky and scratched his head, his voice imitating a dreamy, perplexed man. "Now what type of person would risk the two most important things: their life and their liberty...with *those* kinds of odds?"

He jabbed Delware's chest with his finger. "I'll tell you who. Idiots and psychos!" Jack paced, waving his arms. "You know what an idiot is? That's a guy who thinks he's smart. Knows it for a fact! Sees everyone else getting caught or killed and thinks – *what a bunch of suckers, but not me.* He's smarter than all of us – the only shitbird criminal on God's Green Earth who *isn't* gonna get caught. That, my friend, is a genuine, blue-blooded *idiot.* Certified and guaranteed! And the jails are full of them." Jack stopped and whispered directly into Delware's face. "Know what a psycho is? A guy who doesn't care about death or jail. Know why?" Jack didn't wait for an answer. "'Cause he's a *psycho!*" He crowded Delware with a wild look in his eyes. "Now you tell me, kid, with those kinds of odds – does crime make *any* sense?"

Delware leaned back. "No."

"And don't expect it to." Jack stepped back and gave Delware some breathing room. "That's why you follow your gut, and the evidence. Because what *they* do will never make sense." He waved a finger. "They don't live like you; they don't think like you. And some days, knowing that ..." Jack spun his finger at his head, "is the only thing that keeps you from losing your fuckin' mind."

Turning, Jack marched on.

Delware's legs went numb. His stomach sank into a bottomless pit. He damned himself. How could he have ever trusted Jack – even for a second? How could he have hoped Jack was a mad genius, a magician who would pull the rabbit out of his hat at the last moment? He regretted being drawn in by the old man. Jack had just crossed the line into irredeemable madness. He watched Jack disappear around a corner, and saw his chance at that gold badge disappear with him.

Coming around the corner, Delware stopped dead in his tracks. The backyard was eerily similar to the Tate's: the in-ground swimming pool, the bushes, the patio almost exactly the same. And then beyond the lawn, the yellow desert valley.

His eyes searched for Jack and found him at the open door of a garden shed. Jack stared inside. "I found it, kid. Just where she said it would be."

Coming to the shed, Delware followed Jack's gaze. He saw it instantly. It was like a moment of déjà vu, except Delware knew exactly where he had seen it before: Cielo Drive. It slapped him in the face. The screen was slit exactly as it had been at the Tate murders. It was not a straight horizontal or vertical slash. It was L-shaped. It was beyond a mental recognition, it was like Jack said it would be: guttural. He knew it with a certainty the mind could never know. Some ancient instinct awoke in him: the hunter.

Delware could not tear his eyes from the screen. "Jesus, Jack."

Jack turned slowly from the screen and looked in the direction the woman said the hippies had run. The green lawn ended at dark emerald bushes, beyond was the yellow sloping desert. Dry and forbidding. Jack became calm and very still, as if listening to distant sounds. He reminded Delware of his uncle's bloodhound in Alabama sniffing the air. There was Jack – on the trail of his prey.

~ ~ ~

The Packard drove on narrow cliff-side roads, down and out of the Hollywood Hills.

Delware looked over at Jack. "I'm not going to sleep tonight ... I admit, I doubted you right up to the moment I saw that screen. Now I know it, Jack. As insane and incredible as it is, you're right. There's a group of killers out there, listening to the White Album." Delware looked at the road ahead. "Jack, they were there, in that residence, in that very room we were standing in."

Jack nodded, "Yes, they were, and they're not going to stop. They've just gotten started."

"Jack, I just knew – like you said."

"That's good. Sometimes when nothing adds up, your gut is the only thing you can trust."

"All the evidence makes more sense now, but it makes who we're looking for...more bizarre."

"That's the number one rule, kid. Suspect everyone."

Delware looked out the window. "And the bloody barefoot print – it's not a female witness. It's one of the suspects."

"Yes. Well, of course they didn't photograph that footprint; it got washed away with the rain. Hell, they're LAPD...why would they want to do a thorough job with murder evidence?" Jack smiled at the road ahead. "You and Dirk would be right ninety-nine percent of the time. It's funny that this is your first case. It's patterns, kid, you learn them. Dirk is looking for the motives that usually work. But acts of passion look one way, premeditated read another way...madness is unmistakable. Its pattern has a fetish feel, like a sick fantasy, almost theatrical, but it's so rare, even when you see it, your routine procedures still kick in. I've made that mistake before – years ago. It took me too long to look in the right direction and by then the trail had grown cold. I vowed never to let that happen again." Jack glanced over at Delware. "I'm going to catch this sumbitch."

Delware looked at Jack with new eyes. "So you could

tell the difference right from the start?"

Jack nodded. "I've had my eyes peeled for this one. Close connections always have the biggest motivation, but this...here the motivation will only make sense to the killers themselves. In this type of case you can only look at the pattern...which is a ritual of sorts."

For the first time, Delware felt something close to respect for the old man. "Jack, how do you do that stare thing?"

Jack gave Delware a questioning glance. "What?"

"You know, when you stare at someone to get the truth, when you don't want a lie. How do you do that really intense stare?"

Jack smiled. "I'm not looking at them, kid."

"What?"

"The first decade on Homicide, I couldn't sleep. I had these reoccurring nightmares. The victims of the cases I was working came to me in dreams, stood over my bed, staring at me as I slept. Scared the shit out of me, I could never get back to sleep. These nightmares felt so real, like these dead people were really there – in my bedroom."

"What did the victims do?"

"Nothing, they just stared."

"That's all?"

"Yeah, I thought they were angry at me for not solving their cases yet, or maybe I was looking in the wrong direction, but then I finally figured it out."

"What?"

Jack shrugged "They wanted to see their killers. But they couldn't. They were on the other side of the grave. They wanted *my eyes*, so they could take one last condemning look at the people who killed them."

Delware shuddered and sat back for a better look at Jack. "That's far out, man. Those nightmares ever go away?"

"No. Since we started this case, I've seen one of our victims a few times."

"Who? One of the Tate victims?"

"Yeah, Sharon. Sharon Tate. In dreams, she showed up, just staring at me. But now I understand and give the dead what they want."

"Jack, what can you give the dead?"

"That stare I do. *I* don't do it, kid. But whenever I want the truth, I lend the dead *my eyes*. When that lady was fucking around this afternoon: *I* didn't stare at her. It was Sharon Tate."

Monday, September 8th, 1969, 8:10 AM

The sun rose over LA's smog and the white tower of City Hall. In Robbery Division, Delware sat shifting through files dredged up from June's reports. More breaking and entering, nothing taken.

Jack hunched over a desk nearby mapping out the break-ins. He studied the pattern. Just like July, all of them were in and around Bel Air.

Delware's eyes popped at the sheet from an old file. He re-read it in disbelief. "Jack, you got to see this!"

Jack came up from his map. "What?"

"We got another eye witness here."

Jack jumped.

Delware waved the page at him. "It's from one of the very first break-ins in early June. Nothing stolen. Koufax didn't work this case." Delware read it again. Jack stood over his shoulder. "Jack, a Cory Willett saw them, all of them – caught a group of people in his living room in the middle of the night ... and one in his hallway. Jack this could be it, a close up look, this could be our ID!"

"Where's the description?"

Delware shifted through the few pages in the file. "It's missing ... or it wasn't even done. All these reports are half blank."

Jack was already grabbing his coat. "You got the address?"

Heading for the door, Delware read the file. "Right here. 701 Stone Canyon Road."

~ ~ ~

The Packard pulled up to a large iron gate. Behind the tall grille were a white Spanish mansion, cupid fountain, rose gardens and sprinklers watering the lawn. Jack buzzed at the gate. They stood impatiently, staring up the drive lined with palm trees. Moments later, a gray-haired woman in a servant uniform came rushing down. She called out, "Sorry, the gate is broken." She arrived at the bars out of breath. Before she could even ask, Jack badged her. "Police business. Is this the home of Cory Willett?"

The woman nodded and opened the gate. Jack and Delware squeezed through before she had it half-open. They passed her without a glance and almost ran, leaving her far behind. The sprinklers' mist made rainbows in the sunlight. Jack hoped it was a good omen.

A blond middle-aged woman waited at the door. Her figure nicely wrapped in a one-piece sheath dress. Her beautiful face worried. "Where's Maria?"

Jack panted slightly, "She's coming. We're in a bit of a rush, Ma'am." Jack flipped open his badge. "Is there a Cory Willett currently residing here?"

"Yes. Is something wrong?"

"No, ma'am, we just need to talk to him."

She straightened her dress and stepped back. "Come in."

Delware spoke as he entered. "We're here about the break-in."

The blonde brushed a stray hair from her face. "That was months ago."

Delware and Jack stood in the foyer surveying what they could of the house. Jack turned to her. "You're Mrs. Willett?"

"Yes."

"Were you here the night of the break-in?"

The woman shuddered. "It was the creepiest thing I've ever seen."

The maid came through the door breathing heavy. Mrs. Willett asked her, "Will you go get Cory, Maria?"

Jack pulled out a pad. "Do you know how they got in?"

"Back service entrance – they slit a screen on an open window. They opened every window, flipped all the paintings upside down, moved all the furniture, the whole living room was backwards. Just creepy. In the kitchen, they emptied all the drawers; every utensil was laid out on the counters." She smiled, nervous. "We've got an alarm now and new locks. It was like something from Alice in Wonderland. You don't know how disturbing it is to wake up in your own house and find nothing where it should be, all helter skelter."

Jack looked up from his notepad. "So your husband saw them?"

She shook her head. "No, he was asleep with me."

Jack frowned at his notes. "The report says a Cory Willett saw the-"

"Oh, yes. Cory saw them."

Down the stairs came Maria holding Cory's hand. Jack and Delware looked up. Cory was five years old.

~ ~ ~

Cory sat, his large blue eyes staring at the two strange men. He leaned his small body into his mother who stroked his short blond hair. Jack and Delware sat with their chairs in close. They leaned towards the little boy in his Superman t-shirt. Jack glanced at a framed school picture of Cory: cute tiny white dress shirt, tie and a missing-a-tooth smile. Jack smiled at the boy. Cory moved closer to his mother.

Delware was surprised at how gentle Jack's voice could be. "So, Cory, can you tell us about the strange people who were in your living room?"

The child looked up to his mother. "Do I have to?"

Mrs. Willett hugged the boy. "Just this once, honey." She looked apologetic at the officers. "It still gives him nightmares."

Jack's eyes were soft and understanding. "I'm sorry to remind you of those people, Cory. But you can help me a lot if you can tell me what you remember."

Cory questioned. "About the bogeyman and his friends?"

Jack felt sweat breaking out on his forehead. *Bogeyman, that's our man.* "Yes, just this once, tell me about the bogeyman and we'll make sure he never comes here again."

The boy clutched his mother. "Is he coming back?"

Mrs. Willett wrapped her arms around the small child. "No, no, dear, don't worry. The nice officers are going to put him in jail. They just need you to tell him what he looked like. That's all."

The boy's grip on his mother slackened.

Jack leaned in. "What happened, Cory? Why did you wake up that night?"

The timid boy confessed, "I heard them."

"What did you hear?"

His small hand pointed to the hall. "Noise...outside my door."

"What type of noise?"

"People whispering. And ... something fell on the floor."

"What happened next?"

"I thought mom was making breakfast."

Jack smiled. "Good boy, what did you do?"

"I got up-" The boy hesitated.

Jack gave the child his best assuring smile. "Yes ... "

"I opened my door and the man walked by, I thought it

was my mom so I ran after her, and...the man turned around."

The boy stopped and clung hard to his mother, fingers curling into her dress.

Jack bit the inside of his lip. His voice gently guided the boy through the fear. "What did you see, Cory?"

"People."

"What did they look like?"

"Bogeymen ... and ladies."

The boy was shaking. His mother held him tight.

Jack's heart raced. "Go on, Cory. We're almost finished, and then we can put them all in jail."

"They all stared at me, but the man in the hall ..."

The boy's eyes watered. The shadow of fear wrinkled his small face.

Jack whispered gently, "What did his face look like?"

The boy paused, climbed into his mother's lap and then spoke innocently, "Angry."

Delware looked at Jack, but Jack's eyes stayed on the boy.

"What else did he look like Cory?"

"Like his picture."

"What picture?"

"The picture we have of him."

Jack's eyes went *wide*, but his face did not move. "Where is that picture of the bogeyman, Cory?"

"If I show you, will you put him in jail forever?"

Jack slid from his chair and onto his knees, keeping his face level with the boy. He looked into the scared, yet trusting eyes. "Yes, Cory. I'll do it right away, as soon as you show me the picture of the bogeyman. I'll put him in jail."

The boy leapt from his mother's lap and ran from the living room. The three adults followed him through a short maze of sunlit halls and then up a carpeted flight of stairs.

They entered the little boy's room. He knelt among a few scattered toys and reached under his bed. "I took it down because it scares me. There he is!"

The boy came up with a small-framed picture. The three adults stood in awe. They stared at a man with long hair and a beard. It was a painting of Jesus Christ, who looked back at them with compassionate eyes.

Cory's voice trembled with fear, "That's what the bogeyman looked like. But his eyes weren't nice, they were angry."

In Jack's mind, he saw the little boy standing in the dark hall, looking up at the tall shadows around him. A man in the hallway towering before him: a longhaired, bearded man with murder in his eyes.

Jack felt something pulling on his hand. The small innocent face looked up at him. "Now are you going to put him in jail? I showed you." The little boy pointed at the picture again. "This is him. Evil Jesus."

3:33 PM

Jack drove, his head spinning, the Hollywood Hills roads twisting. It was a vague ID, but it filled in blanks and confirmed the other eyewitness. He re-imagined the night of the murders. He saw them now: hippies with knives, young girls with knives – Evil Jesus with a knife. If only the little boy knew how close his nightmare was to becoming a reality.

Delware stared blankly. His imagination plagued with pictures of a murderous messiah, an anti-Christ standing proudly over the Tate massacre. "How can he, they ... do that? I mean, I get it. You find a guy screwing your wife, some asshole steals your life savings. But ... how do you kill a room full of strangers?"

Jack turned onto Sunset. "Because they weren't people to him. Psychos are loners and other people are just empty puppets to them. It doesn't matter how we feel, what we want ... if we live or die. We're not real. Only he is. To him, we're nothing more than pigs."

"That's why he does it?"

Jack nodded. "That's why we gotta find him."

They drove in silence. Minutes passed. Streets passed. The dazzle of the sun softened as it descended towards the ocean. The air cooled. The streets had that strange just-before-rush-hour quiet. The Packard hit the highway. The weight of silence was too much. Delware flipped on the police radio and was surprised to hear the airwaves were dead. The static was ominous, like the entire LA police force had disappeared. He looked up to see if LA was still there. Then a breathless voice broke out from the static. "Right on Olympic Boulevard! Right on Olympic!"

They exchanged glances. The voice shouted through the tinny speaker. "They're up an alleyway towards San Marino!!"

Jack turned to Delware. "Communications Operator must have cleared the frequency so all units could talk to each other."

The voice cried over the radio, "I lost them!"

Delware and Jack stared down at the speaker.

Another voice shouted from the shortwave. "Got 'em! Five-A-Four in pursuit! '58 Chevrolet heading north on Western Avenue past the plaza!"

They listened as a box-in and roadblock were attempted. Both failed with bursts of gunfire exchanged at each. Jack turned up the radio. Delware recognized the streets, could see the chase like a sports cast. Jack tried to be nonchalant, but after a few close calls, his eyes were more on the radio than the road. Another roadblock. Two cars in pursuit. It looked like the end for the Chevrolet. Jack and Delware leaned towards the radio, silently rooting for their team. It was close, but the Chevrolet slipped through the net. Both men howled.

The suspects were making good use of the nameless alleyways, making a coordinated chase difficult. It looked like they might actually lose their pursuers. Doggedly, the high-speed cat and mouse continued.

Unconsciously, Jack started speeding towards the chase in the downtown core. After a full minute without a sighting, the Chevrolet popped out of an alleyway right in front of a radio car. "Eight-A-Four! We have them on San Marino headed east! In pursuit!" The officer on the radio was now shouting street names as the '58 Chevrolet passed them. They were ripping through the streets; Delware guessed the speed by how quickly the names came. "Westmoreland! Elden! Magnolla! Arapahoe!" The voice competed with the wailing siren and growling engine coming over the radio. "North on Hoover! Christ! They hit a pedestrian at Wilshire!"

Another voice jumped in, the squeal of tires in the background. "Five-A-Four. They're on Wilshire! Chevrolet now north on La Feyette Park!! Jesus! We're taking fire! They've turned on Sixth! Headed east!"

Two patrol cruisers and an unmarked car from Vice starting screaming over each other. They were west on Sixth St. and setting up a roadblock at Alvarado.

Jack laughed, "Vice! The whole Department is getting in on the act!" Jack recognized one of the voices and gave a sporting cheer. "Go Buck!"

The female voice of the Communications operator shouted, "Five-A-Four, what's your 20? Five-A-Four, come in!"

"Still east bound on Sixth-" The squeal of tires interrupted. Breathlessly his voice came back, "Approaching Alvarado!"

Buck's voice at the roadblock came back. "Suspects approaching!"

The short silence that followed seemed an hour. Jack and Delware were not aware they were holding their breath. A terrible voice broke the static, the pop of gunfire in the background. "L10, I'm shot! Officers down! Officers down! Sixth and Alvarado!" The channel stayed open for a second more. Gunfire was all that could be heard, then static.

Communications Operator's voice was pitched up high. "Is that *officer* down, or *officers* down!"

The voice didn't come back. Jack wondered if Buck

was all right. He looked up and hit the brakes. "Damn!" The Packard had been speeding almost out of control down the Hollywood Freeway. He got it to a manageable speed and then raced on.

"Five-A-Four, we lost them." Delware could tell Five-A-Four had crashed. The engine roar in the background was gone. "They cut through MacAuthur Park, heading south."

Once again the '58 Chevrolet was free and eluding radio cars sent to head them off. There was a long silence. Both Delware and Jack listened intently to the static, waiting for a voice. They could feel every cop in the city leaning towards their radios. The suspects had gone under the radar, would they come up again?

Jack whispered, "Come on, you flat foots, where are they?"

A near scream cut through the hissing static. "Wilshire at Witmer, '58 Chevrolet just ducked into an alley south towards 7th!"

Delware's eyes flashed at the off-ramp. "Jack! We're just around the corner!"

Jack did a double take and couldn't believe his eyes: he *had* driven right past the off ramp to City Hall. Easing up on the engine, he turned off the police radio and listened. He could hear it: distant sirens raced through the streets all around them. Jack frowned and shook his head. "Forget it, kid. It's not our call."

Delware shot an arm out the window, pointing. "Jack! We're right there! Eighth is dead ahead!"

His old eyes glanced at the sign over the off ramp, the chase ringing in his ears. Jack tried his best, but he couldn't resist the call of the sirens. He twisted the wheel at the last second. The car skidded and skipped onto the off ramp almost out of control. The Packard swept down the ramp and nearly spun out on Eighth, narrowly missing a head-on collision. Jack gritted his teeth as he sped west on Eighth. "Goddamn it, kid! Now look what you got me into!"

Delware strapped himself in and fumbled for the radio mic.

Jack turned to yell at Delware again, but Delware's window showed a '58 Chevrolet barreling out an alley right at them. Jack tried to step on the gas, but too late. The speeding car clipped their back end and sent the Packard spinning into oncoming traffic.

~ ~ ~

Jack's eyes were trying to open. At first, he only caught glimpses of a frosty window. He thought he was twelve-years-old and on vacation in New York on a December morning, then his eyes cleared enough to see the shattered windshield. The roaring in his ears slowed and he heard Delware shouting far off, "Freeze police!" And another voice, farther away, "Drop your weapons!" followed by the popping of gunfire.

Looking to the empty passenger seat, Jack realized he must have been knocked out for a while because Delware was already out of the car. Beside the Packard, two poles were down and sparking wires danced. A toppled fire hydrant in the side mirror shot a pillar of water ten feet high that rained over everything. Scattered cars and a truck on its side blocked the roadway. Feeling a sharp pain above his right eyes, he lifted his fingers. They came back bloody. Jack kicked his door open. A woman lay face down and bleeding in front of him. Jack pushed himself from the car and spit blood from his mouth. There were bodies everywhere, drivers, passengers tossed from their vehicles. Some lifeless, some moaning. On the north side of the street a red Rambler had jumped the sidewalk and crushed its front end into a brick wall. A woman's leg protruded from the windshield, her stocking and flesh shredded. To the west, somewhere unseen, a woman was screaming bloody murder, a man's voice nearby cried for help. A fat man lay dead on his back on the sidewalk beside an overturned truck.

Jack checked the bloody woman at his feet. She was not breathing. As Jack rose he noticed the sharp metallic chinking of bullets hitting metal. He looked around. Empty black-and-whites clustered by the alleyway to his south, their doors flung open. Delware and uniformed officers took cover there, shooting their service revolvers and pump-action shotguns. To his north, Latino men, scattered along on the north side of the street fired back. Jack stood between them, caught in the crossfire.

Eighth Street by the freeway was a narrow canyon of brick, steel and glass. The .10 gauge shotguns echoed like canons. The reverberations sent people running and ducking, covering their ears. Bullets whistled from both sides of the street. The car window beside Jack popped and cracked. He rubbed his throbbing forehead and glanced down at his holster. His gun was still there.

He couldn't see it, but Jack heard the unmistakable pop of a German Luger. Jack smiled to himself in the hail of bullets. Judging by their weapons and lousy aim, these were Hollenbeck Boys, a gang near Boyle Heights. They were taking wild, one-handed shots sending bullets everywhere. The cops were taking two-handed shots, but weren't landing any.

Jack wanted nothing to do with an out-in-the-open gunfight, even if it was amateur hour at the O.K. Corral. Without drawing his gun, he stumbled through the carnage. Broken windshield glass crackled under his feet. Lead ricocheted all around him, the air was deadly, but Jack didn't give a damn. He hunched his shoulders like it was a walk in the rain. He counted six shooters: Latinos in wife-beaters. A fat Latino wielded a .10 gauge wearing double bullet belts across his chest like Pancho Villa. Pancho waved the others to move back towards the packed parking lot of a small grocery store. A few of the gang followed spraying lead. A lot of it. A young patrolman, not recognizing Jack as an officer, yelled at him to get down. He ignored the warnings and grumbled at the bullets whining through the air and popping into the cars around him.

Jack took note of a Latino in a red baseball cap firing two automatic pistols, one in each hand. One was the WWII Luger. Baseball-cap ignored Jack, mistaking him for a confused old man. Jack bet even money the Latinos were thinking of holing up in the grocery store for cover. He made his way to the north end of the street to an alley beside the grocery store. At the mouth of the alley, Jack looked back, the suspects were now hightailing it across the lot and into the grocery store. Hiding pedestrians now caught in the crossfire ran in every direction to get away. Jack glanced at his car. His trunk had been knocked wide open; the back bumper knocked clean off.

He muttered, "Goddamn. My fuckin' bumper!"

The police had taken back the street and more officers were arriving. The large windows of the grocery store were shattering with shots from both sides. Delware, in a running crouch, dodged between cars taking the parking lot. He had reloaded several times and was now out of bullets. A wounded officer lay behind a black Mercury Comet. He was clutching his shoulder that oozed red. Delware saw a pump shotgun beside him and made a dash to the officer. Bullets trailed him. He tossed his .38 and snatched the shotgun. "You alright?"

The officer howled at him with a twisted face. "Fuck! Fuck! FUCK!" Delware saw the man's gun was still in his holster, grabbed it and put it in his own holster. "I might need this too."

Screams could be heard in the store, Delware feared hostages would be taken.

A black-and-white, siren screaming, roared up the north end sidewalk and scraped several cars as it spun to a halt in the parking lot. Its windows already full of bullet holes, Delware guessed it had been at a failed roadblock. A young officer kicked open the driver's door and, using the door as a shield, starting firing. An older, fat officer sprang out of the passenger door with a shotgun. He bent low behind the hood and began firing and reloading at an amazing rate. Both red-faced officers seemed intent on revenge. Quickly, all gunfire from the store was directed at them. Delware took advantage of the distraction. He charged directly at the front door, a few younger officers joined in. Delware led the charge pumping and firing his shotgun as officers on either side of him fell. He had not proven himself a good shot, but now he was up close. With a single blast to the chest he took down Pancho Villa. The gunfire from the store turned on Delware. The officers from the spun out cruiser took advantage of it and came charging. The young cop stopped mid-charge, raised his gun eye-level, and with one well-placed shot clipped the head of Baseball Cap. The remaining four men firing from the windows retreated deeper into the store. Delware threw down the empty smoking shotgun and burst through the front door. He pulled the wounded officer's gun from his holster. Two bullets snapped by his head. He returned fire only to find the gun was empty. He glanced down at the revolver with horror and disbelief, his finger still squeezing the trigger. Ducking to grab his backup piece on his ankle, the glass above his head shattered.

In the alley the noise of the gun battle was muffled. Jack unclipped his holstered .38 and turned the corner. He found the store's backdoor and leaned against the brick wall, pulled his .38 and kissed it. "Don't fail me now." Blood still ran from his forehead, he dabbed it away. Leveling the gun at the door, he didn't have long to wait. The metal door burst open. A suspect with a gun flew out. Jack squeezed the trigger. Jack's gun clicked, the hammer fell. The gunshot in the narrow brick alley was *loud*. The man's head jerked to one side. The other side of his skull blew apart and hit the inside of the metal door. Red splattered.

The man fell lifeless. His head hit the ground still spouting blood.

Another suspect, firing back into the store and not looking where he was going, came out a split second later. Tripping over the dead man, down he went. Jack fired and missed, chinking the pavement beside the man's shoulder. On the pavement, the man rolled taking a shot that whistled by Jack's head. Jack's second bullet hit him in the temple, spraying blood across the alley. The man twitched and went limp.

Jack whispered, "*Adios.*"

~ ~ ~

Inside, Delware ran crouched behind aisles of fruit, the glass doors of the milk freezers exploding above him, raining shards on his head. He stopped at a bread rack. Across the aisle, a young mother on the floor clutched a six-year-old girl, both crying. Delware peeked around the corner and saw a man firing at officers entering the store. Delware took three shots. The first missed, alerting the man who turned to return fire, but the other two connected with his torso; his feet slipped from under him. Hitting the floor hard, the man did not get up.

Jack waited at the back door. A shotgun came flying out. A voice inside yelled, "OK, man. I give up. I'm coming out!"

Jack stepped away from the door, his gun still trained

on the empty passage.

The first thing to appear was the man's leg. Jack fired. The man fell out of the doorway and rolled on the ground howling, holding his leg. A litany of curses came as he rolled in pain.

A black hand holding a badge appeared at the doorway. Delware shouted, "Police officer."

Jack yelled, "It's OK, Delware! It's me."

Delware stepped out of the doorway, surveying the two dead men and the one howling. He looked up at Jack impressed.

Jack relaxed and walked smiling at Delware. "That's all of them?"

Delware nodded.

The man on the ground interrupted his profanity long enough to shout at Delware. "He fuckin' shot after I fuckin' surrendered!"

Delware dutifully began reading him his Miranda rights, "You have the right to remain silent-"

Jack interrupted. "Hey, kid! That's not the way you do it!"

With a youthful twinkle in his eye, Jack walked up and kicked the man across the mouth. He gave Delware a smile, then bent over the now unconscious man. "Hey screwball, you got the right to shut the fuck up!"

~ ~ ~

The street looked like a battlefield: cars flaming, smoke and the smell of gunpowder still in the air, plate glass windows shot out, shards of broken glass scattered like confetti, trails of spent shotgun shells. The wounded moaned, the corpses silent. Jack sat in his car, his leg resting on the running board. He looked up angrily at Delware. "You stupid kid, they're going to bury us!"

Jack's mood had turned on a dime. The adrenaline rush was over and now he was crashing. Delware, still high on the adrenalin, stared bewildered. "What?"

Jack scowled. "What! *This!* Do you know what *this* means? Paperwork. A bottomless pit of it. This is gonna rob us of days, steal hours from us for weeks! We're on the Tate case now part-time – thanks to you! Because the rest of the time we'll be sorting out what happened here. We fired our guns! That's endless crime reports in triplicates. Reports on everything. Reports on reports!" Disgusted, Jack looked away. "Get lost. Don't bother me, kid. I got things to think about."

Delware stood like a puppy who didn't understand.

Jack jumped at him. "Beat it! Get the hell out of my sight, will ya!"

Turning, Delware ambled away. His head spun as he wandered through the wrecked cars and fallen poles. Ambulance workers loaded up the bleeding. Morgue men lifted corpses onto gurneys. Rounding a corner, he left the chaos, his triumph now a dismal defeat. Had he really screwed them out of solving the case? He walked fast and hard down busy streets not looking where he was going, just wanting Jack and the crime scene far behind. He stopped and sighed, leaning against a wall in a quiet alleyway. His eyes followed normal people living normal lives. They hurried by, things on their minds. Across a street a mother pushing a baby carriage stopped to admire a dress in a window. A black man emerged from a deli eating a sandwich. Three hippies rounded the corner.

Delware immediately noticed them: two men, one woman, looking around furtively. Paying attention to who was around them meant they were up to something. Whispering to each other, the three paused at a lamppost. The young blond girl was their look out, watching both ends of the street. One guy held up a piece of paper and the other taped it to the post: illegal posting of bulletins. Delware smiled to himself, busting these kids would be a laughable attempt at redemption.

They crossed the street towards Delware, but didn't make him for a cop. Passing right in front of him, the blonde in striped pants and a purple vest stopped and blocked his view. Delaware checked out her ass as the boys taped a poster on a pole directly in front of him and moved on.

Before the blonde left, she turned her head with a flick of her long blond hair and winked at Delware.

The moment her pretty face was gone Delware did a double take. He saw the poster. His eyes locked. "*Jesus!*"

He stepped closer, gazing up at it. "That's it. That's how they did it. That's where our killers are!"

~ ~ ~

Jack sat, hanging his legs out of his car, looking miserable, the cut over his eye being bandaged by a medic. He reluctantly raised his eyes. "What is it?"

Delware shook the poster in his face. "Jack, this is what we're looking for, where we can find our killers!"

He pointed to the bold lettering at the top of the poster:

How to Create Your Own Commune.

"Jack, they're isolated. That's why we can't find them." Delware's finger directed Jack's disinterested gaze. "Look at this special guest!"

Dr. Ellroy will present a recent study of over a hundred communes.

"Jack, how could our killers go undetected in the hippie community? Only if they lived outside of it – on the outskirts of town! That's where most communes are. This flyer says Dr. Ellroy has personally visited and studied all those in the Los Angeles area. This is who we need to talk to."

Tuesday, September 9th, 1969, 8:59 PM

Evening darkened into night. The dented Packard pulled onto the Sunset Strip. Its windshield replaced, its back bumper still missing. The street was a blaze of lights, honking cars and hippies spilling out onto the road. As Jack stewed behind the wheel, Delware looked out at the pimps, pushers and prostitutes. Maybe Mrs. Powell was right; maybe he was just a centurion in a neon Rome, looking for evil Jesus.

Jack's head ached from the crash. He felt his cuts and bruises. The day had gone as predicted: wasted behind a desk, writing reports about yesterday's shooting. As he filled out form after form, Delware's poster perched on the edge of his desk. Hundreds of hopeful glances at *How to Create Your Own Commune* kept Jack going. All day he had been waiting for this moment. The Packard pulled up in front of the hippest club on the Strip, illuminated in the glow of its red neon sign: The Looking Glass.

Stepping out, Jack sneered at the clusters of hippies outside: laughing long hairs with sideburns, chatting girls with short hair and granny glasses. One beard wore only rainbow-striped pants and a fringed vest. Three barefooted girls sat cross-legged on the sidewalk passing a joint, enjoying watching each other's tokes as much as their own.

Half on the curb, half on the street, a group of Hell's Angels hung around their choppers. They eyed Jack. He made no pretense and gave them a *yeah-I'm-a-cop* grin. An Angel in a Nazi helmet mocked him with a half salute. Jack noted their Death Head patches: Oakland Chapter – a group of felons if he had ever seen one. He would have enjoyed ruining the rest of their evening.

Jack looked back at the scratches and dents on the back of the Packard, the buckled, warped trunk now tied shut with rope. He gave it a sardonic smile, an old warrior used to new wounds.

Delware came up beside him, staring at the battered car. "I can't believe you got the windshield replaced in a day...for a vintage hunk-of-junk no less."

"I get into a dozen collisions a year; my mechanic makes a small fortune keeping replacement parts in stock...just for me."

"A dozen a year?" Delware couldn't resist a mock. "And *you* – such a safe driver."

Lost in his own thoughts, Jack didn't respond. He looked sadly at where the back bumper should be. "You know, he told me he's out – doesn't know if he can get another bumper." He shook his head. "Guess I should be glad he found one for the front. Yet ... I feel like a cat on his ninth life."

"We're lucky to be alive. I can't believe the car wasn't totaled."

Jack patted the Packard. "This beauty is a tank. Reinforced steel, roll bars in the roof, bullet-proof plates in the doors – you know the original windows were the very first bullet-proof glass ever made for civilian use."

"Jack, how much did that cost?"

"Not a dime. The car used to belong to one of Mickey Cohen's captains. A criminal like that has a lot of enemies. He got plugged full of holes getting out of this beauty on

Sunset Boulevard."

Delware smiled at the old man. "So how'd you get it?"

"It was entered into evidence. But the Department and Mickey were ... sort of relying on each other in those days. So the case got buried; the papers were all hush-hush. When I saw everyone acting like it never happened; I drove this beauty off the lot." He grinned. "Everyone knew, but no one said a word." Jack sighed. "It was a different time to be a cop."

Jack took one step off the sidewalk for a better look at the trunk. The shadows made him a deathly gray, as if he had just put one foot in the grave.

Delware shook off the strange vision and joined the knot of hippies mingling at the club door. Instantly, he blended in.

Jack stood alone on the sidewalk, an outsider, an old man.

A hippie with an open shirt, raised collar and the longest hair Jack had ever seen sat on the sidewalk wearing only a single shoe.

Jack turned to the boy. "Hey, you lost a shoe."

The kid smiled. "No, man. I found one."

Delware stepped out of the crowd and nodded. The man they wanted was inside.

The door was outlined in red neon and shaped like a coffin. Jack stepped into another dimension. They walked a long flashing passage. Strobe lights made all movement look slow motion. A muffled *Tomorrow Never Knows* by The Beatles blared somewhere. Ahead, two shadowy men approached. Reading their body language, Jack knew their slow gait was a cover; these men were headed for trouble.

Jack subtly moved his jacket for a quick reach to his holster. One approaching man did the same. Jack felt his pulse quicken, then, suddenly found his foot dangling in mid-air. Jack pivoted back and saved himself from a fall.

At his feet was a flight of stairs. He did a double take. Only a wall-length mirror at the end of the hallway made it look longer. The approaching men had, in fact, been them.

Down a spiral stairway they went. At the bottom waited two strange figures spotlighted in purple. On Jack's side was a young woman dressed as a sexy Alice in Wonderland. On Delware's, The Red Queen, equally sexy, but instead of red hearts, her white card was numbered with Soviet hammer-and-sickles.

The Queen handed Delware a sugar cube from a silvery tray. As she dropped it in his palm, she said what sounded like, "Feed your head."

Sexy Alice held out a cube to Jack. As she dropped it in his palm, she whispered, "Keep your head."

Passing the women, Delware whispered, "Palm it, Jack. It's LSD."

Delware made a motion as if popping the cube into his mouth, yet slipped it into his pocket. Jack followed suit.

They found themselves in a crowded room. Delware motioned to Jack to stay put as he made inquiries. Once again the old man found he was in an optical illusion. He noticed many people were identical to each other. The small room had mirrored walls surrounding the few people in it. Jack felt disorientated, seeing every movement endlessly echoed in infinite mirrors.

Delware reappeared with an attractive woman in a white Playboy Bunny outfit. She motioned them to follow.

The White Rabbit led them into a house of mirrors. She was hard to follow; her many reflections turned in different directions. The twisting corridors reflected her endlessly. Marijuana smoke drifted through the air. Psychedelic murals appeared at random – under black lights slogans glowed: Women's Lib, You can't jail the Revolution and End the War! The snaking passageways led past cubbyholes and wraparound booths full of hippies. They came across a table of young women, all in pants, not a single dress. They fell silent and watched Jack pass with hateful stares. A sharp twist brought them past a crowded barroom. One hippie in a top hat and a shirt made from an American flag stood on a long table shouting what to Jack's ears was complete nonsense. The hippie ranted about free speech, repeating the word 'fascists' again and again like he had gone mad. As a few hippies noticed Jack, others turned and looked at him out of the corners of their eyes. The song had changed and the music grew closer and clearer. Around another mirrored corner, two very butch women – identical twins in matching striped shirts – stood on either side of a doorway with crossed arms. They eyed Jack as he passed through their door.

The labyrinth opened to a vast crowded dance floor. The music was blaring – *Pictures of Matchstick Men* by Status Quo. The walls were alive with a kaleidoscopic light show, huge moving blobs ever morphing their shape, size and color. The dancers were as wildly dressed as anyone in Wonderland. Their eyes wide, their faces ecstatic in ever changing colors as lights flashed in circles above them.

To Jack, they had gone insane: gone were boys paired with girls or dance steps. Uninhibited and manic, each improvised their own style.

Delware nodded towards the crazed crowd. The man they wanted was on the other side. They waded through the confusion and sensory overload as if two gunfighters advancing down a deserted street towards a showdown, their hands instinctively close to the butts of their guns, protecting them from the swarm slowly parting before them.

At last, emerging from the mob of tripping humanity, they came to a door. Over it was a black light, on the door in glowing letters:

The Magic Theater
For madmen only
Price of Admission: your mind!

They glanced at each other, the mob swirling behind them.

Delware opened the door. The pungent musk of marijuana hit them; silver, blue wisps of smoke hung in the air. The room was dim and bare. At first, they saw nothing, but as their eyes adjusted two figures appeared sitting on opposing couches. Both stared at a table between them. On the table, stacked a foot high, were white sugar cubes.

Delware entered first, Jack closed the door behind them. The couch men remained motionless. Then one whispered from the dark. "Delware, is that you, man?"

Delware nodded. "Hey, Mickey."

Mickey's voice spoke slow and stoned from the shadows. "Hey, man, you ain't here to drag me off to Vietnam, are you?"

Jack noticed a poster on the wall. He could barely read the curving letters: Fight the Rising Tide of Conformity!

Delware's stance relaxed, cocking his hip. "Everything's mellow, man, we're just visiting 'cause we need to talk."

A hand rose from the shadows, Mickey and Delware slapped palms. Mickey grinned. "Right on, brother, lay it on me."

Delware held up the commune poster. Mickey smiled under thick dark curls.

Delware asked. "You the promoter?"

Mickey nodded. "Sure. Communes, man, freeing people from this greedy, materialistic society we live in. Helping them find a new consciousness, a way of life outside of the establishment."

"Where's the Doc?"

"That all? Can't wait till next Friday? Doc Ellroy will be here tomorrow night."

"We need to talk as soon as possible."

"Trouble?"

"No trouble. Just talk."

Jack looked at the silent hippie slouched on the other couch. The stoned man just stared at the police officers through the gloom. Jack was drawn to the man's face, studying it. He placed it – a police bulletin. Jack was staring at Owsley Stanley, wanted for making and distributing LSD throughout California.

Delware started a question, but Jack interrupted him. "Wait a minute." Jack turned and gave Owsley a dangerous smile. "You a drug pusher?"

Turning his head, Delware instantly recognized Owsley.

Owsley gave both officers a friendly smile. "Hey, man, it's not for sale. I'm giving it away. Dig? If you want some ... take some. It's free."

Mickey protested in his slow, stoned cadence. "Hey, man, if you want my help – you ain't busting nobody."

Delware glanced at Jack. Jack nodded.

Delware turned to Mickey. "We're not here to arrest anyone."

Mickey scratched his head through his shaggy hair. "I don't know about tonight, but tomorrow afternoon I know Doc will be at the Free Health Care Clinic in..."

Normally, Jack would have paid close attention, but he kept stealing glances at Owsley Stanley. Jack could smell a drug pusher around the corner, spot them down the street, but there was nothing criminal about this man.

Jack pointed to the large pile of sugar cubes on the table. "So, you make this stuff."

Owsley looked up through his long hair without any

fear in his eyes. "Hey, man, dig it. I'm trying to turn people on, open their minds, free their souls. Dig?"

Jack glanced at the massive pile of sugar cubes, once innocent white sweetness, now ominous.

Owsley eyes fell on the white cubes. "You know, when I make this stuff...I try not to think any negative thoughts, so no bad vibes get into it. So, it's pure good karma, man."

Standing up, Owsley swayed as if on a seaborne boat – a man on a trip, he alone was taking. He took an unsteady step towards Jack. "We're going to save the world with this. You can't pollute when you're aware, man. You can't kill when your heart is open. If you realize you're one with it all, how can you hurt anyone? That's what I'm trying to do. Dig?"

Jack gave Owsley a cynical smile. "Save the world? Look, kid, buy a car, move to the suburbs and spare yourself the trouble – it can't be done. Believe me."

Owsley held up a vial of clear liquid, his fingers suspended it between them. "All the answers are in here, man."

Jack kept his eyes on the clear liquid and called to Delware, "What is this?"

Delware glanced. "It's the LSD they've been dropping on the cubes."

Owsley gave Jack a stoned stare through his long hair. His eyes smiled at the vial. "Everything you need to know is right in this, man. When you're ready, it will reveal *all* the answers."

There was a weird light in Owsley's eyes – a total lack of confrontation. Those watery eyes with wildly dilated pupils were lucid. It reminded Jack of a young priest in the parish his wife had liked. He too had piercing eyes that looked through Jack without aggression, without judgment. Jack could face killers and bullets, but he found Owsley's eyes unnerving.

Owsley grinned wide like Cheshire Cat. "The only obstacles are in your mind, dig? Don't trust your mind, man."

Jack looked confused.

Owsley, with a slight-of-hand, made the vial vanish. "Don't worry. You'll find them – when you're ready, *when* you're ready."

~ ~ ~

Delware led Jack out the back door of the club. The dark narrow alley stank of urine and garbage. The brick walls now muffled the roaring club music. Jack stopped and stared. Spray painted in red: *Don't trust anyone over thirty!*

Jack spit on the ground. "Hold up, kid. You were in Narcotics. Didn't you want to bust that guy?"

Delware turned and wrinkled his nose at the stinking trashcans around them. "Nah, that's why I wanted out of Narcotics."

"Why?"

"'Cause we used to bust heroin pushers, I mean real gangsters destroying the youth in Watts. Now we bust teenagers for smoking a joint, and once you get all the marijuana off the street – know what comes in? All the hard stuff. We're making it worse, Jack. The most harmless stuff is what we're focusing on and all the real criminals are getting a free pass. It's stupid politics."

They headed for the car. A street lamp lit the end of the alley.

Jack's sharp eyes turned on Delware. "He'd be a big catch." Jack lit a cigar. "You did LSD."

"I told you, Jack, in '65 before I was a cop, before it was illegal. It was my last year of college."

"So tell me that story again?"

"The trip I had?"

"Yeah, what happened?"

Delware grinned to himself. "A lot of things...but I had that vision, saw myself with a gun and a badge. It blew my mind, opened it. I applied to the academy that week."

Jack scratched his unshaven chin. "You ever do it again?"

"Acid? No. But I've smoked pot. Look, I'd rather be trapped in a room of potheads than drunks. Drunks are loud and violent. Dopers are lethargic. Believe me, the streets would be safer if pot was legal and alcohol was off limits."

Delware smiled at Jack as they turned the corner back to the street. "But I don't even drink now."

"Yeah?"

"Being a cop is *my* high."

Jack muttered to himself, "You'd be better off drinking."

Delware jumped into the car. A young hippie on the sidewalk called out to Jack. "Hey, man! You're missing a bumper!"

Jack put his foot on his front bumper and imitated Owsley's stoned smile and cadence, "No, man. I found one. Dig?"

The kid smiled and gave the power-to-the-people fist salute. "Right on!"

Jack slid into the car, grinning. Delware kicked his boots up on the dash and continued, "My high is having a clear head and catching the bad guys."

Jack dropped the key into the ignition. "If you had a clear head, you'd get a haircut."

Wednesday, September 10th, 1969, 3:49 PM

The next morning was another of paperwork in triplicate. Every aspect of the shoot out was typed and retyped. Jack resented the way cops were treated like criminals now whenever they discharged their weapons, even in self-defense. Jack and Delware escaped by mid-afternoon and headed for Hollenbeck, the location of LA's Free Clinic.

On the way, Delware thought about the door in Jack's home. The one he wasn't allowed to open. The one not even Jack would open. He wanted to ask what was behind the door. Why he never went in there. Playing out conversations in his mind that might lead to that question – he never saw the answer coming. When Jack let down his walls, it was rare, but always on his terms. Still, Delware would not relent, in his head he continued to play with the maze of words that might lead to an answer.

Along a rundown block of closed stores, they pulled up in front of a small storefront. The weathered sign above still read Bill's Shoes. A smaller hand painted sign in the window read Free Clinic. Crowded inside the grimy waiting room were a few hippies, blacks, but mostly weary Latino mothers with sniffling kids.

Delware and Jack scoped the reception window. No one around. An attractive young blonde in a white smock rushed down a narrow hall. Delware hailed her. "Nurse!"

She turned, and he flashed his badge. Approaching, she gave an impatient, "Can I help you?"

Delware put his badge away. "We're looking for Doctor Ellroy."

She blew a stray strand of hair from her face. "I'm Doctor Ellroy."

Delware, meeting his first woman doctor, fell silent. Jack was caught off guard, but recovered quickly. He dropped a hand on Delware's shoulder. "Excuse my young partner, Doctor; he's not *'with it'*."

~ ~ ~

She made them wait. As she attended her most needy patients, Jack and Delware stood in the packed waiting room. The paint was peeling; the ceiling light had exposed wires. Jack gave half smiles to the staring mothers and sniffling kids.

A half hour later, Dr. Ellroy admitted them into her small office lined with filing cabinets. She flopped down into a creaky chair and drew her long straight hair behind her ears. "How can I help you?"

Jack sat. "We're investigating hippie communes in greater LA. We've heard you were involved with them."

Her blue eyes examined the men before her. "There are over a hundred and fifty around LA alone. I'm heading up a study. I've provided health care to a number of communes since I left med school. I know some of the communities quite well – why are you interested in them?"

Jack pulled out a small black notepad. "We believe one of them may be involved with a homicide."

Laughing, Dr. Ellroy gave Jack a disbelieving once-over. Delware was embarrassed; she was good looking, he was coupled with a bigoted old man.

The doctor gave Jack a dirty look. "Detective, these are subsistence farmers, following various gurus – albeit most are self-appointed. But they're often religious communities, ashrams, covens."

Jack waved off her condescending tone. "So a bunch of weirdos."

She gave Jack a long look. "America has a long history of communal living Detective: the Mennonites, the Amish."

Jack looked up from his notes. "So you see anything unusual?"

"Unusual? By what standards? Hippie communes can be categorized into types: crash pads, drug and non-drug families, group marriages, and self-contained rural communities. But each is unique. There is no usual."

"We're looking for a group that might have a history of violence. Did you see any guns, knives, other weapons? Maybe wire cutters?"

Dr. Ellroy glanced at Delware. The look said – *is he for real?* She gave Jack a dirtier look. "Well, I suppose some might have rifles, most have knives. They are living off the land. Knives *are* a necessity."

"But are all of them peaceful?"

She was amused by Jack's persistence. "I think you have the wrong idea about communes, Detective. These are kids looking for freedom – to wear their hair long and smoke dope without ... facing police *brutality.* These young people are looking for support and are very loving to one another. They are moving the human race forward, expanding their consciousness, exploring and changing themselves, experimenting with new ways of living, wanting to get back to the land. They are mostly farming co-ops struggling to get away from the materialistic values of a consumer society. They pick isolated locations to escape society's norms and values, *but they don't want to harm society* – they want to create their own."

Jack was unimpressed. "So do all these communes have leaders?"

"Most have a spiritual leader or leaders. But there are many democratic co-ops."

"Tell me about the ones with leaders."

"They're so many." She looked confused by Jack's line of questioning. "There's a gay community of men living in geodesic domes. Their guru is...a very charismatic gentleman. There's another commune – the Hog Farm, a man called Wavy Gravy – maybe twenty, thirty people on a perpetual acid trip. They live in converted school buses and have a pig mascot they call Pigasus."

Delware grinned. She smiled at him, then frowned at Jack. "There is a nudist colony, Elysium Fields in Topanga Canyon. Their leader, Ed Lange, allows-" Her lips broke into a slightly embarrassed smile, "orgies, sometimes consisting of almost a hundred people."

Jack grew impatient. "Where are most of these located?"

"In the Santa Monica mountains, but they're scattered far and wide. I just came back from one in Death Valley near Chatsworth. An old movie ranch."

Jack looked up from his notes, surprised. "Spahn Ranch?"

"You know it?"

Jack nodded. "By the Bottomless Pit."

She nodded.

Delware asked. "Bottomless pit?"

She smiled at Delware. "It's a very deep well – an old tourist attraction."

Jack laughed. "My dad took us out there as kids. We'd go horseback-riding." Jack smiled.

The doctor relaxed a bit. "Yes, the commune supports itself by renting horses. They run what's left of the dude ranch in return for living quarters – which are mostly broken down western movie sets."

Jack's memories flooded back, he turned to Delware.

"After riding, my dad would take me to that old well. It was huge – all dried up. It scared me. You look down and there was nothing to see. Just darkness. Couldn't even see the bottom with a flashlight. And if you dropped a rock into it, it would disappear, without so much as a whisper – like it never hit bottom." Jack caught himself excitedly rambling and spoke apologetically, "I was just a kid."

Dr. Ellroy smiled. "Well, you don't want to go there now."

Delware asked. "Why?"

"This heat wave. Death Valley is the hottest desert in the world and its bottom is Spahn Ranch. The commune members say the only things that can live out there are rattlesnakes and scorpions."

The thought of a bunch of long hairs running around the ranch soured Jack's reminiscing. He turned to the doctor. "What's that group like?"

She pulled a file off the top of a cabinet and scanned it. "Age range about 16 to 35, the core group consists of approximately 20 people, mostly women. Although there are a few with a college education, most members disapprove of formal education. They believe it's "brain washing". Manson feels that people should be "open to change" and not indoctrinated by society."

Jack took notes. "Wait a minute. Who's Manson?"

"Their leader – a father figure of sorts. Manson is thirty-five and has a mystical philosophy, but he's not involved in Eastern religion. He's more of a psychedelic philosopher. Manson preaches letting go of all hang-ups from society." She scanned further down one page. "They refer to themselves as 'The Family,' but it's a group marriage – polygamous sexual relations. The members feel no need for conventional marriage. Of the 14 females, two were pregnant at the time of my observation. Another girl gave birth to her son in the group's bus. The child was fairly healthy and did not see a physician until about four months after delivery. He was treated at the Haight-Ashbury Free Clinic.

Jack glanced up from his notes. "A group marriage?"

Dr. Ellroy gave a tolerant smile. "Everyone is free to make love to anyone within the group." She went back to her notes. "Some use of LSD, marijuana. I gave one of the children born at the ranch a checkup. They refused immunization, resist an official birth certificate."

Jack sat back. "Would you hand over your files?"

She slid the file closer to her. "I'm not sure I want to."

"Why?"

"Doctor-patient confidentiality."

Jack knew she wanted to say more. He coaxed her, "Yeessss..."

Dr. Ellroy remained silent.

Jack locked his eyes on hers. "In the State of California, the Rules of Evidence does not recognize doctor-patient privilege in criminal proceedings."

She gave a forced sigh and shot Jack a hateful look. "These groups are positive and creative; you want to paint them like they're homicidal. Why should I help you?"

"Ma'am, have you studied psychology?"

"No, but my study is part of a degree I'm working on in sociology."

Jack leaned back in his chair and stared her down. "Then, you're not qualified to detect a psychopath when you see one. A psychopath is a chameleon. He knows how to fit in with his environment. They can be quite charming and persuasive. Only a trained eye can pick one out. Even police officers can be fooled by these dangerous offenders. You could have been in the company of these killers and not even know it. Now you can refuse us the files for now, but...can you live with yourself if my killers are in your files, if innocent people die...because you did not cooperate?"

She looked hurt and resentful. After a long minute, the hardness in her eyes surrendered.

Cursing under her breath, Dr. Ellroy stood up and looked at her filing cabinets. "I have files on 154 that I've come in contact with. You can make copies. But I have got to say officers, it's mostly cases of VD, general health issues; a few drug ODs, pregnant mothers. No violence related treatments. I don't even recall a fist fight...hippies detest violence."

Delware stood up. "Thank you for your cooperation."

Dr. Ellroy collected her papers and filed them neatly into a cardboard box.

Delware took the box and headed for the door. "We'll get these back to you as soon as they're copied."

Jack stared at the pretty young doctor. He pointed to the waiting room. "Why are you treating these people...for free?"

"Health care is a right, Detective, not a privilege."

Jack shook his head. "You just make 'em lazy if they don't have to pay for it."

Saturday, September 13th, 1969, 11:11 AM

The Santa Monica Mountains were wild. A few minutes off the main road and suddenly you were in a Wild West movie: a mountainous desert of rock, sand and cactus.

The Packard blew up a cloud of dust as it climbed the dirt road. Delware was nervous. Jack had let him pick their first commune to investigate.

"So Delware, why this one?"

"Well, it's remote, but not far from The Tate residence. Just head east and in forty minutes you'll be in the canyons above Hollywood. This commune has a 'back to nature manifesto,' but with an anarchist bent. Real tough talk – used the words "rich capitalist pigs.""

"Pigs."

"It's pretty common talk, but it did strike me."

"No. That's good."

The road leveled off. A plateau opened before them and the sun hit their eyes. A circle of small wooden buildings lay ahead. Large tents dotted the adjacent mountain slope to the south, a sweeping view of the desert opened on the north.

Jack dropped one hand onto a shotgun fastened between them. "Better unclip your holster. We don't know what type of reception we're in for."

They passed tarpaper shacks with roofs of plastic sheet, exposed electric wiring ran from shack to shack.

Jack saw an accident waiting to happen.

Delware squinted in the sunlight and saw the hopeful beginnings of a new America, but unclipped his .38 – just in case.

The Packard stopped in front of a large log ranch house: an old pioneer structure standing sturdy since the Old West. Jack stepped out and found hippies peering from tent flaps and doorways. It was a hot day in LA, it was hotter here. Jack's tongue felt dry. He saw a small scorpion scurry by his foot for the cool shade under his car. He wouldn't be surprised to see a rattlesnake under there by the end of their visit.

Delware came around from his side. Everyone stood still. Delware noticed three tall men with very long hair and beards coming down from gardens on the mountain's slope. With a purposeful stride, they headed towards the two officers.

All three bore a passing resemblance to Jesus Christ, except they wore tight blue jeans and beads. They even towered over Jack. One asked, "What's your scene, man?"

Jack watched their faces as he flashed his badge. "Police business. We're here to talk to a Timothy Benton."

The three men looked at each other, silently debating whether to comply. Reluctantly, the tallest, dirty blond Jesus spoke, "Wait here."

Jack pointed after the departing hippie. "Delware, you go with him. Make sure he's not going for a shotgun."

The hippie turned and now stood his ground.

Jack shouted at him, "Don't worry. Officer Hicks is one of you – a hippie dippy peace lover!"

The man glanced at Delware, then walked on. Delware followed, uninvited.

Jack leaned back on his car and surveyed the

commune. He already felt the sand in his shoes and dust in his jacket. He side-glanced the two tall hippies with disgust. "How can you live like this?"

~ ~ ~

The blond hippie looked back at Delware. "I've never seen a black detective."

"I'm not one yet."

"We have lots of brothers living here, why you here?"

"We just want to talk to Mr. Benton, that's all."

"You from Narcotics?"

"No, man, it's homicide."

The hippie turned, stunned.

~ ~ ~

Jack leaned back on the Packard, eyeing the hippies like unwanted foreigners invading his beloved America.

Delware reappeared, waving. "Jack, this way!"

They came along the side of the ranch house to an ill-fitted screen door. Delware entered, Jack paused. Delware popped his head out. "You coming?"

Jack pointed to a field of marijuana in the back of the ranch house. "Look at that."

The tall, leafy plants swayed in the breeze. Delware stepped out, surveying the field. Dark soil had been brought in. It looked well tended and watered. Delware admired the hard work, but shrugged his shoulders. "I've seen bigger."

They entered a dim room with a Christian Cross on one wall and a goat's head in a pentagram on the opposite. A round altar was in the centre, candles arranged to point to the four cardinal directions. Meditation cushions circled the altar. Frankincense burned somewhere in the room. Against another wall leaned three acoustic guitars and a sitar, but Jack's eyes fell on a balding man with long gray hair sitting crossed-legged.

Jack gave the man a snide smile that barely lifted the

corners of his mouth. "You Mr. Benton?"

The old man smiled peaceful with shining eyes. "Yes."

"I have a message for you. It's from God: stop fucking around and set a better example for these young people."

Jack turned and walked out. Delware looked after him, mystified.

He caught up to Jack outside. "What the fuck?"

Jack turned. "He's not our guy. This isn't the group we're looking for." He eyed the field of marijuana.

"How do you know?"

"I just do. Years of experience, kid...they save you from wasting your time with horseshit that goes nowhere. I'll know our guy the moment I see him."

"How?"

"Like I said, he'll call me 'pig.'"

Delware rolled his eyes.

They popped back into the Packard.

Jack looked back at the ranch house. "That's a lot of marijuana back there."

"It's called pot now."

They sat for a silent moment. Jack looked around. "This desert is a snake pit. Nothing good could ever come out of it." He turned to Delware. "Well, are you going to bust these guys for that crop of marijuana or not?"

Delware looked around the commune: mothers chasing toddlers, guys playing guitars. He looked back at Jack. "No, man."

"I thought you were a narcotics officer?"

"They're not hurting anyone."

"They're growing marijuana!"

"They're not trafficking, Jack. There's barely enough for themselves, I'm sure."

"They're breaking *the law*!"

Delware rolled his eyes, then watched Jack pull out his flask.

Jack took a swig. "We just going to let 'em roll?"

"Yeah, Jack. We are."

The old man gave him a sour sneer. "I thought you were *real* police."

"What the fuck? Jack, I thought you wanted to stay focused."

"I don't like these people."

"Well, I don't want to bust them. I told you, that's why I got out of Narcotics. You want to collar them 'cause they've got long hair! Fuck that!"

Jack stared angrily at Delware.

"Jack! You let Owsley Stanley walk with a table full of LSD in front of him, but you want me to bust these people for growing their own?"

Jack's face turned red. "That was different! His friend was *your* informant, so we gave him a helluva pass. But we need nothing from these fuckers. And I don't like their fuckin' attitude. Looking down at me! I'M THE FUCKIN' LAW!"

Delware glared at him. "Jack! You're going to bust these guys for getting high while you drink out of that." He pointed to the flask. "That's some hypocrite bullshit! You can get drop dead drunk, but they can't mellow out on a little pot?" Delware looked out the window and threw up his hands. "That's bullshit!"

Jack's face was scarlet and his eyes murderous and black. "Let me remind you that *I'm* your senior officer. So I'm not asking you, I'm telling you! They're hopheads! And this is *America*! NOT SOME ASIAN PORT, F'CHRISTSAKES!!! Now...are you a cop? Are you even a *man*? You got a set of balls in those pants or a *pussy*?!"

Delware kicked his door open, walked up to a shirtless long hair in ripped jeans. "Empty your pockets!"

"Ah, man."

Delware took a threatening step towards the man. "Do

it, or I'll bust your head open!" He threw the man up against the trunk of the car. "Hands where I can see them!"

Jack craned his neck. Delware jammed his hands deep into the hippie's pockets and pulled out three joints.

Jack got out of the car and came back. "Now *that's* more like it."

Delware looked at Jack with hateful eyes. "OK! He's holding – that's enough to arrest and put this guy behind bars!"

A woman came up with a baby in her arms, screaming, "Leave him alone!"

Other hippies gathered around the car muttering angrily.

Jack pulled his gun. "Stand back!"

The crowd started shouting. Jack fired a shot into the air. They jumped and cowered.

Delware walked up to another hippie and pulled him out of the crowd, pointing to his pocket. "What's that?"

The hippie shrugged.

Delware yanked the guy's arm. "In your pocket!"

"It's just a lighter, man!"

"Give it to me!"

The shaking hippie handed Delware a silver lighter.

Walking back to Jack, Delware stared at him with burning eyes. He popped one of the joints in his mouth and lit it. Puffing on the joint, Delware blew the marijuana smoke into Jack's face.

Jack squinted and pulled back. "What the fuck are you doing?"

"This is what you're doing, Jack! On duty! Every time you take a sip from that thing." Delware pointed to Jack's flask on the driver's seat. "It's no fuckin' different, Jack. Pot isn't damn heroin or fuckin' cocaine. It's the same thing you're doing!"

The hippies' jaws dropped.

A genuine smile crept across Jack's face. He grabbed the joint from Delware's lips and threw it down on the ground. Stomping it out, he laughed. "OK. Fuck this place. You know, Delware, you're one angry sumbitch – once you get to know you. Now partner, get back into the car, will ya."

Delware threw the lighter into the dirt and pulled the hippie off the back of the car. "Get lost!"

Delware popped back in the car. "Am I stoned, or did you just call me 'partner?'"

Jack did a troubled double take. "Did I?"

~ ~ ~

Jack drove away with amused eyes. He had enjoyed Delware's rant.

Delware couldn't take it anymore. "Why you so happy?"

"You."

"What?"

"You did it, kid, with this communist thing."

"You mean *commune*."

"Yeah, whatever, but that's exactly what I was talking about. I can see it now." Jack's eyes glowed as he contemplated the scenario. "A fuckin' hippie commune, all cut off from everything. Off the grid, no one knows what they're up too. No one's watching for miles. This is where some real horseshit could happen."

"Jack, they're here to get away from society."

"Yeah, but that's just it. To you hippies it's a commune. But to a criminal psychopath...it's a hide out." Jack nodded to himself. "It's a perfect disguise too. They all looked up to that old guy. This is exactly what we're looking for. That's who did it. Some psycho grows his hair, makes like a holy man, plays jailhouse mind games on some drugged up kids...*and* all sort of unlawful shit happens. You see that back there? That's not our guy, but he's close: a cult leader. Add a few dimwit followers, some unstable personalities, junkies, and what do you got?" He flashed a grin at Delware. "A nest full of vipers."

Monday, September 15th, 1969, 10:27 AM
Thursday

Barreling down Temple, the Packard weaved between cars. It was another day of commune hunting; they hoped to squeeze in three, maybe four. Without warning, Jack slammed the brakes. The files flew off Delware's lap. The Packard skidded to a stop. A two-tone Plymouth Dart behind them jammed its brakes, but couldn't stop. Its tires squealed and smoked. Jack whipped his head around. Delware braced the dashboard.

The Plymouth hit the Packard *hard*, bumping it more than a few feet. They could hear the front end of the Plymouth crunch and saw the hood pop up. Steam rose from the now exposed engine. The re-enforced Packard and the new bumper looked fine.

Delware turned to Jack. "You just got that bumper replaced an hour ago! You got to stop doing that! Maybe in your day when you drove a horse and buggy –"

Jack protested, "What?! We're fine!"

Curses could be heard from the Plymouth.

Delware glanced back.

Jack kept his eyes on Delware. "What's the date?"

Delware stared at Jack dumbfounded.

Jack asked, "It's the 15th, right?"

"Yeah, so what?!"

"We got to do something first, before any communes."

The driver of the Plymouth appeared in Jack's window, red faced and perspiring. "What the hell are you doing, stopping in the middle of the street like that?!"

Jack looked up at him. "Police business. Step back from the car."

"Police! I want your badge number!"

"Step back from the car!"

"I want to see your *badge*!"

Jack pulled his gun and pointed. "This is my badge."

The man stepped back. The look in Jack's eyes made him break into a run, leaving his car parked half way up the Packard's brand new bumper.

Pulling forward *slowly,* purposely tearing the bumper off of the Plymouth; Jack laughed.

~ ~ ~

Jack took the Harbor Freeway to Century Boulevard. After the ramp, they passed a row of cheap motels infested with hookers and dope fiends. Deeper into the heart of the ghetto the storefronts became rattier: faded homemade signs, dust covered windows, layers of peeling paint. They passed Delware's old all-black school where weeds grew up from the cracks in the pavement. Boarded up windows dotted the homes. Abandoned stripped cars appeared roadside and graffiti covered walls lined with dented garbage cans. Delware looked over at Jack. "Why the hell are we in Watts?"

"I have to do something." He pulled the car over and nosed into an alleyway at 103rd and Compton. "I'll be a minute."

Delware watched Jack walk down the alley. He stood over one spot looking at the pavement, solemn as if in a church.

Minutes passed. Just when a bewildered Delware was about to get out of the car, around the corner came an elderly black woman in her Sunday best: a flowered dress, an old style Jacoll hat with fresh lilies, pin and webbing over her eyes, holding a small bouquet of daisies. She stopped when she saw Jack. Jack's eyes were still on the ground. Approaching, she lightly touched his shoulder. He turned to her. Their hands instinctually touched and they stood holding hands looking at the pavement.

Delware's jaw dropped.

Saying nothing, doing nothing, they looked down. Then the black woman knelt and placed the daisies on the pavement – a tear in her eye. When she rose the two faced each other. The woman gave a weak smile and they shared a few words. She turned to go, but then turned back and gave Jack a light kiss on the cheek. Jack watched her walk away down the alley and around the corner. He looked at the flowers and then walked back to the car.

As Jack entered, Delware demanded, "What was that?"

Jack didn't reply. He started the car and backed out of the alley, absorbed in thought.

"Jack, are you going to explain?"

"One day."

The streets of Watts passed through Jack's eyes. Delware sat thinking about the closed door in Jack's house. How many secrets did Jack have?

Thursday, September 25th, 1969, 3:41 PM

It had been a long haul: two weeks of dusty communes and dirty hippies that turned up nothing. What felt like a break in the case had stalled into another dead end. A hundred and fifty files meant a hundred and fifty communes and a thousand suspects. Jack started an on-the-job bender and turned nasty. For two days, Delware drove the Packard, taking the angry drunk home and picking him up in the morning. Jack's living room was full of files: some organized, some scattered. Pages were food stained and scotch scented. Jack smuggled burglary files out of the station so he could read them as Delware drove. The back seat was full of them.

Delware watched and waited, playing nursemaid like he had to his own father. He had watched his father spiral down to nothing but bad habits. It wasn't lost on him, this instant replay. Strangely, it made him feel closer to Jack and reinforced a sentiment he had with his dad: old men should be careful about what they choose to remember.

They were coming back from another dead end when Delware hit Sixth and Figueroa. Jack demanded Delware pulled over.

Jack stumbled out. "Wait here."

He weaved up the sidewalk towards Mickey's Irish Pub, a few files under his arm. Delware waited ten minutes, then peeped into the big front window. Jack was slumped over the bar ordering straight scotches and downing them in single gulps. Between shots, he poured over files. Delware hit a grocery store across the street and grabbed a coke. When he got out he saw Jack at the car pulling more files out of the back seat and weaving his way back to the bar. He could hear Jack cursing from across the street.

Delware shook his head. "Drunken fool."

He seriously considered calling Pat to get Jack off the street – the old man was edging beyond belligerent – but decided he'd wait for Jack to pass out and just drive him home.

An hour later, Jack emerged from the bar more beast than man, angry and barely standing. Down the street he saw Delware leaning against the Packard, smiling at a white woman. The blond hippie chick stood *way* too close. The body language said it all. They were flirting. Through his drunken haze Jack watched her give Delware playful slaps as they chatted. Jack started to shake. He could feel the heat coming up the back of his neck, his hands balling into fists. The girl took Delware's hand and interlaced her fingers with his. Black fingers entwined in white. Jack's eyes saw red.

Delware gave his female admirer a brief kiss.

Jack stormed towards them. "Get the hell away from her!"

Delware, caught off guard, failed to react. The girl stepped back. Jack pushed Delware *hard*, upended him over the hood. "What do you think this is? Who do you think you are?"

The girl screamed. Jack fumbled for his gun. People down the street stopped and stared. Delware jumped to his feet.

Jack pulled out his .38, walked out into the middle of

the street and shoved the nozzle into Delware's forehead. "Don't you dare touch *her!*"

The girl ran screaming. Cars slowed, drivers rubber necked. In a single swift motion, Delware pulled his service revolver and aimed it square at Jack's forehead. "Don't tell me what I can do, old man!"

"Fuck you!"

"Fuck you!"

Frightened screams came from all around: pedestrians ran for cover, drivers sped away or abandoned their vehicles. All down the street doors slammed, windows shut. With all the blood pumping to their heads, Jack and Delware heard none of it.

Jack's face was turning every shade of red. "I'll kill you, *boy!*"

Delware frowned fiercely back. "I'll fuckin' blow your fuckin' brains out."

"This ain't the fuckin' *jungle!*"

Delware barred his teeth, his whole body seethed like fire. "You're dead, you're fuckin' dead! You think you're going to push me around! Control me!!"

Both men stared down the dark barrels of the other's single-action revolver.

Jack's finger squeezed tighter on the trigger. "Porch monkey!"

Delware squeezed tighter. "Trailer trash!"

"Sambo!"

Delware's face twisted fierce and ugly. "Cracker!"

The cylinders of their .38s shifted slightly, the loaded chambers aligning with their hammers.

"Goddamn spook!"

Fingers squeezed tighter; hammers pulled back.

"Fuckin' redneck!"

Like cobras drawing back to strike, their hammers were closing in on the point of no return. Both their wild, wincing eyes saw far too much daylight between each other's hammers and bullets. But the parts of these men who knew better were drowned out by ego, anger and adrenaline. They could almost hear their guns going off, the quiet click that would release the hammers, the dead thuds of hammers hitting bullets, the loud fiery punch of gunpowder igniting in chambers – rocketing bullets out with a sudden deadly fury into each others' brains.

Delware exploded, "Fuck you, you dumb ass PECKERWOOD!"

The endless drinking, days without sleep, finally took their toll. Jack let out an involuntary burp and his gun fired.

The shot punctured the air and echoed down the street.

Delware's gun went off.

The second shot punched and echoed.

The street fell silent. The doors remained closed. No one came to the windows. Inside people cowered, listening. But there was nothing left to hear.

Inside Mickey's Irish Pub, the hiding bartender peeped over the counter where Jack had left his files. He saw no bullet holes in the front window, but kept his head low just in case. Across the street, an elderly Mrs. Fairfield, who was already on the phone reporting two men with guns outside her apartment, fell speechless against her wall, as the operator asked if she was still there. Finally, the bartender slowly walked to the window and craned his neck to see outside.

He saw two men facing each other, guns drawn.

Jack blinked. Delware opened his eyes slow. Each was surprised to see the other standing. Jack's bullet had only left a hole in Delware's Afro. Jack's hand went to his chest, his fingers blindly felt under his jacket. A second later, he realized Delware must have missed. Neither could see any blood. Delware watched Jack's face. Jack smiled with relief. Delware almost laughed. Like a thunderstorm, the gunfire had killed the tension between them.

Jack steadied himself against the Packard. "Kid." He caught his breath. "You're a lousy shot."

"Me?" Delware pointed at himself. "How about you?"

"Hell, I'm stone drunk. What's your excuse?"

They looked around, surveying for bodies. There was no one even on the street.

A far off siren started. Delware had a *what-now?* look on his face.

Jack held up a finger. "Start the car!" He ran to the bar door and yelled in at the bartender, "Sammy, put those files under the bar! Say it was a white guy and black guy, but you didn't get a good look."

Another distant siren started and another. Jack ran back to the car and jumped in. "Get going!"

The sirens swelled.

Delware hit the gas.

As the Packard raced, Jack kept smiling. Delware looked over at Jack and couldn't hold back a grin. Suddenly, they were both laughing like schoolboys making a get away from the girl's change room.

Delware said in dread and excitement, "Jack, we're fucked!"

Jack shook his head, his speech all a slur. "We're fine. This is LA, kid. No one was hit, so it's just 'shots fired'. Big deal! A patrolman will file a 10-10 report. No corpse, no investigation." Jack convulsed in laughter. He caught his breath and squeezed out, *"Peckerwood."*

Delware stared confused.

Jack repeated, laughing, tearing, *"Peckerwood?!"*

Delware gave a short laugh. "Yeah. So? I called you a peckerwood."

"God, that's the stupidest goddamn word I ever heard.

I swear, it's ri-*goddman*-diculous! I've been meaning to ask youse people for years, what on God's green earth is a *peckerwood*?"

"It means...you got a small white dick, mothafucka!"

Jack laughed so hard, he farted.

Friday, September 26th, 1969, 6:40 PM

Jack drove and hadn't had a drink all day despite a hell of a hangover. They had hit six communes and it had rained through most of it. The skies cleared as the sun sunk into a misty glow over LA. Jack held out an empty palm. "I need a nickel."

"You gonna make a call?"

Jack nodded.

Delware grinned. "It's a dime now."

"Dime then. And forget the station. We've got something to do."

Delware fished his pockets for change. "Jack, where we going?"

"We're off duty. This is extracurricular."

The Packard rolled up to a phone booth. Delware waited while Jack made the call. The conversation was brief. Jack hopped back into the Packard.

Driving through the early dusk, the streets darkened all around. With a crooked smile and a strange glint in his eyes, Jack headed deeper and deeper into the rundown eastside. More and more empty stores and houses appeared. They entered an abandoned industrial park; dilapidated, nameless warehouses flanked them. Delware remembered rumors that one of these old warehouses used to be the unofficial LA Morgue back in the 40s. Jack turned into a short drive that opened up into a large loading yard. The rusted chain linked gates were left open, as if they were expected.

Jack slowed among puddles and potholes. Delware craned his neck, to get a glimpse of an old man in a trench coat waiting at the top of a loading dock. The Packard stopped just below him. Exiting, Delware gazed up at the large man and guessed he was retired police. They made their way up short cement steps and walked towards him. The light was almost gone and shadows filled the yard.

The waiting man eyed Delware suspiciously and raised his chin. "Who's he?"

Jack glanced at Delware. "Don't worry. He's one of us."

The waiting man studied Delware's face – a cop mentally filing a description. He slowly stepped backward and without turning, kicked the large metal door behind him with his heel. The loud hollow sound echoed in the empty yard.

Scuttling feet approached from behind the door. Two large men, retired cops from head to toe, appeared. Between them was a small man handcuffed with a hood over his head. The man shook and whimpered; there was blood on his hood.

Delware turned questioning eyes on Jack, but found Jack was already back at the car, opening its trunk. Without a glance at Delware, the two men moved the hooded man past him. From the top of the loading dock they threw the bound man off the platform and towards the open trunk below. It was a good throw, but the man's forehead clipped the raised lid and his head snapped back before landing in the trunk.

Jack reached in the trunk and felt for the man's pulse – more out of curiosity than concern. He nodded a thank you to the men and looked at Delware, tilting his head towards the car. Delware made his way down the stairs staring at the three men whose eyes followed him.

Delware was glad to be back in the Packard, even though it was not Jack's Packard anymore, not with somebody locked in the trunk it wasn't. Hell, even Jack wasn't Jack anymore and what was happening now, whatever it was, was no longer police work.

They drove through the night, headed north, skirting the Hollywood Hills and then out towards the desert. Delware slumped low in his seat, knowing by the silence of the men at the dock that this was ritual – nothing needed to be explained. And nothing needed to be explained to Delware. He realized what this was; he knew what Jack was doing. This was justice that would never see the light of day.

The desert road was dark. Only the headlights illumined the black asphalt and the endlessly broken yellow lines appearing, approaching and then disappearing underneath the car. Houses had vanished over an hour ago. Delware couldn't do this in silence. He feigned innocence. "Where are we going?"

Jack didn't answer for a long time. Then his voice broke the silence in hoarse deep tones, "Death Valley."

"Why?"

Jack tilted his head towards the trunk. "It's where guys like him end up."

Delware knew the answer, but had to ask. "You gonna kill him?"

Jack ignored the question. He looked at Delware with an emotionless face. Muffled knocks started to come from the trunk. Delware looked across the desert night. There was no end to the darkness.

After a few more minutes, Jack spoke, "You know, kid, when LA was a frontier town our murder rate was ten, even twenty times higher than New York City. Back then there weren't enough jails to hold all the criminals. They needed somewhere to put the undesirables."

Jack said nothing more. The road kept coming. They could hear the man in the trunk whimpering.

The desert road stretched on and on. Delware felt he was in some weird hell and, that for his sins, the road would never end.

In their headlights shone a sign. It was but a speck in the darkness, but slowly it grew until its letters seemed larger than life: Dead End. Jack killed the engine. The full moon appeared low and huge on the horizon.

Jack got out of the car and opened the trunk, pulling the whimpering man out of the back. He was bleeding badly and stumbled as Jack pushed him toward the edge of a dark, deep ravine.

To Delware, the dream of some endless hell ceased. It was all too real. He jumped out of the car. Hearing yipping very close and pebbles running down nearby cliffs, he turned to look. Coyotes darted between shadows.

Jack pushed the man to the ground. He lay at the edge of the ravine which yawned deep and dangerous.

"Jack, don't!" Delware ran to him. "What the hell?"

Jack unclipped his holster, pulled out his revolver and checked its chambers in the moonlight.

"Jack! We're cops. Police don't do this!"

Jack looked around at the desert. A lone coyote sat on a tall cliff, watching them like a judge.

"You know, kid, this is the unofficial graveyard of LA. The first marshals brought scum out here, sparing the public of unwanted trials." Jack looked into the shadows of a ridge where a pack of coyotes were gathering. "Whole generations of desert dogs have been fed and raised on thousands of corpses in this spot. But you won't find a single bone. The desert takes them, like they never existed."

The man on the ground tried to get up, wrestling to his knees, but Jack kicked him hard. He fell moaning.

Delware grabbed Jack's arm. "Jack! Let's go back and we'll lock him up and do this right."

Jack turned to Delware and spoke causally, "You've heard of this place?"

"Jack, I thought it was a legend. I didn't think it was real."

"No. Very few cops come here these days. But *now*, you're one of them."

The hooded man got to his feet and ran. Delware turned towards the running man and felt what every cop feels at the sight of an escaping suspect. His hand went for his gun, but it stopped at his holster. He saw Jack's gun already drawn.

Jack kissed his .38. "Don't fail me now." He leveled the gun at the hooded shadow running into the darkness. Jack squeezed the trigger, slow. The gun clicked, the hammer fell. The shot punched the silent night. The man's head jerked. His hood splattered red. A yelp came through the gag as he fell.

Delware yelled, "Jack!"

Walking to the man, Jack pulled off the hood. The guy's ear was missing, half his face was gore, but he was still breathing. Jack pulled off the gag. The man pleaded, "Oh god, please don't kill me!"

Jack aimed the gun at his head. "*Adios.*"

The .38 rang out in the desert, echoing among the cliff walls. The pleading stopped, but Jack kept pulling the trigger, four more shots and still he pulled, the hammer clicking on empty chambers. "Goddamn it!"

He stormed past Delware, reached under the driver's seat and pulled out another revolver. Walking back to the body, Jack emptied the gun into it. The six shots seemed louder than the first and echoed across the sands. The endless reverberations made Delware feel he was listening to eternity.

Jack stared down at the lifeless man. Delware's eyes were wide and unbelieving. The silence was eerily deafening. It all seemed a dream again, but the pungent smell of burning cordite told him it was real.

They stood for a long moment, two shadows in the desert night.

Delware spoke slow and shocked. "Jack, you shot him...*twelve times*."

Jack holstered his gun and shrugged, his voice soft, almost apologetic, "I know. I ran out of bullets."

Turning, he surveyed the dunes, the stars, the shadows of coyotes running along the ridge and then his eyes fell on the lone coyote on the cliff. It got up on all fours still watching them, a judge, a witness, unafraid. From somewhere in the dark came a long lonely howl.

Jack turned to Delware. "There's a lot of ghosts out here."

~ ~ ~

Delware sat in the still parked Packard, head down, almost comatose. Jack stayed out in the moonlight watching the coyotes feeding, tearing the corpse apart.

Turning, Jack scanned the barren horizons, the long stretches of sand. There was something in the desert wind. He walked away from the Packard towards the horizon. Stopping, he listened to the desert night. Slowly, he squatted, scooped sand, and let it run through his fingers. Like a hound closing in on its prey, he felt them, whispering, "Goddamn Death Valley, where else would they wait out the Apocalypse?"

Jack brushed off his hand and stood. Perfectly still, he listened as if he might hear them: Evil Jesus and his tribe of female disciples.

The wind shifted. The feeling evaporated.

Jack walked back to the Packard and slid in. "Kid, we're narrowing our search. We'll stick to communes located in or around Death Valley."

Delware did not respond.

Jack looked out the window. "They're out here, kid."

~ ~ ~

The way back seemed longer to Delware. Though he had not pulled the trigger, he had not forcibly stopped Jack either. He was an accomplice to murder. Delware wondered if he had pulled his gun to arrest Jack, would his body be lying back there too. In the darkness of the car, he felt a heavy weight around his neck – a crime that would never be cleansed.

They drove for an hour in silence.

Delware didn't even mean to speak, but his thoughts escaped anyways. "We're supposed to be better than that, Jack."

Jack looked over. "What did you say?"

"We're supposed to be better than *that*."

Jack stared, sizing him up. "You think you're better than me?"

Delware didn't answer.

Jack was offended by his silence. He turned his eyes back on the road. "Well, quit your bellyaching, will ya! '*Cause you're not*. You're *just* like me – only younger, you still got dreams, you ain't sick of it yet. Just wait."

Delware pointed back to Death Valley. "That's fucked up!"

Jack barked, "The world's fucked up!"

Delware turned away.

Jack glared at him. "Look, a dozen younger officers would squeal, but you won't. I know that. You don't think I can read you? I know exactly the type of cop you are and the type you're going to be: respectable up front, but when the coast is clear, you'll drive out *here*...to make sure...that justice is served."

"You call that justice?!"

"Damn right! Absolutely! I'm not afraid of what justice demands. I will do *whatever* it takes."

"Justice isn't just for *victims*, Jack. It's for everyone!"

"Yeah, but the innocent deserve it more."

"Everyone's innocent until proven guilty! How can you live with yourself? We're cops. We're supposed to be civilized."

"Let me ask you, do you honestly think we can clean up those streets following *every* procedure, *every* Departmental regulation? Horseshit. It's a fuckin' war out there! What do you think we're doing on the street?"

"Keeping law and order!"

"That's right, and it only works because every cop is legally sanctioned to use whatever violence necessary. A man don't stop beating his wife 'cause I ask politely. He stops 'cause I'm wearing a night stick and gun, and knows I have the license to use 'em."

Miles passed.

The lights of civilization appeared on the horizon. Jack broke. "When I came home from WWII, they gave me a parade, medals, kisses ... respect. Not like now. Now they call returning soldiers from Vietnam 'baby killers.'

"After my plane got all shot up, I just laid there in a hospital bed...for months. We didn't have TV back then and there was no goddamn radio on my ward. So I laid there – thinking – about the war, about my job: dropping bombs. You know, I dropped a hell of a lot of ordnance over Berlin, Dresden, a dozen cities. We carpet bombed Hamburg – 40,000 died in a single night. There must have been some soldiers there: on leave, a few guards, but who was *I* really killing? Women and children. School girls. A lot of old men and babies are dead because of me. But I was a hero for killing thousands of innocent people.

They didn't deserve to die. But that guy! That degenerate scumbag! Don't think I'm going to lose a wink of sleep over rubbing out a rat like that!"

Delware didn't answer, his silence more condemning than words.

Jack stared at the dark road ahead. "If tonight was made public, I'd go to jail ... who knows, with all you hippie communists today, I might even get the chair. But I was a hero for killing thousands of innocent children." Jack looked out across the desert night. "Know why I killed him?"

Delware didn't respond, but he wanted to know.

Jack spit out the window. "'Cause one day, you're gonna find yourself a woman who's going to tame you. And you're going to like it. Then you'll have a baby – a baby girl who walks to school every day. And you know what? She'll be safe, because of what I did tonight. She won't be raped or molested because *he* won't be waiting and watching on the street corner for her. No jury could do that for you. No jail could keep him locked up forever. The law would let him go, sooner or later. You can judge me *now*. But you wait, a few years of this racket – you'll be watching guys like that go free, on technicalities, because a pinko, hippie-loving jury can't recognize a psychopath when they see one, because they can't tell when someone's lying ... or telling the truth."

Delware barked, "Fuck you, Jack!"

Jack smiled. "You're not mad at me, kid. You're mad at yourself – 'cause I showed you what type of cop you are. You know why I took you? Because I wanted to show you how it's done. Because that's what I said to the old cop who showed me Death Valley, I said 'fuck you' to my first partner on Homicide. And you know what? He didn't kill the pervert. He let him go to trial...because of me. And you know what happened? Years later, I was working a case, this dead little girl. We never found her killer. It broke my fuckin' heart. And I wondered, I always wondered if it was him: the pervert I begged my partner to let get away with mere jail time.

"The case was over and I still couldn't get that thought out of my head. So I searched and found him. I broke into his house when he was at work. He had a dirt basement and the only thing down there was a shovel. Not one goddamn thing down there. Just a dirt floor and a long-handled shovel. I found five, maybe six...corpses, small ones. Children. I just waited with that shovel in my hand. When he came home, I beat him with it. I took him to Death Valley, and did what I should have let my partner do all those years ago. I shot him.

"To make sure...he didn't get off.

"That guy back there tonight, he *wasn't* innocent.

"So, judge me tonight. But this racket will show you sides of yourself you never believed existed. Put you in situations where you do things you never imagined – you'd rather forget. Just wait, kid. LA ain't through with you yet. Welcome to The White Man's Burden. And if I'm right about you, if you really care about what you're supposed to be doing out here with that badge and gun, then one day ... you'll make sure.

"You'll make sure rats like that meet with justice ... head on."

The Packard entered the city. When they parked out front of headquarters, the desert seemed like just a bad dream. Dawn was breaking.

Delware opened his door, got out and paused. He was a dark shadow in the twilight. It seemed he might just walk away, but finally he turned to Jack. "You don't know what justice looks like."

Jack looked up. "Kid, there's plenty of justice at the end of a gun."

Delware rested an elbow on the open door, the other on the roof. Shaking his head, he dropped it. "You're right about me, Jack. I won't squeal. But you're wrong about the cop I'm going to be. I'll never do what you did, because I'm black.

"I had an uncle lynched in Alabama. He was with me and my father when a mob grabbed him. They said he raped a white woman that evening – but he was with *us* – the whole night. They hung him ... right in front of me. I was *nine* years old, Jack. No trial, no lawyer, no due process. We tried to tell them he had been with us. No one listened. I knew my uncle all my life and I watched him dangling at the end of that rope – an intelligent, innocent man. That's why my father got us out of the south. Because any hysterical white woman could have you lynched. Any guy who committed a crime could claim he saw you, a *black* man, do it. No trial, Jack, just vigilante lynching. My uncle was a chief organizer of the black vote in my county. Isn't that interesting? Almost convenient, wouldn't you say?"

Delware looked into Jack's eyes. "Well, Jack, both you and I know it was and *never* will be investigated. So there's another side to *your* type of justice, Jack. There always is."

Delware slammed the door.

Thursday, October 2nd, 1969, 3:10 PM

The desert was blinding, its dunes distorted by rippling waves of heat. Even with the windows down, nothing but hot air hit their faces. Sweat dripped from Delware's forehead onto Dr. Ellroy's files as he crosschecked commune members' names with arrest reports from Robbery Division. Jack was bleary-eyed, his jacket dusty with sand.

Delware took a long hateful look at Death Valley. "That's it, Jack. That's all the communes. Let's get the hell out of here."

Jack laughed. "This place *is* Hell. Only the Devil himself could stand it, but, kid, we got one more."

"Shit, Jack! I'm outta files."

"Hey, we're out here, aren't we?! We haven't done Spahn Ranch."

Delware rolled his eyes and threw up his hands. "You're trying to kill me!"

Jack just smiled.

Delware sneered. "I don't have *that* file. We'll do it tomorrow."

"No, we'll do it today. It's on our way back. Kid, it's right over the hill there."

"No, Jack! I'm gonna lose my mind out here. We're so far from LA, the radio's been dead for hours. And I can't take one more commune. I'm thirsty as hell and we're out of water!"

"What, you tired?"

"Yeah!"

Jack laughed. "Kid, you're soft. Back in my day there was no such thing as tired. My mother use to push a broom and scrub a wooden floor till it sparkled. You kids got washing machines, vacuum cleaners, and whine that you're tired."

Delware pointed an accusatory finger. "You just want to see that wishing well thing, don't you? Don't think I don't remember!"

Jack grinned. "It's called the Bottomless Pit."

Delware threw himself back in his seat. "Bottomless Pit?! It's a fuckin' well! I'm dying in the desert and you wanna stroll down memory lane!"

"Hey! It's on our list, isn't it?"

"Not today! Christ!"

"Well, it is now. Besides, this will be quick. I know the ranch. My dad took me horseback riding here all the time *and-*" He added gleefully, "we'll see if the Bottomless Pit is still there."

The sign came out of the dunes. A wooden plank job with faded paint: Spahn Ranch.

The radio spurted, "Detective Middleton, are you there?"

Jack hit the brakes, the Packard skidded and disappeared in a cloud of dust. Inside, Jack grabbed the mic. "Middleton here."

"Detective, we've been trying you all day. We have another 185 – bloody messages on the walls. At 3301 Waverly Drive."

Jack looked up, stunned. The dust cleared and the Spahn Ranch sign reappeared. "Shit! It's just around the bend." Jack didn't feel it before, but now he did. It was more than just seeing the Bottomless Pit; his gut told him this place was important.

"Holy shit, Jack! What are you doing? Turn this thing around!"

Jack didn't move.

"Jack! We gotta go!"

Jack's eyes fixed on the sign. "I got a feeling, kid."

"What?"

"I'm not sure, but I think we should check out this commune first."

"Are you kidding? There's been another murder. Dirk, the entire Department, is at the scene now, probably trampling all the evidence as we speak."

Jack nodded, his eyes still on the sign. "That's right, kid. But-"

Delware punched the dashboard. 'Damn you!"

Jack snapped out of it. "Hey, be careful with the car!" He met Delware's fierce stare and saw his partner was clearly at his edge. Jack shook his head. "OK, OK, kid. We're going."

He spun the car around, consoling himself that the ranch would still be there tomorrow.

~ ~ ~

Jack sped. Delware stewed.

Jack glanced over. "Calm down, kid. We're getting there."

Delware curled his lip at Jack.

"Kid, even at this speed, we're still an hour out, so CALM DOWN!"

Delware punched the dashboard. "I'm sick of this case and I'm sick of *you*! You're a criminal, Jack – with a badge and gun! And here I'm chained to a madman in the middle of the desert when the action is miles away in LA! And all your secrecy bullshit! Never telling me anything! Following your mysterious hunches! I'm sick of it!"

"OK, kid! Relax before you blow a gasket! You wanna know something? Well, go ahead! Ask away! We got all the time in the world."

"What happened in that alley way?! Who was that goddamn black church lady who kissed you?"

"Kissed me!?" Jack looked at Delware like he was crazy, then it dawned on him, "Oh, she did." He got defensive. "That was a peck on the cheek, don't go around saying-"

"Tell me! What happened in Watts?"

Jacked turned to Delware, looked him over, and surrendered. "Gwynette Sanders."

"Who?"

"She was eight-years-old in '47. That alleyway is where we found her."

"And the lady that kissed you?"

"That was her mother. That day was the anniversary of her death. Patty was my old partner then, for many years we went there together on the anniversary."

"Why?"

"We never solved it. It got a lot of press for a colored girl – on her way home from Sunday school, father was a famous jazz musician. My first big case. We worked it for over a year, hundreds of leads, field interviews, endless interrogations, same suspects again and again. But it never broke. We were young and we made mistakes. I didn't read it right from the beginning."

Jack looked tired, sad beaten eyes.

Delware whispered, "You give up?"

Jack shook his head. "The newspapers forgot Gwynette. The community leaders moved on to other issues. The Department cut Patty loose and sent him on another case. For a while it was just me. Then, the Department pulled the plug." He shrugged. "That was it."

"That was it?"

"My sergeant walked in and told me to clear off my desk. I thought I was through in Homicide, but he sent me on a new squeal. When I protested, my sergeant said, 'She's just another colored girl from Watts. She's not important, Jack.'"

~ ~ ~

The Packard pulled up to Waverly Drive. The street was cordoned off, a growing crowd packing behind the barricades.

Jack pulled over and glanced up at the houses sloping up the hill. "There's no use trying to get through, we'll park here."

~ ~ ~

The afternoon was fading fast. Jack and Delware made their way through the crowd held back by a line of police sawhorses. They passed into the grim carnival of what was death in LA. A dozen patrol cars choked the street, a few up on the sidewalks – lights still flashing. Neighbors rubbernecked out windows and the end of driveways where they were held at bay by bleary-eyed patrolmen, sergeants pulling news photographers off the mansion gate – cameras flashing. Crime Lab guys grabbing equipment from their van, two deputies smoking inside a photo car and the crew from the L.A. County Coroner pulling gurneys from their wagon.

Up the driveway, the traffic was just as bad. Jack turned to Delware, "Well, they're doing a bang-up job of trampling any evidence in the front of the house. Let's circle round back."

The driveway extended behind the house. They saw a small sailboat up on a trailer. No one was around. Jack took his time, looking for signs of passage in the grass near the backstairs. He looked at all the windows: no slashed screens.

They entered through the back door. Stepping into the

kitchen, Jack paused. There on the white fridge door, written in blood, were the words, "Helter Skelter."

Stepping into the crowded living room, they saw a body on the floor. The police photographers were there, flashbulbs going off. A man in his fifties lay beside a couch: a carving fork jutting from his stomach, a steak knife deep into his throat. Through a doorway Jack saw a bedroom with a woman in her forties sprawled on the floor. "Pigs" and "Rise" written in blood on the walls. Dirk eyed Jack. Dirk's team turned their heads and their talk stopped.

Jack walked by the man's body, glancing at the stab wounds, too numerous to count. He entered the bedroom, estimating over 40 stab wounds on the female.

Stepping back into the living room, Dirk stood waiting.

Jack smiled. Dirk half smiled.

Jack rubbed his gray crew cut. "It's a series."

Dirk gave a silent laugh. "At a glance, but we've been here all day."

Jack jabbed a finger into Dirk's chest. "This *proves* me right. It's the same MO!!"

"That's what they want us to think – the two cases are unrelated."

Jack looked at Dirk with unbelieving eyes.

Dirk grinned. "It's a copycat, to throw us off. I'm going to let Duran and Millis take this one."

"Are you blind? You're saying these are unrelated?"

"Beyond the multiple victims, bloody lyrics..." He pointed to the red letters on the walls. "No, I don't see any connection, these victims and the Tate murders are too widely removed. There are no similarities linking the victims. You're really late on the scene, maybe you should have arrived sooner and-"

"Shut up, will ya!" Jack paced. "Are we not standing in a mansion in LA?"

"I wouldn't call this 'a mansion.' We're a long way

from Hollywood, Jack, a long way. Right now, we found no links between these victims and the Tate murders. They ...” he pointed to the bodies, “aren’t movies stars and ... no drugs were found in this house.” Dirk gave Jack an all-knowing look. “I know you’ve been off on your own, but we got a good lead and suspects on the Tate murders. You’re the only one in the Department looking for a series. The rest of us are basing our investigation on facts. Maybe if you were working a little closer with my team-”

Jack pointed to the body. “They used kitchen knives.” He pointed toward the kitchen. “Those knives are from *that* kitchen!”

Dirk placed his hands on his hips. “All that means is the killer arrived unarmed.”

Jack stood staring at Dirk with incredulous eyes.

“Like I said, Jack, it’s a copycat.”

“No, our guy wants credit for his kills.”

Dirk was going red. “These details were all over the papers. Anyone could make like the Tate murders, after the fact, to cover their trail!”

Jack fumed, “Just wait a minute!”

Jack disappeared into the bedroom, then rummaged through the living room. Forensics and photographers jumped out of his way grumbling and protesting. Everyone stopped and watched.

Dirk watched Jack enter a bathroom with amusement. He taunted, “Jack, be sure not to disturb the evidence in there too.”

Jack called from the bathroom. “Dirk!”

Dirk stepped into the bathroom.

Jack pointed to the wastebasket. “Look”

In the basket was a bloody page from the Bible. “It’s from the Apocalypse. Just like at the other murders.”

Dirk shrugged and walked out into the living room.

Jack followed. “Don’t walk away from me you

sumbitch. That's a bloody page from the Bible, it's the same MO!"

"Jack, it doesn't mean anything." Dirk turned on Jack. "I don't see the telephone lines cut!"

"The bloody pages from the Bible!"

"Jack, *that* was in every paper! It leaked Monday! Everyone in LA knows that by now and that's why the killers thought they could copy-cat their way out of this!"

Jack stood stunned.

Dirk caught Jack's confused expression. He mocked in a loud voice that silenced what little chatter there was left in the room, "What, Jack? Don't you the read the papers?"

Jack turned. The whole room was watching: forensics men, detectives, patrolmen, photographers.

Jack turned back to Dirk. "Wait a minute. *That* detail is out?"

Dirk's voice was a mix of frustration and mockery. "Yes, Jack, *on every front page of every paper in the city!*"

There were snickers among Dirk's team. Delware, watching from the kitchen, dropped his head, embarrassed.

Dirk enjoyed the lost look on Jack's face. "You don't read the papers? Jack, what's the matter with you?! Christ, it's the case you're assigned to!"

Snickers spread throughout the room. Jack went red with embarrassment.

Dirk grinned. "The only case you've worked effectively on this year is...is a case of scotch!"

The room burst into laughter. Jack looked around. The young men laughed, an older detective gave him an uncomfortable look of pity.

Jack fumed and turned on Dirk. "Every last detail is out! You're *head* of the investigation! It's your *job* to make sure *that* doesn't happen. So you just fucked us big time and you're fucking laughing!"

Dirk hissed. "Every reporter in the country is jumping on this investigation. How can you expect-"

"How can we know if we have good leads now?! If every detail is public, how can we confirm anything! *You've* completely fucked us!"

"Jack!"

Jack flushed redder. "You stupid, goddamn punk. You call yourself a detective!" Jack shoved his finger in Dirk's face. "It's your goddamn job to keep shit out of the fuckin' papers!"

"I didn't-"

"*You* didn't do your job! Do you even fuckin' know how to handle a big case, you stupid fuckin' moron! Now we can't rule anything out. You've left us in the goddamn dark!"

Dirk jumped in Jack's face. "Fuck you, you've never been a part of this investigation, old man! Pat's letting you play private dick for your last few months before retirement to keep you outta the way! With a partner no one in the Department even wants to touch! If it wasn't for Pat, you'd be on skid row! When was the last time you solved a case, old man!"

Jack turned and stormed towards the door. Dirk fired a parting shot. "When was it, Jack? That last time you solved a case? Good thing Pat keeps you in Watts, where no one important dies!"

Jack halted at the front door. He saw the face of eight year old Gwynette Sanders, her missing-a-tooth smile, his old sergeant: "-just another colored girl – she's not important, Jack."

With those words ringing in his head, he spun around. Jack sprang at Dirk. No one had time to react. His reflexes from decades of police work made him a dangerous man. Jack drew his gun, turned it in his hand, and smashed the butt into Dirk's face.

Dirk went down like a rag doll, unconscious before he hit the floor. He lay motionless, blood trickled from his nose and ear. The room stood motionless, not believing what they had seen. Like another body, Dirk was out cold on the crime scene.

Jack bent over Dirk and hissed, "They're *all* important!"

~ ~ ~

Jack burst out of the front door, almost knocking it off its hinges.

Delware followed him across the lawn. "What the fuck, man! What the hell were you thinking? Do you know what you've done! You screwed us!!"

His ranting was only on the fringes of Jack's consciousness. Jack's head was boiling with rage, his stomach sinking into a bottomless pit of foreboding. He had not fully formulated it, but his gut knew he had just torpedoed his own ship.

Frustrated that Jack would not even acknowledge him, Delware stopped and shouted, "Do you ever stop to think of what it's like to be a goddamn Negro in this Department?!"

That word, 'Negro' pierced Jack's mind. He turned to his partner and did not recognize him. Never could Jack have imagined the word Negro coming from Delware's mouth, but before him was another Delware, one he'd never seen: a scared, twisted face, a wretched man who had just lost everything.

"I have to work twice as hard as any white man to earn half his pay. Now I'm going down with *you*. Another *Negro* in blue, out on the street!"

As his adrenalin and anger subsided, Jack felt his age. His years came on, weighing him down. Delware's voice echoed down the street. Cops came to the windows. The street stared.

Delware could barely keep his feet on the ground. "You square, up tight mothafucka! Everything you did that was any good was twenty years ago. So what?! So what that you're even fuckin' right about this case? What the fuck does that even matter because you're still going round in circles. 'Cause you're OLD! You just don't dig it, man. You don't read the newspapers, you don't watch TV! The whole world is changing, everything is changing, except *you*! You may have been great two decades ago, but now you're too old to be any good to anybody!!"

Delware stood panting, his hand on his holster, waiting for Jack to go for his gun.

But Jack just stared. Turning his old eyes towards the blood-red sunset in the smog, he saw its fleeting light sweeping back from LA, sinking into the ocean. The last of its rays scattered across the sky.

Jack walked away.

Delware watched the Packard speed off.

Two detectives watched from a window. One turned to the other, "You know, I like Delware. He's alright."

~ ~ ~

Jack burst through the door of his home, grabbed the framed glossy of his wife off the wall and tossed the picture across the room. The glass burst into shards. Grabbing a fresh bottle of scotch from the kitchen, he sank into his chair. He took a swig. He sat. The darkness deepened. The phone rang many times. Never moving, he knew it was Pat and then the Chief of Police. They were going to throw him off the case and then dismiss him from the Department. There might be charges, even jail time. Jack sat. Even the bottle remained untouched. The living room grew darker still. Not reaching for a light, he let the darkness fall.

Finally, in the pitch black, he let out a long, sad sigh.

Slowly standing, he walked into his grease-spattered

kitchen. He turned on the light. The bare bulb illuminated a small room, faded floral wallpaper peeling off the walls. The open pantry doors revealed bare shelves except for a few dusty cans of corn and beans. The dishes were gone, heaped high and dirty in the sink. Jack surveyed hundreds of unwrapped newspapers piled about his feet.

Searching the stacks, he found the one he wanted. Grabbing the pile with both arms, he poured it across the kitchen table. Jack picked through the tightly wound papers until he held the one he wanted. Slowly, he slipped the rubber band off. Newsprint unrolled across the table. The bold headline:

RITUALISTIC SLAYINGS
Sharon Tate, Ten Others Murdered.

The page featured an aerial shot of the Tate grounds paired with a crude blueprint of the mansion with Xs representing each victim. Page 2 had more photos. He mulled over the articles and then opened another paper. Finding the follow up stories, he was surprised the press was connecting the evidence as he had. Jack wasn't consoled. Newspapers were famous for wild speculation – laughed at by detectives – always proven wrong. Now, he fully understood how foolish he had looked that afternoon.

He sat still and silent. Numb.

An hour later, he began systematically opening up every newspaper.

There before him in print and pictures was a decade he had done his best to ignore: the Vietnam War, anti-war demonstrations in every major city across America. 250,000 marched on Washington in protest, burning draft cards and the American flag. There were protests from coast to coast: blacks, women, gays marching in the streets of America demanding equal rights.

Page after page saw a country in conflict. A protest at

Columbia University escalated into an invasion of the Dean's office, three school officials taken hostage. A picture showed a confident longhair in the Dean's chair, his feet up on the prestigious mahogany desk, smoking one of the Dean's cigars.

There was a week's worth of pages and pictures of Detroit in flames, a seven-day riot by blacks, sparked by police brutality. 43 people dead, 2,000 injured and 5,000 left homeless.

On the steps of the Oakland courthouse, Black Panthers donning large Afros, black leather and dark sunglasses escorted their leader Huey Newton to freedom with shotguns cocked on their hips.

Chicago Democratic National Convention: the surrounding streets were full of turmoil and confrontations between police and hundreds of anti-war protesters chanting, "The world is watching!" Mayor Richard Daley gave riot police instructions: "Shoot to kill." Cops moved in with clubs, beating indiscriminately, clobbering tourists, newsmen and people on their way home from work.

An April paper showed the civil rights leader Martin Luther King Jr. shot dead on the balcony of a Memphis motel. The papers that followed showed reactionary racial violence in cities nationwide.

A June paper had a picture of Robert Kennedy shot down just after announcing his victory in the California primary. A nation mourned as they had the assassination of his brother, JFK, five years earlier.

In New York, gays and lesbians outside the Stonewall Inn in Greenwich Village rioted and marched in violent demonstrations against police brutality, openly protesting their persecution as homosexuals.

A September front page featured a picture of a young woman with a placard: Cattle Parades are Degrading to

Human Beings. The headline: Miss America Beauty Pageant Waylaid by Women's Lib Movement. Millions of viewers were shocked as the live national broadcast was interrupted for 10 minutes. A banner was unfurled from the theater's balcony proclaiming "Women's Liberation," stink bombs and chanting of "Freedom for Women!" "No More Male Chauvinism!" and "Stop the Oppression of Women!" followed. The paper claimed protesters outside burned their bras.

An August paper had aerial photos of 500,000 hippies gathered at the Woodstock Music & Art Festival. The larger than expected crowds turned the three-day open-air concert into an impromptu city with National Guard helicopters bringing in food and medicine. Smaller photos showed open drug use by performers, naked fans sliding in the mud and more awe-inspiring shots of a half a million longhairs.

Jack wandered to the living room and stared at his console black-and-white TV. He dropped to his knees and reached under for the plug. Once in the socket, he stood and wondered if the set still worked. Cautiously, he turned it on and walked back to his seat. Slowly, the tube hummed, flickered, then popped on.

NBC was broadcasting a special report on the Vietnam War and the My Lai Massacre. 109 defenseless Vietnamese civilians in My Lai had been murdered by US troops. The footage was graphic: huts burning, scores of women, children and infants lying dead in dirt roads.

A British reporter came on the screen. "Soldiers went berserk, gunning down unarmed men, women, children and babies. Families which huddled together for safety in huts or bunkers were shown no mercy. Those who emerged with hands held high were murdered. Elsewhere in the village, other atrocities were in progress. Women were gang raped; Vietnamese who had bowed to greet the

Americans were beaten with fists and tortured, clubbed with rifle butts and stabbed with bayonets. Some victims were mutilated with the signature "C Company" carved into the chest. By late morning word had got back to higher authorities and a cease-fire was ordered. My Lai was in a state of carnage. Bodies were strewn through the village."

They flashed back to The Tet Offensive. Viet Cong forces launching a series of surprise attacks in South Vietnam, even taking the U.S. embassy, two thousand US troops killed in a single day.

Jack stood up, walked over to the TV and reached behind it. He pulled the plug and the TV went silent. The picture blinked off.

He looked down at his hand holding the plug. It trembled.

~ ~ ~

The door hung crooked, its aged, faded wood covered in dust. In the dark night, in the dim hallway, Jack stood before it. Delware had always wondered about this door, the one no one was allowed to enter, not even Jack.

His aged eyes stared at the rusting, dented doorknob. He had lost everything. The full realization was sinking in. He could almost hear his dismissal being typed up in City Hall. Fear pulled at the muscles of his face.

A sweeping desperation moved Jack's hand towards the handle that had not been turned in six years, but stopped before it touched. His hand hung there in the silence of the night.

Then he consented, surrendered. Clutching the cool handle as if it would unleash demons, his hand turned. The knob creaked. The door swung open.

Jack stood in the doorway; a shaft of dim living room light fell onto the floorboards. He stared at the darkness beyond. Stale air and the odor of mothballs hit him.

Stepping inside, his eyes widened, searching in the dark. Vague outlines emerged: a bed, a bare mattress – the sheets gone with its occupant.

Jack did not visit the grave at the back of the cemetery, the black stone with her name on it. Because his wife was *here*, silently waiting for him.

Stepping deeper into the room, he felt her presence again, the last good thing in his life. The only person he knew who had nothing to do with murder and crime.

Objects slowly came into focus: frilly drapes over the window, a framed mirror over a make-up table, neatly arranged perfume bottles, a round pearl hairbrush – all covered in thick dust. A pair of faded pink slippers with matching bathrobe draped over a chair; on the wall, framed black-and-white baby pictures of their daughter, a young smiling Jack and Martha on a ship's deck on their honeymoon, Jack looking slim and sharp in his Air Force blues.

A tear formed. It swelled and rolled along the deep, mean wrinkles around his eye.

Sitting on the musty bed, it squeaked beneath him. The shaft of light from the doorway fell on his legs, but the rest of him was a dim silhouette in the dark room.

Bowing his head, his fingers felt the bed, longing to touch her, to feel her as real – not just a memory.

He let out a whimper as he remembered her embrace. The lone tear fell from his face. His chest heaved, emotion shook him as it had when she was beside him on dark nights like these.

The words heaved from him. "It's over, Martha.

"There's no way back. I'm leaving a failure.

"The Department tried to put me out to pasture. They had no right to do that. No right. But I hung on and I was going to break the case ..."

He turned to the mirror hoping to see her face

reflected there as it had been so many times before, but only his shadow appeared in the frame. He was still alone. "We're losing our country, Martha. Men look like women; women act like men. Can't even take a walk down our street no more – homos, coloreds, hippies everywhere. There's no order to things. No one's got any respect for authority. They don't want any rules ... any laws.

"It's just not America anymore. All my buddies in WWII, dying on the beaches, Holland, the Ardennes ... for what? So those longhairs could make America a communist haven?

"And guys like me. We're the enemy – they used to call me officer, now they call me *pig*. Those longhaired bums got no respect.

"Why?

"Is it my fault?

"I did everything my country asked: when it went to war, I went to war. When my city needed men to take bad guys off the streets, I signed up. I did *everything* to take them down. I did my job! I defended my country! And now they call me *pig*.

"Twenty years ago, I would have had this psycho locked up by now – but the world we lived in is gone, Martha.

"It just doesn't make sense: the victims, the murderers, the clues. They're right in front of me, but ... I can't understand them."

He dropped his head and shook it slow and sad. A long minute passed.

"I'm tired. Tired of this world."

~ ~ ~

Jack's chin rested on his chest, moving as he breathed. His mind was a black bottomless pit. Then a thought wandered out of that dark: a memory of Delware on the lawn today yelling 'Negro.' That kid. He might have done it. Maybe not this year, but if Jack hadn't blown it, the kid might of made detective ... someday. But not now. He would be busted back into blue, walking a beat in Watts. Back to the ghetto he worked so hard to escape. Delware was out there in the night lying in his own personal abyss, his losses stinging him like scorpions. *Negro*. Delware had used that word today to describe himself. The word he so loathed and longed to overcome. Jack knew that was the heaviest weight, that Delware was shackled to that word tonight, sinking under its weight.

Jack looked up through the doorway from the black room. His .38 holstered on his chair. He eyed the gun and thought it might be the easiest way out. No tomorrow, no facing Delware or hearing about his fate. No facing the Department or Pat. No sad looks or jeering grins. No lonely days with nothing to do, but to think about how he failed and what he had done: to himself, to others.

His father and grandfather had died by the gun. Maybe *that* was the Middleton curse. He stood up and walked back into the light.

Jack moved like a man to the gallows, passing the chair, his hand swept out, his fingers embracing the butt of the .38. His arm hung limp as he passed, but his fingers held. The gun slipped out of its holster, swinging by his side.

Sinking into his chair, he stared at his World War II shelf: a citation for bravery, purple heart, medal of good conduct, a jar holding a piece of shrapnel taken from his leg, a Congressional Medal of Honor wrapped around tarnished brass knuckles.

His eyes turned to the table of empty scotch bottles.

His head turned to the antique television set on legs, blank, its plug still on the carpet. Its rounded glass screen darkly reflecting his elderly body in his worn out chair. His reflection stared back at him.

Jack muttered, "I am old. *Too old.*"

The gun hung loose at the end of his arm. The trigger finger rose and spun the cylinder. The clicking of the whirling bullet chamber was the only sound in the room.

Jack looked dead, his eyes lifeless, a corpse slumped back in a chair. Only a whisper of life, enough to take his own, remained.

His head slid to one side, those dead eyes fell on the console stereo. There lay the black Bible and the White Album. He whispered to them. "I am a useless, old, man."

The gun rose slowly, silently through the air. His arm had a life of its own, as if a cobra, its deadly head the .38, sneaking up on the weary man.

The finger rolled the cylinder again, sounding like a rattlesnake about to strike. Jack's head lolled over and he kissed the barrel of the .38. "Don't fail me now."

He turned his head away from the loaded gun and squinted. The black hole of the barrel rested on the hollow of his temple like it too was tired.

His finger curled around the trigger. The hammer began to draw back. Jack held the black Bible in one eye, the White Album in the other, but there was no intelligence in his pupils. He was already dead.

His withered lips whispered, *"Adios."*

His eyes slid down.

Something glittered. He faintly wondered what it was, but his eyes continued to drop and closed. Jack stared into the black infinity behind his lids, waiting for the bang. His finger, slow and steady, squeezing. The bullet chamber aligned with the drawn hammer.

His last thought: *what the hell?!*

A single eye popped open. It glittered again. Something was under the old Victor Victrola gramophone, near the back leg.

Studying it for a moment, he still couldn't decipher

what he saw, but it wasn't supposed to be there.

He gave up. He didn't care. Closing his eye, squinting, he waited for the blast, but his finger eased up.

Both eyes popped opened. "What the hell is *that*?!"

Tilting his head back for a better view, anger straightened his spine. In one swift, annoyed motion, he was down on his hands and knees. Popping his head under the Victrola, he leaned on one elbow and reached under with a single hand.

His fingertips touch something soft and plastic. Pulling it out, he came up grimacing on his knees. He held a clear plastic bag; at the bottom dangled four white sugar cubes.

His mind raced, how did he know this? Then he remembered: Julia, his granddaughter in San Francisco, handing the bag to him as he left, him getting home and realizing it was LSD, then tossing it. He hadn't thought of it since. Anger mixed in with the memory: *this* was her present to him! He detested her for that. How could she?!

Coming to his feet, he held his knees and groaned.

Tossing the bag on top of the record player, it landed on The White Album. There it was, his bane: The White Album. He stared at its all white jacket: a twelve inch by twelve inch wall of hippiedom, it might as well have been eight miles high and long – it was never going to let him in.

Jack whispered, "I know you're in there, you psycho. You hid the clues in the most public place, you goddamn sumbitch! Where everyone could see 'em, but no one could understand – not the way you do!"

Reaching down, he flipped open the double sleeve. The motion knocked the cubes from the bag and shattered them on the surface of the console. The light sparkled on the white sugar.

Glaring down at the cubes, he remembered his

granddaughter's eyes, sparkling as she handed him these cubes: they were like Martha's eyes – full of caring.

"*Oh my god.*"

He went back to the chair, his breathing labored.

"Oh my god."

His heart raced.

"That's it."

Sweat popped on his brow. His eyes looked back at the album and the four white cubes. His shaking hands gripped the chair handles. "*That's it!*"

He whispered. "I can't do this.

"But it's the only way.

"No, no."

He looked at the cubes with helpless eyes. "Please forgive me." Jack stood up and sat right back down again. "No!

"Oh my god!

"Don't do it. Don't!

"But that's the key...that opens the door."

He rose and walked over to the stereo, his eyes moving back and forth: the white cubes, the White Album.

A trembling hand came forward, pinching a cube, dropping it into his palm. Holding it like a communion wafer, his eyes widened with fear: the innocent cube of sugar: white like death itself.

He closed his eyes. His lips parted. As if bringing a poisoned chalice to his lips, both arms shook. The cube rolled in the shaking palm. He held his breath. His hand paused on touching his trembling lips. The cube rolled and stopped at his bottom lip. His nostrils flared at the sweet smell. His hand hung there. Jack's entire body shook.

With one last effort, like plunging a dagger into his own heart, he pushed the cube into his mouth. His eyes shot open wide with surprise, but it was too late. On reflex, he swallowed the sweet, melting sugar laced with LSD.

~ ~ ~

The White Album opened with the whining whistle of a jet plane landing in the left speaker and skidding to the right. The band kicked into *Back in the USSR*. Jack sat expectantly, his hands clutching the worn, upholstered arms of his chair. The bouncing beat faded out into the quiet, tentative *Dear Prudence*, Lennon coaxing a reticent girl to come out and play. The slightly off-center *Glass Onion* rolled by and then *Ob-La-Di, Ob-La-Da*. Jack sat thinking something had gone wrong. The first side of the record had finished with the fractured *Happiness Is a Warm Gun*, but he felt nothing.

Walking to the stereo, he stared down at the three white sugar cubes, thinking he had taken too weak a dose. Delware would have warned Jack that LSD can take up to forty minutes to take effect and that he had already taken a huge dose. But Delware wasn't there.

Jack popped two cubes into his mouth like candy. Clumsily, he flipped the record over to Side Two. Glancing down at the remaining cube, he frowned and then popped it into his mouth. Sitting back, he swallowed the last of the melting sugar laden with LSD.

As Paul McCartney kicked off side two, Jack felt something creeping up on him. He couldn't tell what it was at first, but it was ominous, like the darkening of the sky before a storm. Pushing himself deeper into his chair, his shoulders tensed.

As Lennon dragged his feet through the last verse of *I'm So Tired*, full paranoia set in. Jack's eyes darted about the room. The strange notion that the entire LAPD, *somehow*, knew he had taken LSD haunted him. Images of officers lurking outside his house plagued his imagination. He thought he could hear whispering in the kitchen.

Checking the kitchen, the windows, he found them all clear. But he still couldn't escape the feeling that someone was watching. Where was this faceless, disembodied surveillance? What did they want? Who were they?

Jack didn't realize it, but the first dose of LSD had just begun to take effect and three more were on the way.

As *Blackbird* snuck into the room, the music seemed to warp as if the turntable was wobbling. Jack felt a desperate need to escape. Sitting in his chair, he held himself there, fighting the urge to run screaming into the streets.

Then came the oink of pigs from the stereo, the song *Piggies* began, and so did the hallucinations. As the harpsichord played, Jack's eyes were drawn to the imitation Persian rug at his feet, an object he hadn't noticed in twenty years. In the intricate patterns, a little tendril started to curl and uncurl as if alive. A moment later, all the interlacing designs looped around each other. Pulling his eyes from the carpet, the walls moved as if breathing. The windows grew very large then very small. Jack wondered: *are they really moving?*

By *Rocky Raccoon*, the patterns on the carpet, drapes and wallpaper pulsed and swirled in ever larger flowing circles. Jack slid down in his chair, eyes wide and pupils broadly dilating.

The stereo needle finished Side Two. Pulling out the second disc, Jack's fumbling hands let four photos fall to the floor from the album's sleeve. Included in every copy of the White Album were 8'x10' glossies of each Beatle. Jack stared at them, the Beatles stared back.

Not realizing he was skipping Side Three, he put on Side Four. It took a number of laborious attempts to drop the needle correctly on the spinning disc.

Revolution #1 kicked off. Instruments whirled around him, notes fading in and out. Jack dropped to his knees. He no longer remembered why he was listening to the record. By *Honey Pie*, Jack didn't even comprehend he was listening to The Beatles. He only experienced chords, notes, melodies. The other three doses were kicking in. Everything in the room was in motion. Tables, chairs, bottles, pictures were alive, radiant with energy. The black-and-white picture of his wife followed him with her eyes as he crawled back to his seat. Sadly gazing at his shelf of medals, for the first time, he didn't feel fierce pride. They seemed dead: faded ribbons; neglected, dusty pieces of metal.

The walls and floor rippled like water. Jack kept sliding from his chair. He had no choice, but to lay on the swirling carpet. There was no center anymore, nothing left to hold on to. The world was a swarm of sensation, a stream of surging, shifting color and sound, melting and moving, morphing endlessly. Feeling his body sinking into the floor, he lay there amazed.

Then it began: *Revolution #9.*

It wasn't a song. It was a sound collage, a patchwork of random audio: a plaintive piano wandered across the speakers, a somber man's voice repeated, "Number nine, number nine, number nine..." An orchestra played backwards, John Lennon spoke over it in a flat, monotone, "and everyone knew that as time went by, he'd get a little bit older and a little bit slower ... "

Sounds continued to morph: a girl's laughter into a baby crying, a choir's lamenting chant into the somber man repeating, "number nine, number nine" shifting from one speaker to the other. Jack's eyes widened: insane, uncontrolled. *Revolution #9* grew more chaotic. Cars honked, traffic barged in. A cocktail party emerged. Football crowds chanted, "Hold the line! Hold the line!" Unintelligible speech turned into George Harrison's voice: " ... there were four of them ... "

Suddenly, Jack saw the lawn of the Tate mansion in the middle of the night and the backs of four hippies facing the mansion. The hallucination was vividly real. Harrison continued, " ... only to find the night watchman, unaware of their presence ... " The hippies snuck up to an open window, cutting the screen. Following them to the kitchen, Jack watched them taking knives from the drawers. Instantly, John Lennon screamed like a maniac, "Rise! Riise! Riiiise! Riiiiiiiiiiise!!" Jack saw the word being written by a bloody page on the white walls.

New sounds appeared: the crackle and snap of fire, interrupted by a barrage of radio static, bursts of gunfire jumped from nowhere. The somber voice swung again and again from speaker to speaker, "number nine, number nine,"

George's voice whispered, " ... pushing it between her shoulder blades ... " Jack saw a blade plunged into a woman's back repeatedly, blood spraying. The stereo gave a painful scream which descended into a low, manic mumbling.

Jack's dry tongue flickered like a lizard's, trying to moisten his chapped lips. His teeth hummed like electricity. A voice came from the stereo, "There were lots of stab wounds."

"Number nine, number nine, number nine,"

Abruptly, Jack sat ramrod straight, his eyes wide with some mad revelation. Rising unsteadily, he rocked on his feet like a mad man on a seaborne boat. His pupils outrageously dilated like they might rupture. Strange tics pulled at his face, as if he might weep one moment, then fly into a murderous rampage the next. On and on, contorted and pale, his face twitched out of control, an impossible expression...from murderous to suicidal, suicidal to murderous, murderous *and* suicidal!

"Number nine, number nine, number nine, number nine,"

Jack stumbled toward the stereo, torn with some

violent, bizarre, god-awful idea.

Beside the White Album: the black Bible. As he picked up the Bible, John Lennon spoke from one speaker, "Take this, brother, may it serve you well ... "

Jack, thinking the voice was in the room, dropped the Bible and violently turned, frenzied with fear. Sounds multiplied: shouting men, women choirs singing backwards, the burst of machinegun fire erupted all around him. The Bible lay open on the floor.

Falling onto his hands and knees, he wept and laughed wildly, desperately turning pages, sweat dripping from his forehead onto the Bible.

The somber man began again, from speaker to speaker, "number nine, number nine,"

His trembling finger could not grasp the thin pages. He tore as many pages as he turned, until he clawed them out of the Bible, grinding his teeth while orchestras climaxed and spun around him. Tearing away page after page, he finally reached the last book: The Book of Revelations.

His trembling hand moved more slowly now, carefully ripping pages from The Apocalypse, until he reached the chapter he was looking for: Number Nine.

His shaking, claw-like hands withdrew from the shredded Bible, afraid to touch it again. Staring wildly, his eyes attempted to read, but they could not. Words with watery letters bounced up and down the page and from side to side.

The phrase: *four angels,* jumped out at him. Jack glanced at the pictures of the four Beatles on the floor.

Angels. The Beatles' long angelic hair framed their solemn, contemplative eyes staring quietly from their photos.

He glanced back at the Bible; two words moved in and out of focus. *The Locust.* They grew larger and larger, then faded back, only to grow again: *The Locust*. Vanishing into the jumble of letters, they emerged once more: *The Locust*. Jack almost screamed, "Beetles!"

Jack whispered to himself, "Locusts are beetles. Beetles! Beetles!"

He looked back at the pictures that lay on the swirling carpet. John Lennon, Paul McCartney, George Harrison, Ringo Starr. He whispered, "The Beatles!"

Struggling, Jack managed to read the passage: *The Locust came and their faces were as the faces of men and they had hair as the hair of women*. He glanced back at the four faces framed by long hair.

His eyes returned to the Bible, *And they had a king over them which is the angel of the Bottomless Pit*.

Jack froze. His eyes fixed on two words: *Bottomless Pit*. There it was! What he had never seen.

Suddenly, Jack was at Spahn Ranch in Death Valley watching his father and a ten-year-old Jack dropping stones into a deep well. Beside the well, a sign: The Bottomless Pit.

It all flashed back: the Free Clinic, Doctor Ellroy's office, her mentioning a commune at Spahn Ranch. He even remembered their leader's last name: Manson.

Unexpectedly, an evil energy awoke in the room. Feeling a menacing presence, Jack looked up and saw a shadow rising in the air. He knew where it was from: Death Valley. The shadow became a man with wild murderous eyes. The staring eyes of Evil Jesus knew Jack had found him. The centurions were coming. The prophecy would be fulfilled.

Yoko Ono spoke from the stereo, " ... then ... you become naked."

~ ~ ~

The walls took hours to stop moving, but finally the floors became solid again. Jack fumbled with the phone and, after many attempts, dialed Delware's number. Twenty rings later, Delware picked up. After minutes of fragmented sentences, Delware realized the strange voice was Jack saying he knew where the killers were. Delware arrived expecting to find Jack stoned drunk, but was surprised to see a mellow Jack lying on the floor listening to The Beatles' *Honey Pie*.

Jack looked up with glazed, lysergic eyes. "You know...*this* song ain't so bad."

In the car, Jack explained while Delware drove. Years in Narcotics allowed Delware to decipher Jack's incoherent ramblings. Ten minutes into the drive, Delware realized it all made sense. The killers were at Spahn Ranch.

~ ~ ~

They found Homicide empty. Delware had no choice. Without permission and sidestepping chain of command, he jumped on the phones to organize a raiding party. Arriving officers were shocked to see a black officer in Homicide and it took them a moment to realize they had just followed his orders. Jack sat quietly watching the commotion with wide innocent eyes, seeing men he had known for years, as if for the first time. Pat arrived, demanding an explanation. He got the rundown from Delware, and got on the phone. "We'll need a Helicopter. I don't want anyone getting away."

Pat called Dirk, "Better get down here. We have a suspect. We're going to pick him up."

Dirk protested, "I want a name!"

Pat handed the phone to Delware. "He wants a name."

Delware grabbed the receiver. "Manson, Charles. Records is pulling his file right now. It should be up here anytime-."

"Tell Records to hold that file, I'll be there in five minutes, I'm picking that file up myself. Goddamn

Delware, I got nothing against you, but if this is just a wild goose chase..." Dirk hung up.

Pat turned to Delware and pointed at a dog-eared Rolodex. "Get on the phone to County. Tell them we're coming and where we're going."

District Attorney Vincent Burgess swept in at full steam, barging through officers arming themselves with shotguns. "Pat! Calling a raid without me? You looking for photo ops? Goddamn thing in the middle of the night!" He barked, "Who called this raid and who thought I wouldn't find out about it?!" Vince was genuinely stunned to find a black man conferring with Pat at the center of Homicide. He asked with surprising sincerity, "Who the hell are you?"

"Officer Hicks, I called the raid on orders of Detective Middleton."

Vince leaned past Delware to see Jack. He did a consternated double take. "Jack, what the hell is the matter with you? You look," he searched for the words, "... *relaxed.*"

Vince snapped at Pat, "I thought you threw him off this case?"

Delware stared at Jack, his eyes demanding him to say something. Jack was daydreaming. Delware stepped up. "We've broken the Tate *and* the La Bianca murders."

Vince's eyebrows shot up. "Holy Christ! They *are* connected?" He inched back and blinked – realizing an unknown black officer had just informed him of the most important news he might hear in his whole career.

Waylon Hampton, Mr. Ku Klux Klan, came up with a group of officers carrying pump-action shotguns. He was two-hundred-and-fifty pounds of puffing flesh and led tactical operations for all LAPD raids. He saw Delware, phone still in hand, at the center of activity. Approaching him like a steam train, he eyed Delware giving orders.

Waylon turned a few shades of red, his puffing face about to explode, his massive body tensing, fists balling. He spit out the words into Delware's face. "What the fuck is this nappy headed coon doing on the third floor giving orders! No self-respecting officer gonna take order from no uppity cotton picker!!"

Delware took a step back and the busy room fell absolutely silent. Waylon eyed Delware for a murderous minute, their hands inching towards their guns.

It was as loud as a gunshot and just as startling: the crash of breaking glass. The whole room jumped and turned. There in the corner, sat Jack, a toppled water cooler at his feet. His grin said he had kicked it over purposely. Broken shards lay about, the now large pool of water expanded slowly like blood across the dirty linoleum.

Jack spoke quietly, but with such intensity his words could be heard clearly to the back of the room. "Waylon. Sit down, before I knock you down." Jack stood slowly.

Forty men watched Jack and he defiantly eyed each and every one. Then his eyes narrowed. "Waylon!" He pointed at Delware. "That's a *black* man!"

In a single swift motion, Jack drew his gun. Everyone gave a collective "Whoa!"

The men closest to Waylon took cover. The rest of the room bobbed and weaved to stay out of the wavering gun sight.

Jack walked slow, closing in on Waylon. "And he's an officer of the LAPD acting on my orders."

Waylon remained frozen; amazed that Jack was waving a gun in his direction.

Jack sneered. "You know, I never liked you. And I've known you for twenty years...so that's saying something."

Waylon snapped out of it and spat. "You're smashed out of your head, you goddamn drunk!"

"Maybe, but tomorrow I'll be sober and you'll *still* be an asshole."

Vince was about to step in when Pat made a small hand motion, warning Vince to keep out of it.

Grimacing at the now nervous Waylon, Jack shook his gun like a scolding finger. "You know that story you tell about your father burning down that church full of coloreds? And the other Klansmen locking the doors so they couldn't get out? That story always made me sick...it's the way you tell it too, like you're proud of it: killing a bunch of defenseless women and children and old men." He shook his head. "Bunch of men in sheets, covering their faces – always struck me as cowardly."

Jack made a lazy glance at Delware. "You see Officer Hicks? He's a better cop than you've ever been, Waylon. And that's why you hate coloreds...because you're afraid, given half a chance, they might prove themselves better than you." He closed his eyes in disgust. "I'd kill you, but I don't like you that much." Jack sat and slid his .38 back into his holster, slow, like he was dreaming.

Waylon grabbed for his gun on his hip, but found the holster empty. He spun around to find Delware pointing his own gun at him. His finger wound tight around the trigger, his eyes filled with the rage of four hundred years of slavery, white brutality and segregation.

A voice from the back of the room startled everyone. "Jack, you're a disgrace!"

Every head turned to find Dirk standing in the doorway, black-eyed, swollen faced, his head bandaged – a large file in his hand. Jack glanced up, then dropped his eyes.

Dirk entered the room. "You *are* a drunk, Jack! I hope you're enjoying this night up here because it's your last."

Jack bowed his head – no comeback, no dirty looks – a silent confession. Dirk just stared at the old man.

Turning to Pat and Vince, Dirk weighed the heavy file in his hand. He spoke under his breath, "They found our killer."

The pair of men stood astonished. Pat stepped forward and barked. "Dirk! Jack! Waylon! In my office!"

As Pat marched past Delware, he whispered, "You'd better come too."

He stopped at Waylon who stood dangerously still, containing his rage, his eyes murderous. "Waylon, you're in the office with us."

The motley crew filed into the small room: blood-shot middle-of-the-night eyes, crooked ties, unshaven faces. Pat sank behind his desk; Vince perched on top of it. Dirk and Delware straddled chairs at opposite ends of the room. Jack slumped into a corner chair where a dozen clipboards hung on the wall.

The moment Waylon closed the door, he turned his eyes on Delware. "I'm not staying in an office with *him*!"

The declaration hung in the air. With every second, the pressure in the room increased. Pat dropped his head. Everyone did side glances to take a read on his face, but it was down, out of sight. Vince felt the temptation to throw his weight around, but resisted. It was Pat's command, his call.

Finally, Pat surged out of his chair, red faced. "Well, then get the fuck out, Waylon!"

Waylon was shocked, so was everyone else. In the stunned silence, Waylon remained wide-eyed.

Pat pointed a finger in Waylon's face. "Do you know where the killers are?"

Waylon's face was blank. His shoulders shrugged.

Pat frowned fiercely. "Then get the fuck out!"

Dumbly, Waylon turned and exited.

Jack spoke softly to no one in particular, "One day I'm going to put his head right ... with a baseball bat."

Dirk pointed at Jack, protesting, "He's not officially in the Bureau!"

Jack laughed. "Yeah, but I'm the only cop in this room who found our killers."

Pat spoke softly, but with authority, "I'll decide who's on the force or not."

Jack jabbed, "While the rest of you were running around like chickens with their heads cut off."

Pat's voice cut the air. "Which one of you wants to be the next holding his balls outside with Waylon?!"

Dirk rose and dropped the heavy file on a desk. The boom made everyone flinch.

"That's the jacket right there. I've gone through it. Jack's not fit to wear a badge, but he is right. This is our killer."

Vince got up from the edge of the desk. "Jesus Christ! It's thick as a Bible."

Dirk threw open the file and tapped on the mug shot clipped to the first page. "That's our guy."

Jack stood very slowly. The room melted away and everyone in it. For Jack, he faced the picture – alone: that was his man, the one he'd been hunting. He would have recognized him anywhere, even though he had never seen him before, he would have been able to pick him out of any line up, or any busy street. Jack recognized the face; the hunter in him was fully awake now, fully in control. He read that face like ordinary people read a road map. This was a psychopath. Beyond his dirty good looks and boyish con-man grin, Jack read his story. A heartless childhood, abused, raised not by parents, but by institutions. Rejection and loneliness had destroyed all that was human in him – a man who saw other people only as puppets in his play. He could cut them as easily as a child tears apart paper dolls. He was the man Jack was always looking for, the question behind every unsolved murder: the man without a motivation, except the need to destroy.

A ghoulish, devilish grin took possession of Jack's face. He whispered, "I gotcha, you *sumbitch*."

Delware's eyes remained on the photo of the longhaired criminal, amazed at the accuracy of five-year-old Cory Willett's description. It was perfect: Evil Jesus.

Pat's eyes came up wide. "Jesus, Mary and Joseph!" His fingers flipped through the bloated file. "Vince you should see this. The rap sheet alone is twenty pages. This guy's no hippie. He's been in and out of the system most of his life. First arrest when he was ten for arson!" He pulled a sheet and gawked. "He actually begged the parole board at his last hearing *not* to release him!"

Delware looked to Jack, but his partner stood silent, staring into another world. Delware piped in, "This lunatic's out there *now*, in control of a hippie commune. He's their leader."

Vince asked Pat, "Who is this guy?"

Pat read it off the file to make sure he got it right, "Manson, Charles."

Vince started pulling pages.

Pat turned to Dirk. "You really think this is our guy?"

"If this man has followers, LA's not safe."

Vince gasped, his hands full of arrest reports. "Where the hell is this maniac?"

Jack whispered. "I know."

Everyone turned. Jack seemed to tower over all of them. "I know exactly where he is."

~ ~ ~

Waylon popped his head in. "The team's ready to go."

Vince, Dirk and Delware filed out. Pat grabbed his jacket and was halfway out the door, when he stopped and turned. Jack sat in the corner, head bowed.

"Jack! You coming?"

"Yeah, I just wanted to say something."

Pat gave him a curious look and closed the door. The two men faced each other in the empty room.

Jack half mumbled, *"Sorry*...for the last six years."

Pat's jaw dropped. He tried to say something, but just mouthed. Once he got his air back, he asked. "Jack? What *the hell* did you do tonight?"

Friday, October 3rd, 1969, 2:01 AM

Delware drove the Packard along a dirt road that wound into a big nowhere, the great abandoned heart of Death Valley. Jack looked out at the shadowy dunes. In the moonlit night, he glanced back at the caravan following them: a long line of police cars raising dust into the silvery sky.

Jack was coming down, but still had uncontrolled flashes of powerful, vivid hallucination. He saw Manson's hippies winding down this same road on their way to Cielo Drive: a tall hippie with a beard driving a pickup into the desert night, three smaller hippie girls squeezed in beside him. He imagined no talk as their faces glowed by the dashboard light, knowing where they were going and what they planned to do. They would leave the crime scene that would draw him back down this very same road.

Jack knew the officers following him were silent. He pictured those men. They too had plans.

The Packard came to a turn in the road where the dunes rose high. Jack's hand shot up. "Stop!"

The car halted throwing up a cloud of dust. In the headlights, a dilapidated sign: three planks of rotting wood. The bottom plank hung lopsided by a single nail. The faded letters: Spahn Ranch.

Jack peered through the windshield. "The ranch is just over the hill."

The caravan slowed behind them, closing ranks. Jack's imagination flashed the hippies slowing the pickup down the road from Cielo Dr. – far enough away to take their victims by surprise. He saw the pickup pull to the side of the canyon road. Its headlights died.

Pat appeared at the window.

Jack rolled it down. "This is it."

Pat nodded. "We'll set up a perimeter."

In his rearview mirror, Jack watched the officers getting out of their cars. His mind flashed: the tall hippie and the three girls getting out of their truck. As he watched a young officer checking his gun, Jack saw the tall hippie popping out the cylinder of his revolver, making sure the chambers were loaded.

Delware opened his door. "Come on, Jack. We're going to miss it."

Jack snapped from his vision. "No, wait. Close that door."

Delware slammed it shut. "Damn it, Jack. What is it?!"

"Hey, wait a minute, will ya. We won't miss a thing."

Delware tried to sit, but fidgeted. "Come on, Jack!"

"I have to tell you something."

"What!"

"You've made it."

"What?"

"I overheard Patty and Vince talking in the parking lot. They've been watching you. They're going to give it to you. You're going to make detective, kid."

Delware sat back stunned, his eyes wide, his head swaying as if he didn't know what hit him.

A whisper of a smile crossed Jack's lips as he watched. "You're going to be LAPD's first neg-...*black* Homicide detective." Jack smiled. "Kid, your commune hunch, it was right as rain. That was some good hunting."

Jack turned, pretending to look out the window.

Delware looked over at him. A long silent minute passed. He was about to ask Jack what was wrong when the words escaped Jack's lips. "*Now* I can...go out." Jack whispered so close to the window, his words left fog on the glass. "Thanks...partner."

Delware stared at the old man a long moment, his face darkened with doubt. "But, Jack, what if we're wrong?"

Jack smirked. "Take it easy, kid. We're holding all the aces this time."

Delware thought about his new life with that gold shield. In that quiet moment, Delware confessed. "Jack, I got to tell you something."

Jack turned.

"You know how I told you my uncle was lynched?"

Jack nodded. "Sure, kid. I remember, in the heart of Dixie, the buckle on the Bible belt. I don't forget anything."

"Well, you're right about me – what you said after that night in the desert. It had crossed my mind that getting into Homicide would teach me how to commit the perfect murder. To kill...and not get caught." Delware looked away. "I've thought about it from time to time. Going back one day and getting the sonvabitch who led the mob that lynched my uncle."

Jack nodded and sat there a full minute. "There's a file, in cold cases. Look under 1957, June 7th, an informant gone wrong called William Lee. You follow the details in that report like a set of instructions. If you do, they'll never catch you."

Delware turned to ask if the William Lee file was one of Jack's kills, but he didn't have to, the answer was already on Jack's face.

Delware asked, "You're not surprised?"

Frowning, Jack shook his head. "I read you, kid. Had you pegged from that first day in my living room, confirmed it that day in the morgue when you pulled your gun. It's in your eyes. You don't hold a gun like a man who doesn't mean to use it."

Looking up through the windshield, Jack gazed at the desert stars. "Let me tell you something." After a silent moment, Jack looked at Delware in earnest. "Before you go messing around with the past, you gotta ask yourself...do you really want to end up like me?" Jack opened his door and paused. "You got a future, kid. There's hope for you yet."

Jack left the door open.

Delware watched him walk into the darkness and had a sudden premonition that the old man would not live through the night.

~ ~ ~

Watching the waves of officers scrambling up the dunes in the moonlight, Jack's mind flashed with the shadowy figures of four hippies scrambling up the long driveway of the Tate mansion.

When the signal came that the perimeter had been secured. Jack made his way to the top of a dune. He looked down at the moonlit ranch. It was still an Old West ghost town, an abandoned movie set, a cluster of dilapidated buildings nestled into the foothills. Jack scanned the scene. There were no lights on. The street was deserted. Beyond was nothing but sand stretching to the horizon.

Creeping around the corners came shadows. The first wave of officers moved slowly among the buildings. Detectives lay on the dunes and watched. It was October 3rd, 1969 and they were witnessing the first significant deployment of LAPD's new SWAT unit. With tactics more like soldiers than cops, the SWAT unit searched the barn and smaller buildings, but found no one. They now surrounded the scatter sheds. Three officers were at the windows of the ranch house, checking inside. Flashing through Jack's mind were the Manson Family, creeping across the lawn and peeping into the windows of the Tate mansion.

As if in a dream, as if he were there on the night of the murders, he stood up and began to walk towards his vision of hippies outside the mansion.

Delware noticed first; he whispered fiercely, "Jack!"

Jack walked down the dune towards the ranch house. Delware tried to follow, but Pat grabbed his arm. "Keep down, stay where you are." Pat shook his head and whispered, "Jesus Christ! What the hell is Jack doing? He's going to get himself *killed.*"

Delware thought of the Middleton curse. Jack's father and grandfather had died in the line of duty. Was that what Jack meant when he said '*Now he* can...*go out?*'

Jack walked straight towards the front door of the ranch house. In his mind, he was walking the grounds of the Tate mansion. Two SWAT team members with rifles and helmets silently waved him away. Jack stared at the door, for a moment he thought he saw the word 'pig' scrawled in blood on it. He blinked in the moonlight and it was gone. A young SWAT officer looked at the old man in disbelief and whispered to his crouching partner, "What the hell is he doing?"

The young officer saw Delware running down the dune towards Jack and whispered urgently, "Come on Dave, do it before these lunatics blow our cover."

Someone hit the lights inside of the ranch house. A voice came from within, "Do you hear someone outside?"

Dave rose with resolved eyes and kicked the door open. There was a moment of stunned silence as the hippies inside turned their heads. The walls were spray painted with the words, *piggy, rise!*

Cops poured in through the doorway. Naked teenage girls jumped from sleeping bags, the air was stabbed with screams. Longhaired guys grabbed knives, pistols, anything that could be a weapon. The boom and thud of doors being broken brought more cops bursting into the ranch house. A redheaded girl rose up naked in the middle of chaos and let loose a breathless, psychotic laugh. Naked girls ran helter skelter, cops knocked them down and clubbed and pistol-whipped their boyfriends. Heads cracked and clubbed kids hit the floor. Grating, out of tune screams came from every direction and swirled around. The sergeants tried to shout orders, but they could not be heard over the dim. Girls plunged at cops, clawing their faces; frantic fists relentlessly smashing.

Outside, black-and-whites roared in flashing red. Shouts and gunshots rang throughout the compound. A helicopter flew overhead, a searchlight shone down bright as daylight.

Jack stepped into the midst of the screaming, but to him it sounded like one thing and one thing only: murder. He was hearing the screams in the Tate mansion on the night of the murders. He heard the song Helter Skelter: the ripping guitars, the smashing cymbals.

A tall hippie came from behind the front door, the SWAT team had missed him in the confusion. He rose tall with a gun in his hand, slowly, deliberately his arm rose and he took aim at the back of Jack's head.

Delware burst through the doorway, "Drop your weapon!"

Jack turned to stare down the barrel of the gun.

The tall man ducked and shot at Delware. The doorframe exploded into splinters by Delware's head. The hippie rolled and shot again. Delware fired, but a naked girl ran by, knocking him to one side. Hearing another shot, Delware felt a pain in his shoulder, so powerful he dropped to his knees. In the blur of motion, Delware aimed at the now standing hippie and fired three rapid shots, each one connected. The hippie stumbled back and fell lifeless.

Jack watched the gun battle like a dream, then turned and walked through the confusion.

To Jack, he was still walking through the blood spattered Tate murders. He saw and heard it all: the boy trying to escape in his car, the gunshots shattering his windshield, piercing the boy, who after opening the car door, fell out dead. A long haired blonde, covered in blood running to the mansion's door screaming, falling in the doorway, her beautiful summer dress: red. The man managing to make it to the front lawn, bloody and beaten, being swarmed and stabbed, blades piercing him, falling to the ground, crawling away, until a tall hippie shot him and plunged a carving knife into the back of his neck. Jack saw Sharon Tate, a screaming pregnant woman being thrown to the ground and the Manson Family holding her down, stabbing, blood spraying through the air, blades rising and falling, the sound of them entering flesh, and the screaming mouths of victims. In the ranch house, naked girls screeched as they were wrestled to the ground and handcuffed. Jack saw blood soaking into the Tate's carpets, the bloody pages of the Bible being used to scrawl RISE across the walls.

Jack felt him, very close: Manson. Then he saw it on a bedroom door inside the ranch house, the word written on it with multi-colored paints: Helter Skelter. Jack walked, staring at those words. He stood before the door, raised his .38. He almost saw through the door into the black room beyond. There was a dark devil inside, waiting for him.

He gave the door a solid kick.

Before him were only shadows. Black. Jack stepped in, temporarily blinded. He stumbled; his gun wavered trying to find a suspect to fix on. His eyes shot wide open like he'd seen a ghost. His hair stood on end. Standing in the center of the room was the butchered body of Sharon Tate. He stared into her blood-covered face. Her bloody finger pointed to a corner of the room and vanished. He turned. His pupils widened, he saw the dark outline of a bed, on it a man with long hair perched like an animal. In a split second, Jack saw there were no other doors and one tiny window. He trained his gun on the shadowy figure. He had him! There was no escape. Jack felt dark, poisonous eyes staring. Slowly, the man rose, knocking the curtain from the window. The moonlight fell on the rising man who loomed ever larger. To Jack's lysergic eyes he was a great shadowy demon, a black avenging angel. At full length, he towered over Jack. Jack tried to speak, but couldn't, as if this devil had snatched his breath. Jack half-expected the black angel to swing a white sword and lop off his head. He saw this demon dragging his soul into the depths of Hell for all his sins. Jack stood transfixed by the set of dark eyes, a murderous, insane stare, concentrating all their power and poison on him.

Suddenly, the man's arm burst forth with a vehement, damning finger at Jack. A guttural voice shrieked an unholy condemnation, unleashing all the pent-up fury of Hell,

"PIG!"

Epilogue

1970

Jack Middleton played a key role in providing evidence and testifying at the trial of Charles Manson and the Manson Family. Jack passed away peacefully in his sleep on December 8th, the day after the conviction of Charles Manson.

1992

Delware Hicks was named Chief of the Los Angeles Police Department. He was the first African-American police commissioner of the LAPD, taking over after Chief Daryl Gates' resignation following the 1992 Los Angeles riots. He tried to create a positive image of the Department and close the rift created between the police and black neighborhoods by the violent arrest of Rodney King in 1991.

Newspapers around the U.S. featured his official LAPD portrait with the exception of the *San Francisco Chronicle* which ran a color photo of a young Delware Hicks in 1969. The picture was taken at Spahn Ranch. It showed the sun coming up. In the background was Charles Manson being led away in handcuffs; in the foreground, a bandaged, but smiling Delware Hicks with a shotgun cocked on his hip, leaning back against a black-and-white.

About the Author

Neal Arbic's life was the inspiration for the Bruce McDonald film *Road Kill*, which won Best Canadian Feature Film at the 1989 Toronto International Film Festival and today is considered a seminal film in Canadian cinema. He has appeared on CBC radio and Bravo and Star!TV.

Thank you for reading.
Please write a review of this book.
Reviews help others find newpulppress.com
And inspire us to keep bringing you
the best in crime noir.

http://www.newpulppress.com/